PICKING
up the Pieces

E.L GREEN

Copyright 2015 by Emma Green

All rights reserved, including the right to reproduce this book or portions thereof in any form whatsoever.

Cover Design by Mayhem Cover Creations
mayhemcovercreations.com

Copyedited by Cassie McCown:
gatheringleavesediting.com

This book is the work of fiction. Names, characters, places, and incidents either are products of the author's imagination or are used fictitiously. Any resemblance to actual events, locales, or persons, living or dead, is entirely coincidental.

Table of Contents

Prologue	1
Chapter One	6
Chapter Two	15
Chapter Three	24
Chapter Four	30
Chapter Five	34
Chapter Six	43
Chapter Seven	50
Chapter Eight	56
Chapter Nine	62
Chapter Ten	71
Chapter Eleven	78
Chapter Twelve	86
Chapter Thirteen	92
Chapter Fourteen	97
Chapter Fifteen	104
Chapter Sixteen	116
Chapter Seventeen	129
Chapter Eighteen	138
Chapter Nineteen	143
Chapter Twenty	149
Chapter Twenty-One	155
Chapter Twenty-Two	162
Chapter Twenty-Three	172
Chapter Twenty-Four	183

Chapter Twenty-Five	190
Chapter Twenty-Six	200
Chapter Twenty-Seven	210
Chapter Twenty-Eight	223
Chapter Twenty-Nine	230
Chapter Thirty	236
Chapter Thirty-One	245
Chapter Thirty-Two	254
Chapter Thirty-Three	261
Chapter Thirty-Four	269
Chapter Thirty-Five	276
Chapter Thirty-Six	281
Epilogue	293
Acknowledgements	298

Prologue

After the last of our luggage was loaded into the back of the car, I shut and locked the door of our new home and did a quick scan of the windows and garden before turning my attention to the gorgeous man sitting in the front seat of our new family car parked in the driveway. My cheeks hurt from smiling so much as Jake fidgeted in his seat and played with the gadgets. He was like a big kid with a shiny new toy, and I doubted even standing naked before him would distract him from pressing the multiple buttons. It was a good few minutes before he realised I was even standing there. His smile matched my own as he reached for my hand and pulled me gently into the passenger seat. I got lost in the depths of his gorgeous blue eyes. They'd captivated me the first time I'd seen them, and four years later, they still had the same effect. The smirk he flashed when he realised I was staring had me giddy like a schoolgirl over her first crush. This wonderful specimen of a man was all mine, and I was the luckiest girl alive.

"Our last holiday before our angel arrives. Just so you know, I intend to make sure we don't leave the hotel room." He pulled me across the car in one fluid movement, but I was abruptly stopped when the gear stick got in the way of my very large, rounded belly. The heat of the moment quickly evaporated, and we both burst out laughing. "Things were so much easier on the bike." He sighed.

I adjusted myself back on my side of the car and fastened my seatbelt.

Yes, things were easier on the bike. I looked down at my baby bump and smiled at the memory.

"As tempting as that sounds, I do want to do a bit of sightseeing, you know," I said, referring to his earlier comment. I was still slightly flustered, so I opened the window to let in some fresh air. Sticking my arm out, I felt the warmth of the spring sun settle on my skin. There was hardly a cloud in the sky. I relaxed back into my seat and became lost in thought as I watched the birds, wondering what it would be like to be truly free, soaring above the earth.

"Yeah, yeah. Let's get this show on the road. I have a beautiful pregnant wife to ravish for a whole weekend. I also plan on making good use of the hot tub," Jake said, pulling me back to reality.

"Really? That sounds pretty amazing. If I were her, I'd be anxious for you to get there as soon as possible."

Jake reversed out of the driveway quickly, prompting me to hold on to the door handle and scream with delight. He stopped and looked me over before grinning from ear to ear, lust evident in those beautiful eyes, but the love that shone from them was just as fierce. As if our angel sensed it too, she somersaulted, causing a ripple across my stomach. He pulled away from the curb safely, and as we headed off for our last weekend of freedom, we both wore matching expressions. It had taken me a while, but finally, my life was exactly how I wanted it to be. I was happy. I was safe.

Unfortunately, fate had other plans.

Seconds. It took *seconds* for my whole world to shatter and collapse around me. To be torn from a life I had worked so hard to achieve and thrown straight back to the depths of despair and the existence I'd fought so hard to forget. *Seconds* to slip back into that broken girl all over again.

An earth-shattering scream, the sickening sound of crunching metal on metal, and such intense pain I wasn't capable of stringing together a coherent thought. The world fizzled out around me, an incessant ringing in my ears drowning out the chaos, and then absolute deafening silence consumed me before I was completely swallowed by darkness.

I drifted in the darkness for minutes, hours, days, weeks... Distant voices asked me to wake up. Sometimes I could hear sobs, but I knew, deep down, none of those voices belonged to him. I knew I didn't want to wake up if he wasn't there.

For a while, the darkness kept me protected.

There was no pain, just peace. I was safe in my own bubble. It was as if I knew if I headed toward the light, the pain would rip me open like it never had before. It would be so intense I was certain I wouldn't survive. Yet the light persisted, and soon, the compulsion to leave the darkness became too much.

It wasn't the sort of light you hear about in stories. There was no one standing there waiting for me to step through and join them on the other side. I was trapped in a darkness, in between, and rather than being drawn to the afterlife, something shoved me completely in the other direction, pushing me to wake up. Someone was urging me to fight, telling me it wasn't time to give up now no matter the challenges I would face. I was a survivor.

I made that final step and walked into the light.

A relentless *beep, beep, beep* in the distance had me stirring from my slumber and was seriously pissing me off. God, I was so tired. The beeping came louder and louder. It was literally driving me insane. I *needed* it to stop. A hammer should do the job. Preferably a very large one. I tried to turn, but I couldn't move. I was completely frozen to the spot, and panic replaced any annoyance I had over the awful sound.

All my senses screamed at me to open my eyes, but my eyelids felt like lead. I finally managed to flutter them, but as soon as they were fully open, I had to shut them quickly. It was too bright. The beeping sped up and became a more erratic.

What the hell is happening?

Even with my eyes firmly shut, I felt disorientated and, my God… that noise! I lifted my eyelids more gradually so I could adjust to the light and then allowed myself take in my surroundings. My throat tightened and I struggled to breathe, not just because there was a tube shoved down it. My arms felt less like lead and more like jelly now, but I moved them slowly and gagged as I pulled at the tube. Tears pooled in my eyes and I squeezed them shut, letting the moisture spill down my cheeks. Flashes of the accident violently assaulted my thoughts, causing me to whimper in pain. *Please no, please no.* I moved my hand to my now flat stomach, confirming what I already knew. *Oh God, no.* In one final attempt, I yanked the tube free and let out a silent scream.

Chapter One

ELLIE

"Hey, Els. How you doing?" Cassie walked into the private hospital room, clutching my chart and wheeling in a blood pressure machine. It was time to check my vitals again. She needn't have bothered. I knew she was just doing her job, but she was smothering me, using it as an excuse to check up on the patient who'd lost her mind.

You see, I might have been physically healing well, but mentally—not so much. At least I'd started eating and speaking again. For three weeks, I'd refused my meals and ended up being fed through a tube. Being manhandled in order to insert said feeding tube was degrading, but I was in no state to feel shame. I also refused my pain medication. The whole ordeal was nasty, but I endured the discomfort. No one could understand the pain was the only thing keeping me remotely sane. I needed it to help me feel alive. I needed it as a distraction from what was really going through my mind. If I didn't feel the pain, then I wouldn't feel *anything*. I would be numb. Dead like Jake and Lyla Rose.

I might have come back into the light, but the darkness still consumed me.

"Fine. When can I get out of here?" I asked. I tried, but I couldn't even manage a smile.

Cassie wasn't just my nurse; she was my best friend since primary school and probably the only person, apart from Jake, who really knew me. She'd been my critical care nurse, but unable to let go, managed to pick up some agency shifts when I was transferred to the private hospital two weeks ago.

"Probably a couple more days. Did you see Dr. Cole today?" she asked.

Dr. Cole was the shrink assigned to me when I first showed signs of mental instability. Not sure how you're *supposed* to act when your husband and daughter are killed tragically, leaving not only your body, but heart and soul completely in pieces, but apparently not talking, not breaking down every five minutes, not eating, and refusing meds gets you labelled a mental health risk pretty quickly. If only they knew.

I'd been in hospital for three months, one of those in a coma. He'd visited every day for the past five weeks. Often sporting a tweed jacket, delicate glasses perched on the end of his nose, and a head full of fuzzy silver hair, he resembled a nutty professor and probably should have retired years ago. He was nice enough, I suppose. My appointments were valuable in the sense it gave me something to do and meant I didn't have to spend time with unwanted visitors. As for the actual purpose of the sessions, they probably didn't do much to help, and to be honest, I wasn't ready for whatever else they were meant to expose. Most of my life, I'd managed to deal with my problems on my own. I didn't need to start relying on anyone else now. I'd relied on Jake, and look where that got me.

"I said I was fine, and I'm fine."

Cassie wrapped the blood pressure sleeve around my arm and pressed the button to inflate it. "Your BP is one-twenty over eighty, so absolutely spot on. We'll make our way down to physio at two, and then Matt will be able to sort out an outpatient schedule."

I nodded. Matt was okay for an arsehole. He either didn't know my husband had just died or didn't know how to think with anything other than his dick.

"Good, you're awake!" My mother swept in as if she owned the place and chucked her bag on a chair. I looked on expressionless and waited for her normal theatrics. Cassie immediately made herself scarce.

On cue, the woman who called herself my mother wiped her eyes as she shed the crocodile tears she'd perfected over the years. "You are looking so rested. I must look a mess. I mean, look at the bags under my eyes. I haven't been able to sleep for days. All this stress is wearing me down, and my blood pressure is going through the roof! You have it so easy in here, resting up while the rest of us have to just get on with it, but still, it's not like you know much different, is it? You've always had the easy life."

And there we have it... My mother, the bane of my existence.

Since waking from my coma, I had daily visits from my parents. I would like to say I welcomed them, but I'd be lying. My father would turn up and hardly say a word. My mother made it her mission to inform me every day about how hard everything had been on her. Like always, I was the cause of her lack of sleep, loss of appetite, and the increase in dosage of her blood pressure medication. Anyone would think it was her whose husband and daughter had died.

It's not like her behaviour was unfamiliar to me. She was selfish, a control freak, a master of emotional blackmail and insults. I would never be good enough to meet her standards, no matter how hard I tried. You would think being twenty-four, I'd be able to move on from this by now, but no matter how hard I tried to forget, her comments haunted me every day. I suppose I should have been grateful she wasn't throwing her usual insults at me. I could take the selfish comments; it was the other stuff I found harder to handle, and right now, my frame of mind was beyond fragile.

The idea of ever confronting my parents or defying them in any way had always scared the hell out of me. They had influence over everything I ever did, whether I liked it or not. Even if I managed to make my own decision, they would have to have their say in some way.

The decision to go into nursing was easy. I wanted to help people, and if I were honest, I thought this would be a profession that would make my parents proud, make them happy, but like everything I wanted to do, they tried to talk me out of it. It was apparently hard work, underpaid, and I didn't have the patience or brains.

Really, Ellie? Only bright people become doctors and nurses, dear.

I winced at the memory and shoved it back in the box with the rest of them. They fought me every step of the way, but for the first time in my life, I fought back. When I said they wouldn't have to pay a penny, they finally agreed I could go to uni to train to be a nurse. I'd been planning my escape since getting a job at fourteen, so luckily, I had savings. From an early age, I knew I had to break free of their overbearing hold and control before it killed me.

It was during my training to become a nurse that I met Jake. I was twenty. He was eight years older, a police officer in the local armed response unit, and raced motorbikes for a hobby. I thought my parents would love him, but once again, I was wrong. According to my mother, he wasn't husband or family material. What they actually didn't like was he had his own mind and stood up to them. They, or rather my mother, didn't talk to me for two weeks when I told them we were getting married. I should have taken that as my chance to run, but still, I did everything in my power to try and make them accept me again. It was as if I craved their attention, whether good or bad. I was a glutton for punishment.

Still, I defied my parents and married Jake anyway because I couldn't lose what I had with him. He made me feel safe in his strong arms, his smile made me go weak at the knees, and he loved me for who I was, but deep down, I also knew he was my chance to escape.

A single stray tear rolled down my left cheek and I wiped it away quickly. I wouldn't cry in front of her.

"Ellie. Are you even listening to me?" I turned around and faced my now red-faced mother. Admittedly, I had zoned out seconds into her one-sided conversation. "Stop being so selfish. We're doing everything for you, and you just sit back and ignore me! I know it has been hard, but you need sort yourself out. Jake is dead, and count yourself lucky you never met Lyla Rose and got the chance to love her like I did. You have always been such a selfish little bitch. I can't believe you are *my* child."

I'm not sure why I ever expected any different. Over the years, I'd perfected blocking out her hurtful comments. In truth, I'd always known she had the capability to be a cold-hearted bitch, but never in my life had she stooped so low. Whatever she said after that was lost on me as I processed the last sentence. The room became hollow as the whooshing sound of my blood pumping through my veins drowned out everything around me. I could feel it boiling right down to my marrow as white-hot fury replaced any complacency I might normally have found in my mother's company. To say I was shocked and angry was an understatement.

My poor, sweet Lyla Rose came into the world too soon. Born by emergency caesarean at twenty-eight weeks gestation and weighing just over two pounds, she fought hard for two days, but her lungs just weren't strong enough. I never got to see my angel and never got to say a proper good-bye, as both hers and her dad's funeral had taken place while I was in the coma. Despite this, I loved her with all my heart. I might not have ever held her in my arms or kissed her delicate little face, but the love I had for her was there the instant I saw those two pale-blue lines. I only had the photos the neonatal unit gave me, but my C-section scar would be a constant reminder of what I loved and lost.

The resentment I now felt for my mother went beyond anything I'd ever felt before, and considering what she'd done in the past, this was quite an achievement. *How dare she!*

My body was stronger now. Regular physiotherapy had gotten my muscles working properly again, and even though I still needed to use crutches, only a slight limp remained as evidence of the injuries I sustained to my left hip and leg. I pulled myself up and grabbed the crutches. My mother stopped her rant and narrowed her gaze as she watched me approach. I remained calm even though my whole body felt charged with electricity. I was ready to combust. *Just one more word…*

"What the hell do you think you're doing? Get back in bed," she snapped.

"Get out," I whispered through clenched teeth. She didn't react quickly enough, so I repeated my words loud enough for her to hear the warning in my voice.

"You don't know what you're saying, Ellie. It's the head injury. You haven't been the same since," she argued.

"NO SHIT!" I yelled.

Cassie ran into the room but stood back when she realised what was happening. She wouldn't stop me yet. She knew this was a long time coming, and even though she probably would have preferred it a long time ago, the look her face told me she was relieved. I'd finally found something resembling a backbone.

"JAKE IS DEAD! MY DAUGHTER IS DEAD!" My dear old mother flinched at my words, but she stood her ground. Only just clearing five feet, she was a force to be reckoned with, but push me too far and so was I.

"You might have hated Jake, but he was still my husband and I loved him. You might have met Lyla Rose, but I am still her mother and I loved her the moment she was conceived. They were my life. THEY WERE MY LIFE! SO DON'T YOU DARE FUCKING TELL ME HOW MUCH YOU LOVED MY DAUGHTER MORE!" I screamed.

Her eyes glistened, and I think for the first time in her miserable life, real tears streamed down her cheeks. I didn't care. The strain in my legs grew the longer I stood, and I stumbled slightly. Cassie moved quickly and supported me by my waist and led me back toward my bed.

My mother's sobs echoed around my room. "Oh,

Mother, pull yourself together. What did you tell me once? Crying shows weakness," I snapped.

For once, my mother stood speechless as she wiped away her tears and stared at me. She suddenly looked small and fragile, but that was exactly how she managed to manipulate me all my life, and I wouldn't be manipulated now. It was the image she showed everyone to make them believe she wasn't the cold, vindictive cow she really was.

I'd already started, so I decided to add to the carnage.

"I want you to leave and not come back." She went to speak, but I held up my hand to stop her. She flinched and her eyes turned into tiny slits as she tried to come up with a way to salvage control of the situation. She was back to the woman I'd grown to despise, but right now, she wasn't going to have control. It was mine, and it felt bloody good. "NOW!"

She nodded, anger still radiating from her, grabbed her bags, and walked swiftly from my room —with any luck, from my life, but I doubted it. I still didn't cry, because if I did, the dam would break and an ocean of tears would follow and my already ruined heart would shatter into a thousand more pieces.

Chapter Two

ELLIE

I propped my feet on the coffee table and slunk back into the depths of the cushion-covered sofa. Cassie sauntered in with two tubs of ice cream and a couple spoons, throwing herself down next to me. When I was discharged from hospital, I moved into her apartment. I couldn't face going back to the house and what could have been.

After my showdown with my mother, I managed to portray confidence and bravado for a good month, until guilt consumed me. My parents ignored me the entire time, but as if she could suddenly sense my vulnerability, I got a text from my father suggesting I contact her because all the stress hadn't been good for her health. All of a sudden, I was that child again, desperately seeking forgiveness for being a horrible person. Of course, the adult version of myself argued my actions were just and she wasn't really sick, but it didn't stop me from going through the motions that were so deeply rooted they were second nature.

I'd been living with Cassie now for about two months, and during that time, apart from trips back to the hospital for physio and to see Dr. Cole, I'd spent roughly six weeks hidden in my room. I was grateful my sessions with Dr. Cole had been reduced to fortnightly now, as he was happy with my progress. He was obviously not as good at his job as he thought, or he needed to clear room on his schedule, because my mind was far from healed. Hiding away in my room was surely evidence of this, but I must admit I didn't exactly tell him everything. I nodded and agreed in all the right places, and sure enough, my discharge was imminent. It's a pity I was too self-conscious to appear on stage, because my acting skills were truly Oscar-worthy.

"How was work?" I asked Cassie between mouthfuls of Chocolate Chip. Who needs antidepressants when you have Häagen-Daz?

"Good. Everyone says hi by the way."

I nodded. Before the accident, I worked as staff nurse in the accident and emergency department at the local hospital. Signed off sick indefinitely, no one knew when I would return.

"Maybe you can catch up with them when we go for my farewell drinks?" She continued.

Cassie had recently handed in her notice. She'd applied for her visa and landed herself a job in

Vancouver. Yes, my best friend was also deserting me for a better life in almighty British Columbia, Canada. I didn't blame her. A new start was highly appealing. She grew up in the care system, so she didn't have any family. Well, not any who gave a shit anyway. Maybe she was running away from her problems, or maybe she truly was after a fresh start. Regardless, it was what she wanted, and I said I would support her all the way. I was just gutted she had to move so far away to do it. She was more than just my best friend; she was like the sister I never had.

"We'll see. Not sure if I want to see everyone just yet," I replied. She sighed and went to protest, but I cut her off before she could say anything. "So. Dad came round. Mum still doesn't want to talk to me until I apologise. I nearly gave in."

Cassie choked on the ice cream she'd just shoved in her mouth.

"You can't be serious," she replied after righting herself. "Sometimes I'm really grateful I don't have a family. You don't need to apologise, Els. Remember that. You don't owe that woman *anything*."

"So what're we watching?" My mother was another subject I was happy to avoid right now. I grabbed a couple DVDs from the table and examined the back covers. It was a choice between the latest *Marvel* film or Denzel Washington. I secretly hoped the superheroes won. Rom-coms hadn't been in the running for a long time now because, frankly, I still didn't feel like laughing

"Cas?" I looked up when she didn't answer. She was playing with her ice cream, avoiding looking me in the eyes. She would never make a poker player. Her face gave away everything. She reached behind a cushion and pulled out a white envelope, gingerly handing it over to me.

"Ted dropped it round this morning." Ted was the landlord of my house. Despite not having returned since coming home from hospital, I was anxious to know what it was about. I noticed the envelope already had been opened, and I gave her a questioning glance.

"Sorry, hun. I opened it because I wanted to know if it was anything bad." In other words, she didn't want to be unprepared in case I finally had the meltdown she expected when the shell I'd erected around my fragile mind finally cracked.

I opened the envelope and pulled out the crisp white paper. As I read the note from Ted, I crunched it up and threw it at the bin. I felt sick to my stomach and a pain ripped right through my heart. Returning home hadn't been on my list of priorities. I knew I would have to go back eventually, but right now, I didn't feel like I could face it. Not that it mattered anymore; the decision had been made for me.

"It'll be okay, sweetie." She pulled me into a hug, and I reluctantly let her. I'd never been a huggy person. The concept was foreign to me, even when I was with Jake, but Cassie had always been a hugger and wouldn't let me pull away even if I tried. "I spoke to Ted after I read the letter. He feels awful. He really does, especially after… you know, everything. He's getting a divorce and needs to sell the house. His bitch of a wife is taking the poor guy for every penny he's got, even though she was the one who went all *Desperate Housewives* and screwed the gardener."

"I know." I curled up and leaned farther into Cassie's arms, and she held me as I finally broke down and cried.

"You know you can always stay here." I did know I could stay with her, but she would soon be leaving too. What would I do then? There was no way I was moving back to my childhood home. When Cassie left, I would truly be on my own. That shell cracked, and piece by piece, my past caught up with me, unravelling everything I'd accomplished over the past four years.

"Come on, Els. Just one more step."

I stumbled on the last step and fell head first through the now open front door. I swore profusely as pain jolted up my shin. I still walked with a limp, but that wasn't what caused me to fall. I was pissed. So incredibly drunk I couldn't see straight and the world was just one giant merry-go-round. Three concerned faces looked down at me with sadness. I blinked and tried to focus again. Scrap that, only one face looked down at me, and it wasn't just sadness that radiated from those big blue eyes like a glowing beacon. It was pity. After just twenty-four hours from receiving Ted's letter, I'd effectively gone back four years and picked up where I officially left off. Numbing out the pain at the end of a bottle… or two. It's amazing how you revert to old habits when things get hard.

Cassie has had to help me get home after drinking way too many shots on far too many occasions. My shitty family and her shitty life threw us into the world of drinking and partying at the tender age of sixteen. Even though I didn't look a day over twelve with my petite frame and serious lack of height, Cassie was blond, tall, curvy, and easily passed as being older than her years. The joys of fake ID and knowing the right people meant access to alcohol was easy. I didn't care so long as I got drunk. I enjoyed the buzz, the sense of freedom, and the fact I could numb away all the shit going on in my life, no matter how brief the effect was.

For two whole weeks, rather than locking myself away in my room or going on a mass spending spree, I numbed out the pain with alcohol. Cider, tequila, beer, wine… whatever was offered. Eighteen-year-old Ellie was breaking loose again. Any semblance of the calm-natured, responsible Ellie was gone, and self-destructive Ellie was back with a vengeance, barely clutching onto life through a permanent drunken haze.

On the last night of my drinking spree, I ended up visiting my old colleagues at the hospital. I would like to say it was to catch up for old times' sake, but I wasn't conscious enough to mutter a single coherent word, let alone string together a whole sentence. There was also the fact they were busy pumping my stomach at the time. To be fair, that day I'd finally spoken to my mother, which would be enough to send any sane person over the edge. Not once during the hour-long conversation did she ask how I was or what my plans were. She did successfully remind me what a failure I was and how my husband and daughter were dead, though.

Even they couldn't bear to stick around you!

I think those were the last words she said before I hung up and decided to hit the town. Again. This time, I didn't want to just become numb. I wanted to forget. Everything. I think I lost at least two hours that evening. I had no recollection of absolutely anything. I know this might have been my intention, but it was utterly stupid and didn't have the overall effect I was after. The alcohol didn't wipe out the memory of the conversation I had about six hours before.

I suppose you could say one good thing came out of my hospital visit, though. It temporarily sobered me up and made me look at what I was doing with my life. I had been saved from that accident for a reason. I just didn't know it yet.

Three weeks passed slowly, but not slow enough. The day had finally come where I would have to take the next step. Cassie stood with me at the threshold of my old house. The home I would have shared with my husband and baby daughter—all a distant and shattered memory now. She held my hand as she walked me to the door and then helped me go from room to room, painstakingly packing away my old life. No matter how hard I tried, I couldn't prevent the floodgates from opening.

I'd made the decision before going back that most of the furniture and furnishings would be collected by the Salvation Army so they could be donated to families in need. That decision had been easy. Going through Jake's things, however, was more pain than I could bear. I sobbed hard as I hugged his favourite football shirt close to my chest and inhaled his smell. He'd worn it to a match the day before the accident. Even though months had passed, it still smelled like his Calvin Klein aftershave and the crafty cigarettes he would smoke, believing I was none the wiser. The softness of the fabric and the scent that was purely Jake was comforting and soul destroying at the same time. The familiarity pierced my chest and hit me straight in the heart, and once again, I found myself choking on months of pent-up emotion.

Once the tears subsided, I pushed back the pain until it was like the distant memory of metal crunching on metal and packed up the rest of his belongings. Most could be picked up along with the furniture, but I placed the shirt, along with a few other select items, neatly in a box to bring home with me.

There was just one room left to go through, and I knew without a shadow of doubt, this would be the room that would break me. I slowly opened the door to Lyla's nursery and crumbled to my knees at the sight of her Winnie the Pooh cot and matching furnishings. Stacks of nappies, sleep suits, vests, and other bits and pieces sat in the corner, still in the carrier bags we'd left them in the day before we left for our trip. The pram we'd bought a week earlier was still packed in its box beside the rocking chair I'd fallen in love with. I cried until my body shook with uncontrollable spasms. I cried until there were no more tears to cry.

When I'd finally gained control over my body and mind, I set to work packing up Lyla Rose's nursery, all the while remembering my pregnancy. At first we didn't want to know the sex of the baby, but at the twenty-week scan, we were given the option to find out, and we suddenly found ourselves not wanting the surprise. When they told us we were having a girl, Jake's grin rivalled that of the Cheshire Cat. He never told me, but I knew he secretly wanted a little girl. I only cared that the baby was healthy, but I was still overcome with emotion. We laughed all the way to the hardware store, one thing at the forefront of both our minds: we were going to paint the walls pink.

Running the parcel tape over the last box, I wiped away a few stray tears. My life was now packed into five boxes and the suitcase currently in my room at Cassie's. There was one box for Jake, one box for Lyla Rose, one box of memories, and the other two filled with other belongings I couldn't go without. It's amazing how a life full of promise and hope can be reduced to just a few photos and belongings.

Chapter Three

ELLIE

My head pounded, and if I moved a fraction, I was going to be sick. My alarm suddenly going off next to my head sounded like a jackhammer. I'd given in to temptation and had a few glasses of wine. Okay, maybe it was actually a couple bottles. Cassie was at work, and I was alone with my boxes and text messages from my mother.

Cassie appeared in my doorway in a onesie, looking as fresh as a daisy, holding a glass of water and two little miracle white tablets. Suddenly, the need to be sick outweighed the need to not move my head, and I legged it to the bathroom. Cassie followed after me and waited patiently while I finished puking and rinsed my mouth out using water from the tap.

"You've got to stop this, Ellie," she said as she handed me the painkillers. As much as I hated to admit it, she was right. Jake was no longer around to help me get through this mess, and Cassie would soon be gone too. There would be no one left to help scoop me up off the pavement, get me home safely, and look after me while I recovered from my stupidity.

I rolled off my stool and stumbled as I tried plant both feet firmly on the floor. The floor was moving. When the hell did I board a boat? Nope, still at the club. The stench of stale smoke, alcohol, and sweat was starting to turn my stomach.

Where's Cas?

I needed to go home and sleep it off. I had a shift at the hospital in the morning, and I couldn't go in still drunk. I giggled. I would most definitely still be drunk. I searched the crowds of sweaty dancing bodies for my best friend and then remembered she had a date with… Nope, couldn't remember his name. He was an arsehole anyway. His name could just be prick for all I cared. He would end up hurting her. They always did.

Finding my feet and gingerly placing one in front of the other, I headed toward the exit. I was thankful I wasn't the short skirt and heels kind of girl, considering the walk was proving to be difficult in skinny jeans and my favourite pair of purple Docs. I shoved past the people still entering the club and finally made it outside. I sucked in the fresh air and instantly regretted it. The world spun, my knees wobbled, and my stomach heaved.

I quickly dashed around the side of the club and relieved myself of my liquid dinner.

"You okay there?" A deep, sexy voice travelled down the alleyway and met my drunken ears. I ignored him and hoped he would go away. My stomach heaved again as I puked up some more, my gagging echoing off the brick walls. I hated being sick. My mother always told me I could wake the dead with my retching. I think for the first time in my life, I had to agree.

A warm hand reached around and pulled back my hair and the other rested on my shoulder.

I blinked back the memory of meeting Jake four years ago. Like most of the more serious of my binges, I'd had a run-in with my mother and decided to go out for a drink… or ten. Needless to say, after sinking several pints of cider and following them up with quite a few more shots of tequila, I was slightly worse for wear when Jake discovered me. He'd recognised me from the hospital where he'd brought in a young lad in his custody. Although we never spoke much during that time, apparently, I'd left an impression, because he was hoping to run into me again.

He never elaborated on what he saw in me that day. I used to wonder why he would want to see me again. He was older, had a good job, was gorgeous, and could have his pick of any girl he wanted. Why me? At first, I was convinced it was all some sort of sick prank, but after a while, I realised me puking my guts up in a dark alley was hardly the most romantic of reunions, and he didn't seem to care as he held back my hair. Without even realising it, Jake had put the ball in motion and started the road to my recovery.

"I've been thinking," Cassie said, sitting herself down next to me on the bathroom floor, disrupting my thoughts.

"Now, now, Cas. That could be considered dangerous." I teased. I held the damp glass to my forehead, welcoming the cold. I was feeling better, but my head still hurt.

"You're coming with me."

"I'm ill, Cas, and I'm going back to bed. I'm not going anywhere today," I replied.

"No doubt you want to stay in bed, but I'm not going to let you. I'm not going to let you destroy your life. Jake wouldn't want you to keep doing this to yourself, Ellie. So I figure there's only one way I can keep an eye on you. You're coming with me."

I sat and watched as my friend rambled on. I really had no idea what the hell she was talking about, but whatever it was had her looking too serious for a Sunday morning, and my head hurt too much to ask questions. She looked tired. Dark circles appeared under her eyes, indicating she hadn't slept in a while. She looked like she'd lost a little weight and the spark that was normally forever present in her big blue eyes had diminished.

I was a shit friend. I was so busy wrapped up in my own little bubble I'd failed to see Cassie was suffering as a result of my self-destructive behaviour.

You've always been a selfish bitch.

I lowered my head and avoided making eye contact with her while I fought the steady rolls of guilt enveloping me. I leaned back on the bathtub and stretched my short legs in front of me. I was still wearing last night's clothes, and I stunk of stale beer and cigarettes. Classy. I counted to ten in my head and then exhaled slowly. With each breath, I pushed out some of the guilt and self-loathing.

"Where am I going, Cassie?" I asked.

"You're coming with me to Canada." I opened my mouth, but before I could cut in, she shoved her hand in my face, causing me to stop. "I can't stay here. I need to leave, but it doesn't feel right leaving without you, especially when you're like this. We only have each other. I want you to come with me. I know Jake and Lyla Rose are buried here, but I honestly think moving away would be good for you too. It would be a completely fresh start. I mean, let's face it. Would you miss your family?" *No, I wouldn't.* "And what were you planning on doing for money? You gave up your job, and Jake's life insurance money won't last forever. The hospital I'm going to in Vancouver was looking for nurses in all departments. You would get a job easy, and we would still be together, watching each other's backs as always." She paused a moment to let it all sink in. "Fresh start. What do you say?"

I sat dumbfounded, staring at my best friend. Fresh start. Clean slate. No one apart from Cassie would know who I was. Maybe this was the opportunity I was looking for. Jake and Lyla Rose would live forever in my heart. I didn't need a headstone to remind me of their existence. The answer was easier than I expected.

"Yes. I'll come with you."

Chapter Four

ELLIE

Five months later...

I strolled through arrivals, rolling my suitcase behind me, and heard the scream before I saw her. Cassie jumped up and down like an excited toddler, waving her arms around like a crazy person. I smiled. She looked well and incredibly happy. She'd been in Vancouver four months now. Before leaving, she'd nailed me a job in the emergency department at the same hospital. Part of me toyed with the idea of doing something different, but emergency medicine was what I was good at. She might have landed me the job, but applying for visas took time, so I couldn't fly out with her.

Cassie launched herself at me, nearly knocking

me off my feet. "I can't believe you're here!"

"Me either. I've missed you, Cas."

She hugged me tighter and let out a light sob. She hadn't changed a bit. She pulled away and wiped her eyes on her sleeve.

"So did you get all my stuff?"

"Yep. It's all still in boxes in your new room. You're going to love the apartment, and you're going to love working at the hospital. Everyone is so friendly, and my God, there are some fit doctors. I always thought *Grey's Anatomy* was too farfetched. I mean, surely there could never be that much talent *and* looks in one place, especially a hospital, but I was wrong." Cassie became all dreamy eyed, and I laughed.

I'd missed her so much. Talking on Skype wasn't the same as seeing her smiley face in person. She continued to talk a hundred miles per hour, giving me a rundown of every single eligible bachelor in town. I was more than happy for her to check out all the "talent" in the area. She could dream all she wanted about double-dating and meeting new guys, but that was all it would be right now. A dream. I was starting to get my life back on track, and I didn't need anyone, especially a guy, complicating things. I was happy being on my own.

Cassie was right. The apartment was lovely and homely. I smiled a real smile, something I'd been doing more lately. I could see myself happy here. I headed to my new bedroom and saw my boxes piled neatly along the wall. I knelt down in front of them and pulled them toward me, then peeled off my coat and placed it in a heap behind me. Cassie had warned me about the heat, and I was grateful I'd worn a spaghetti strap top underneath.

An intake of breath caught my attention, and I turned to see Cassie in the doorway, looking at my shoulder blades.

"Oh, Els. It's beautiful. Skype didn't do it justice." Absentminded, I ran my fingers along one of the angel wings I'd tattooed across my shoulder blades. Cassie came across for a better look. "So how are things now, really?"

She didn't have to press any harder. I knew what she was talking about. My binge drinking had continued after she left and my life continued to spiral out of control. I still wasn't speaking to my parents much, my best friend had moved away, I celebrated my twenty-fifth birthday alone, and to top things off, it had been a year since Jake and Lyla Rose died. Once again, I'd gone out drinking and found myself the following morning in a strange bed and in the company of my ex-colleagues at the hospital.

It was the second time they'd had to pump my stomach in a matter of months. It took everything I had to convince them I didn't warrant a visit with Dr. Cole. My ex-colleagues looked down at me in sympathy as they explained I'd drunk so much I passed out and nearly choked on my own vomit outside a club. Thankfully, someone discovered me on the pathway and called for an ambulance. I was then subsequently whisked off to hospital, where they treated me and left me to sleep off the effects of the alcohol.

When I was discharged, I went home to the empty apartment and started opening my boxes from the house. I'd had another close call. Jake would have been so angry with me, and what would Lyla Rose have thought of her messed-up mother? I found my photos of Lyla and Jake and thought about how disappointed they would be. Finding strength I never realised I had, I pulled myself together and started looking at how I was going to live the rest of my life.

The following day, I went to my local tattoo parlour and discussed ideas with Claire, the lady who eventually tattooed the intricate angel wings across my shoulder blades. Jake's name was inscribed on one and Lyla Rose's on the other. It was perfect and fitting. As for the drinking… I hadn't touched a drop since waking up that morning in the hospital.

"I'm doing okay." For the first time in a long time, I said it and meant it. I might have left my family in England, but I was with the person who now meant most to me in the whole world. The person who'd stuck with me through thick and thin since primary school.

I grabbed hold of Cassie's hand and squeezed it tight. "We are going to be okay."

Together we unpacked my boxes. Together we were moving on.

Chapter Five

ELLIE

I hated to admit it, but Cassie was right. I thought returning to an accident and emergency department would be hard for me, but I was loving every minute of it. My colleagues were mostly great. I'd made some really good friends. There were a couple of people I struggled with. I often thought of sinking my fist in to their pretty faces, but I'd always prided myself on my professionalism and I wasn't going to rock the boat now. Cassie had hooked up with a doctor, and I couldn't be any more pleased for her. Although, he didn't seem to be her usual type—rough around the edges—he genuinely seemed to be a nice guy. Unfortunately, this meant she kept pointing out single guys at the hospital whether they worked there or not. She meant well, but I still wasn't ready to make that last and final step.

I shoved my things in my locker. It was the end of a long dayshift, and I was eager to get home and sink into a nice hot bath. My hip was playing up, and all I wanted to do was get off my feet.

"Sheesh, my feet bloody hurt." Paulie came crashing through the locker room door and sat down. Taking off her shoes, she started rubbing the soles of her feet. "Remind me to not wear these bloody things ever again. Comfort should seriously take precedence over style. I am a fucking moron if I thought these shoes would get me a date with Dr. H.O.T."

I laughed. She was just as bad as Cassie when it came to needing a guy on her elbow. She was fresh out of training and an absolute hoot. She made it very clear from the start the only reason she got into nursing was because she had every intention of snagging herself a rich doctor. Right now, she had her eye on a new intern.

"You should have taken my advice, hun. You could be wearing killer hooker heels and it wouldn't have made a lot of difference."

"Trish has legs up to her neck and huge boobs. I may have the boobs, but he looks like a leg man to me, so I figured I'd try and make myself taller."

I laughed even harder. Like me, Paulie was vertically challenged, but unlike me, she hated it.

"Trish has zero personality. You, on the other hand, have an abundance. Lay off the heels and charm him with your amazing sense of humour and of course… your boobs." I ducked as one the offending shoes sailed across the locker room.

"Of course you're right, as much as I hate you for it. So you want a lift home?"

"Nah, I'm good. Thanks. It's just down the road and it's a lovely evening."

My and Cassie's apartment was just across the other side of the water, surrounded by Stanley Park, and I always welcomed the walk. Come rain or shine, the park was beautiful. If it were later, though, I'd have taken her up on the ride. Like most places, it still wasn't safe to be walking the streets on your own. The areas surrounding the park were busy—numerous bars, cafés, and restaurants lined the streets, each popular in their own right and not necessarily full of nice people.

"You'll be out later, though, right? Cassie's finally free this evening, and we figured we'd hit the new place in town." Paulie slammed her locker shut and we both headed toward the door and the exit.

"Planning on staying home tonight. It's a difficult time at the moment." She nodded in understanding. I hadn't intended in telling anyone my story, but after she offloaded her life story to me one day, I divulged as much information as I was happy with. Plus, she'd seen my angel wings, which obviously attracted her attention.

It was coming upon the anniversary of Lyla Rose's "due date." *There is always a reminder.* If the accident had never happened and she was born when she was supposed to be, she would have been one. Considering my history, I wanted to avoid the temptation of drowning my sorrows. I often turned down nights out for this reason. It was also easier to become a social recluse than explain why I was drinking orange juice all night.

We stopped in our tracks just before the emergency department exit. We heard the rumbling sounds of motorbikes approaching fast before we saw them. Paulie muttered under her breath and the colour drained from her face. It was then I noticed the anxiety levels increasing in the waiting room, rolling off the patients and staff in waves.

"I need to go," Paulie stuttered and ran from the building just as the bikes rode into the ambulance bay. I made a mental note to ask her about it later.

I stood curious more than anything as I watched the motorcycle crew drive in and take over. I'd heard several stories about the local gangs and treated a few members already in the department, but I'd never witnessed such a sight. The sound of roaring engines cut abruptly and shouts eagerly took their place. A muscular tattooed man grabbed hold of a teenage boy who was clumsily slumped against an even bigger tattooed man on a different bike. The first man cradled the teenager in his arms protectively and ran toward the entrance. The other bikers followed after him. You could quite literally cut the atmosphere with a knife. Like everyone else in the room, I stood frozen, until I noticed the blood pouring from the region of the teenager's stomach, and all my training kicked into place.

"Need some fucking help here!" shouted the man holding the boy.

I grabbed the nearest empty gurney and headed

toward them. Unlike most medical dramas, nurses and doctors weren't readily available. Instead, curious bystanders crowded the area like vultures circling their prey. Thankfully, the patient came with bodyguards so the looming crowd moved back quickly. Admittedly, if I hadn't been trying to stop the blood pouring out of the poor boy's gut, I would have backed off too. These guys were scary.

"What's his name?" I asked.

"Junior," replied Mr. Tattoo.

"Okay, Junior, I'm Ellie, and you're going to be just fine."

The poor boy couldn't hear me. He'd pretty much passed out on arrival, either from loss of blood, pain, or both. With my scissors, I made quick work of his soaked red T-shirt and gasped. It wasn't a pretty sight. I was grateful when backup came in the form of Tamara, another nurse, and Dr. H.O.T.

"Gunshot. Shit, no exit wound." It was a statement rather than a question. I grabbed supplies from an abandoned trolley nearby and started packing the wound. "Was he shot anywhere else?" I asked no one in particular.

"I don't know. It happened too fast," Mr. Tattoo said, running his bloody hands through his hair. Crimson streaked his tanned face, which was gradually losing its colour. The man who held on to Junior on his bike approached cautiously.

"What the fuck do you want, Tiny?" Mr. Tattoo snapped.

Tiny? Surely I heard him wrong. The man was bloody huge, at least six feet five and twenty stone of muscle. His long dark hair was tied back in a pony and his beard was braided. Both arms were exposed and revealed two complete tattooed sleeves. The man was kind of intimidating, and Mr. Tattoo just called him Tiny. *WTF?*

"Red and Bear have headed out," he said.

"FUCK!" Mr. Tattoo hit the closest wall in temper, and I jumped. "Tell them not to fucking go there. We need to plan, but right now, I need to stay with Junior. I do not need another one of my fucking crew in here."

"Oi!" I shouted, temporarily attracting the attention of one of scariest men on the planet. "Tone it down or get the hell out."

No reply, just death glares.

"DO YOU UNDERSTAND ME?" I shouted even louder. This time I was grateful for the nod in response. The glares beforehand were frightening. I didn't want to provoke them more than necessary.

I pushed down the bile steadily creeping up my throat. Why the hell did I just shout at them? Did I have a death wish? I'd always had a fiery temper, but this usually only surfaced when I felt threatened. It was my shield. My warning for people to back the hell off. Did I feel threatened? *No.*

While the mini war in my head continued, I finished packing the wound and ran my eyes over the rest of the kid's body, searching for more injuries. Thankfully, there were none.

Happy with the temporary patch-up, James, also known as Dr. Hot, gave the all clear, and Junior was wheeled quickly to the nearest trauma room. I'd done all I could, but I followed behind and watched the scene unfold before me.

Heavy footsteps fell in close behind. Mr. Tattoo anxiously ran his hands through his short black hair, and despite the moment being highly inappropriate, everything about him had me captivated and completely gawping. Ignoring the fact blood streaked his face, he was strikingly handsome in a rugged sort of way. His features weren't perfect. He had a slight crook to his nose, which made me think it might have been broken in the past. A five o'clock shadow lined his jaw. Normally, this wouldn't do anything for me, but admittedly, he made it work. I'm an eye person, so naturally, I tried to get a look at his eyes. Turns out this was quite difficult when the person's eyes you were trying to look at weren't exactly looking in your direction.

As if sensing my ogling, he briefly turned in my direction, causing me to blush at the embarrassment of being caught. I held his stare as long as I felt comfortable, which to be honest, wasn't very long. His eyes were dark brown and so intense. For that brief moment, it felt like he had the power to look deep within my soul. They were slightly intimidating but beautiful at the same time.

When I was sure he was no longer looking, I secretly admired the rest of the view. His T-shirt hugged his heavily tattooed biceps, and every time he anxiously ran his fingers through his hair, it rose and revealed a perfectly sculpted stomach. My fingers itched to run along every contour, every line. Surely, he wasn't old enough to be the boy's father? Junior was probably about fifteen, and this guy was probably about four years older than me, but I suppose he could have become a dad early. Teenage pregnancies weren't exactly uncommon these days. Uncle? Big brother maybe? Why did I even care?

James, Tamara, and the others looked like they had everything under control, and from the looks of the monitors, Junior was stable. I looked down at my bloodstained hands and ruined clothing and sighed. I would have to clean up and go home in scrubs. It wasn't the first time and certainly wouldn't be the last.

I looked at tattoo guy and the two friends who followed him, wondering if they would cause any problems. Okay, despite their appearances and everyone's reaction when they arrived, they'd all behaved like perfect gentlemen. So why did the attitude I had from earlier resurface? Why did I feel the need to say something before I left?

"Don't cause any shit and let them do their job. That means staying out of that room no matter what you see."

Mr. Tattoo's expression looked like he didn't know whether to clench his jaw or smirk. Either way, he remained silent while he assessed me. I tried not to squirm under the heat of his stare as his eyes roamed from my face to every inch of my body, lingering on my boobs and my arse. His stare was predatory and I was his prey. It had been a long time since a man had looked at me that way, and my body reacted in ways that only told me I liked it. My heart, however, told me to run. Run from the feelings this man managed to produce with one sultry look. Run from the ache that now pierced my chest as I realised for the first time since Jake's death I'd actually dared to look at another man

Chapter Six

KYLE

Why today of all days did the fuckers break the truce? Someone was going to die for shooting Junior, but not now. Right now, my little brother was having the bullet in his stomach removed. *The bullet they put there.* Shit, this was bad. The need for revenge coursed through my veins, right down to my core. It would be so easy to gather the brothers and hit them hard, but I needed to think. I wouldn't act in haste—not this time. Acting without thinking could lead to more casualties, and I wasn't sure if I'd keep my shit together if someone else took a bullet. My father learned the hard way, and I was not my father.

"How's he doing?" I turned to my VP, my right-hand man Saint. He'd run down from the maternity ward, where I assumed he'd left his ol' lady pushing out his kid. He had a death wish if he did. Sadie had a ball chained to his ankle the moment he clapped eyes on the bitch. I only hoped he waited until the kid was born; otherwise, he might as well pull up a bed beside Junior.

"They're removing the bullet from his gut. Internal bleeding and all that shit, but he should be okay." The anger burning in his eyes reflected that of my own. Saint might not have been related to Junior by blood, but he'd known the kid since he was in diapers, and although it might be unconventional, we were all one big family.

"Saw Tiny before I came here. He called back Bear and Red. They were pissed." He clenched his fists as he fought against hitting something. "They nearly had 'em, Kyle."

I squared up to Saint and looked him straight in the eyes. "Those fuckers are mine," I said through gritted teeth.

He didn't need to reply. His grim expression told me he understood.

I sat in the family room on my own. Saint had gone back upstairs to see Sadie and his new daughter Saige. I sent the others back to the club. I didn't want company. I was stewing in a whirlpool of emotions, ready to explode. I felt sorry for the fucker who got in my way.

The day had started out to be a good one. We'd enjoyed a few beers and barbecue on the beach, lapping up the glorious summer sun as we engaged in some good old banter and trips down memory lane. It was our first ride out as a club for months and for good reason. Today we celebrated the first anniversary of my dad's death. A year ago, he acted in haste and paid with his life, but even though his death tore me to pieces, I knew he wouldn't have wanted to go any other way. The club was his life. He might have been full of holes, but the old man went out smiling.

We were heading back to the club when shots started firing. Everything happened so quickly I didn't even see any other bikes. As soon as Junior went down, I lost all reasonable train of thought. Rage consumed me as he fell from the back of my bike. If it weren't for Tiny grabbing him from the dirt and getting him on his bike, he would have probably bled out with me standing there like a fucking idiot. Now I was consumed by guilt. Why didn't I get to him sooner? Was I so fucked up I could only see rage instead of seeing my own brother needed me? With Dad dead and a mom who fucked off years ago, I was all he had left, and I just stood there like the shit I am.

I ran my hands through my hair and inwardly screamed at my cowardice. I had to use my brain rather than jump straight to thoughts of rage and violence.

I needed to learn control. Like the bitch who commanded the emergency room when we ran, all guns blazing, into the hospital. At first, she stood frozen, taking it all in as we roared into the ambulance bay on our Harleys. I could understand why she would be afraid. We had a rep, and even if we didn't, I was pretty sure the sight would have been daunting in itself. I didn't see any evidence of fear in her eyes, though, just curiosity. And then out of nowhere, a spark ignited, as if a switch had just been turned on and she'd come alive that very moment. As soon as she spotted Junior, she grabbed that gurney and wheeled it like a pro. Not once did she hesitate as she ripped open his shirt and packed the wound. Even when backup arrived, she continued to treat Junior until she was happy they could take over.

Then, when she'd overheard our conversation, she shot Tiny and me down in flames like we were misbehaving toddlers. She shot ME down. It had been a long time since anyone had even had the audacity to try. I'd like to say I was too wrapped up in what was going on and I didn't notice, but I did. And if I'm honest, it didn't wind me up like it should have. It was refreshing. Her lack of fear, her bravery, confidence—whatever you want to call it—was like a breath of fresh air. I was fed up with the way people looked at me all the time, the way people walked on eggshells, concerned I would slit their throat or plant a bullet in their head for talking. It was nice to be treated like a human again.

I followed her when Junior was wheeled to the trauma room, not solely because that's where my brother was going, but because I was curious to see what she did next. I wondered if she even noticed I was there. Someone like her wouldn't normally bother to look at someone like me, so catching her giving me the onceover stirred the animal inside. I caught her eye and held her gaze in a secret challenge. She held my attention longer than most before dropping it to the floor, a blush rising up her cheeks.

She was feisty for sure, but I sensed there was much more to this little firecracker than met the eye. There was something fragile about her. Broken.

My attention returned to Junior and, for a brief second, all my thoughts focused on him, until the little firecracker spun her tiny body with such ferocity she nearly had me landing on my ass. With absolutely no resolve, she laid out her instructions, loud and clear. I didn't know whether to be pissed or laugh, but overall, I found her confidence sexy as hell. The animal inside stirred once more as my eyes travelled over her perfect little body. She was tiny. I could probably wrap both hands around her waist, but she was most definitely filled out in all the right places. Her hair was a silky black, tied haphazardly on top of her head, a few loose strands framing her delicate, pale face, and all I could think about in that moment was yanking the rest free and giving my fingers free rein.

"Kyle Slater?"

I snapped out of my thoughts and focused on the young doctor calling my name. The poor guy looked like he was going to shit himself. Any other day, this reaction would satisfy me, but today, I couldn't care less. I nodded in answer, and he anxiously walked closer.

"We removed the bullet without complications. Junior lost a lot of blood, but he'll be fine. He was incredibly lucky."

The tension I didn't know I was holding released from my shoulders slowly, and I stood to shake the good doctor's hand, but he didn't take it. The nervousness in his face had me stepping back, my shoulders instantly tense again. He wasn't finished. I sensed a *but* coming.

"Spit it out, doc," I snapped.

"It was a complicated surgery and he'll be in the hospital for a little while to recover, but we're concerned about where he'll be going when he's released. He'll need a lot of care once he's home, and…"

Shit! I knew where this conversation was heading and I didn't like it one fucking bit.

"He'll be coming home with me and I'll be the one looking after him," I grated out, not giving him the chance to finish.

"Do you think it's wise considering your… your, um… lifestyle? I mean, look at the circumstances that led him here to begin with. It's not right for a child to be caught up in your activities." *Activities?* "I understand your father passed away and your mother left. Unfortunately, we've had to notify family services, and the police want to talk to you about the incident."

In one stride, I stood jaw to jaw with the man who just probably saved my brother's life. That was the only reason he was still standing. I might be a lot of things, but my father taught me respect and honour. The doc did right by me, so by rights, I owed him, but he was treading a very thin, dangerous line.

"He'll be coming home with me. To. Our. House. I'll look after him, and if I can't do it because I'm at the club, a very good friend of mine will stay at our house or he'll go stay with her. She's like a mother to us anyway. So, doc, Junior comes home with me.

You got that?"

"Yes, Mr Slater, I understand perfectly, but the police and family services still want to talk to you. Now, have I made *myself* clear?"

I'll be damned. The young doctor had some balls after all. I shouldered past him and stood still at the family room door when he didn't follow. He stood straight and adjusted his white coat before walking in my direction.

I pushed the door open so he could walk out first. "Lead the fucking way."

Chapter Seven

ELLIE

Lyla Rose's official due date would have been in two days, two years ago, and needless to say, I wasn't my normal self. She was all I could think about. If I were in England, I would have visited her grave, but no, I'd decided to run away. Today, her memory and my photos just didn't seem enough. I thought I was over the self-pity, but apparently, I was wrong. The temptation to have a drink was killing me. I'd just finished a shift, and like usual, Paulie joined me in the locker room.

"Ready to head out?" she asked, slamming her locker shut.

"Not yet. Going to head up to the kids ward and check on Junior," I replied. Two days had passed since the incident, and Junior was apparently doing well, but something at the back of my brain was nagging for me to go see him.

Paulie sighed. "I don't think that's a good idea, Ellie. You need to steer clear from that lot. You don't want to get caught up in all that shit."

"Is that why you legged it?" I asked. I'm the last person to judge, so I kept my tone light, but I was curious.

"I grew up with a couple of the crew and I just didn't want to see them. Last time I saw Bear, it didn't go too well. I'm trying to move on from that part of my life."

Fair enough. I nodded, not needing to add to the conversation, and we said our good-byes.

I headed up to the children's ward and then made my way to the nurse's station. I could hear Estelle belting out a laugh before I even saw her. She was a large black lady in her fifties and one of the nicest people I'd ever met. She was a regular in the emergency department when the youngsters came in, always wanting to make their trip up to the ward as easy as possible. The fear in their eyes would evaporate the instant she started to sing. She had the voice of an angel. Despite my usual musical tastes, I could listen to her all day.

"Hey there, sugar. What you doing up here, girl?" She pulled me in for a squeeze, and I laughed as she nearly choked the life out of me with her breasts.

"Hi, Estelle. Just thought I'd check on Junior. The kid with the gunshot wound," I said, still readjusting my clothes after she released me.

"He's doing just fine, sugar. Quiet little soul, but then I would be too if I had all those big burly men rock up every five minutes. They cuss like I've never heard in my life and look scary as hell, but teddy bears all of them. The way they look after that kid, you'd think they were all family."

Teddy bears. Not quite sure that's how I would describe them, but what did I know?

"Anyone with him now?" A feeling of unease settled in my stomach. I was confused about how I wanted her to answer. Did I want to run into them, or more specifically *him*, again? For two whole days, my mind had played tug-of-war between thinking about Lyla Rose and those intense brown eyes and intricate tattoos covering perfectly sculpted arms attached to an equally perfect body. As his image came to mind, guilt consumed me once again, and I quickly quashed my thoughts.

"Nah, sugar, he's alone, but no doubt that brother will be back soon. Family services was sticking their noses in, so he's a bit overprotective."

I smiled and headed to Junior's room, indeed feeling disappointed he didn't have company.

I poked my head around the door of Junior's private room. Due to his age and probably his "family," they didn't want to place him in an open ward with other children. Arms folded behind his head, he watched some action film on TV, absorbed in violence and bloodshed. I wondered if the staff knew he probably wasn't watching an age-appropriate film and then silently laughed at the ridiculous thought. The kid came in with a gunshot wound. An adult-rated film was probably nothing he hadn't witnessed in real life.

"Hey, Junior, how are you?" I asked.

He turned in my direction and gave me a hesitant smile. His eyes turned cold as he eyed me from head to toe cautiously. It hadn't even crossed my mind he wouldn't recognise me, let alone welcome me with open arms.

Waiting patiently to be invited farther into his room, I glimpsed a tattoo of a Celtic cross on the inside of his left arm. He sat up straighter and crossed his arms across his chest, raising his chin in a challenge. I recognised the defensive stance as one of my own and smiled. No longer covered in blood and with colour in his cheeks, he was a ringer of his brother. He had the same profound brown eyes and gorgeously long eyelashes that should be illegal for a man. His brown hair was slightly longer and lighter and he was yet to grow into his body properly, but there was no denying the family connection.

"Who are you? You don't look like no social worker. What do you want?"

I didn't know whether to be offended or laugh. Not sure what social workers looked like these days, I decided to take his comment as a compliment. "Sorry, Junior. I should have introduced myself when I first popped in. You were kind of half dead when we first met, so I'm not surprised you don't know me." I stepped farther into the room and held out my hand. "I'm Ellie, one of the nurses downstairs in emergency. I treated you when you first arrived at the hospital." I smiled as he visibly relaxed and shook my hand. I pulled up a chair and threw my jacket over the back. "So how are you?"

It's amazing how a conversation with a complete stranger can temporarily remove you from the shit going on in your own life. Listening to Junior talk about the music and films he liked, the staff and other kids on the ward, and his unorthodox family was better than any counselling session with Dr. Cole. Although obviously holding back on certain aspects about his life, he spoke with ease, and I found myself truly interested in what he had to say. I think deep down, he was using me as much as I was using him. For a brief moment, we could just forget about what was going on in the real world and talk about mindless nonsense. He had a wicked sense of humour and charisma that probably charmed the pants off many a girl. He was sixteen and lived in a predominantly male environment. You didn't need to be a rocket scientist to work out he wasn't a virgin. Despite his losses, for such a young man, he was grounded and insightful, and I found myself envying the kid who grew up in a gang of bikers. It might not be a life full of hugs and kisses, but he was loved. Regardless of how he was brought up and who had done it, they'd done a good job.

I looked at my phone and saw it was time for me to head out. I'd been so engrossed in conversation I hadn't realised I'd been with Junior for nearly two hours. I stood and pulled him into a hug, gentle so as not to hurt his side, and promised I would return with ice cream. I was completely oblivious to the figure looming in the background.

"Whatcha doing, bitch?" a voice boomed from behind me.

Chapter Eight

KYLE

She practically jumped out of her skin, and it took all I had not to laugh. The death glare she levelled at me made it even harder. If looks could kill, I'd be joining my dad six feet under. She hadn't noticed, but I'd been watching her for a while from the doorway. Junior had spotted me, but I put my finger to my lips, silencing him. When she leaned in to give him a hug, jealousy crashed over me like the waves of a tsunami. Hell, my brother was just a kid, but I didn't want him touching her. It was pretty obvious he was more than happy to receive the attention. He had the perfect view of her cleavage, after all. The little shit probably thought all his Christmases had come at once.

The skintight jeans and tank she wore perfectly accentuated her tiny hourglass figure. As she moved away from the chair, I noticed the biker boots on her feet and the leather jacket she cradled like a lost puppy. The sight had me quietly intrigued. Her long black hair trailed over her naked pale shoulders like layers of silk. Could I see the tips of a tattoo across each shoulder blade? The temptation to pull her straps down and see for myself was fierce.

"Bitch? Do I look like a bloody dog to you?" she snapped.

Thoughts of running my fingers along her soft pale skin were quickly pushed aside, and I broke out in a huge grin. I hadn't noticed she was English before and had never cared much for the accent, until now.

"Not from where I'm standing, sweetheart." I sauntered into the room and grabbed Junior's medical chart from the end of his bed, desperate to have something to do with my hands. "I asked what you were doing."

"Not that it's any of your bloody business, but I was coming to check if Junior was okay. I should imagine it's quite a rough deal being shot."

Having been shot myself, she wasn't wrong. The pain's excruciating, but I decided I wasn't going to satisfy her with a reply.

"How you doing, kiddo?"

Junior smirked. The kid looked at me like he knew something I didn't. Hell, maybe he did, judging by the smug expression on his face.

"I'm good. Ellie here obviously can't resist the Slater charm," he said with a wink, causing her to blush profusely and play with the edge of her jacket. She looked at everything but me, and damn, I'd be lying if I said I didn't like her reaction.

"That right? Well, as you've got the charm of a dead fish, it must be *this* Slater she can't resist. Ain't that right, angel?" I watched as her blush deepened and she made a beeline for the door.

"What's wrong, Ellie? You don't think I'm charming?" I said, following her with my eyes. She stopped at the door and turned to look directly at me. Her cheeks were still slightly pink and she looked a little flustered, but I swear a smile was threatening. She was trying her damnedest not to turn the corners of those luscious pink lips up at the sides, but it was her big aquamarine eyes that gave her away. The mischievous twinkle in them floored me.

So she likes to play.

"Well now, Mr. Slater, Junior's got charm in abundance. You, on the other hand..." She touched her right forefinger to her chin and tilted her head as if deep in thought. That action alone had me captivated and wanting more. Finally, that smile broke free and those unusual yet beautiful eyes smiled too. "I can think of other words to describe you, and sorry, charming isn't one of them."

Junior shouted a, "Hell yeah," and she replied with a wink of her own. She looked back at me and watched as I secured Junior's medical chart back on the end of his bed. The heat from her stare burned into my flesh as she watched me take every single step toward her, my heart hammering against my chest wall.

Never in my life had I wanted to be as close to a woman as I did now. I wanted to stroke that black silky hair away from her face, run my fingers down the side of her neck, and then pull those pink plump lips to mine. Standing toe to toe, I looked down at her and watched her suck in sharp intake of breath. Her chest rose and fell as she worked hard at keeping steady breaths, but not once did she drop her eyes. As clear as a hot summer's day, she fought hard to keep control of her emotions. Fear, determination, lust flashed across her eyes, but above all else, underneath that false layer of confidence, I saw uncertainty. She was vulnerable right now but refused to back down, and I silently commended her for it.

The tension continued to bounce between us like highly charged electricity, and I was certain if I touched her skin, I'd feel the shock. I leaned down so my lips were close enough to lightly brush against her ear, but not actually touch. Her eyes twinkled mischievously and she shivered as my warm breath travelled down the naked skin of her neck. The reaction hit me hard in the pants department, and it took all I had not to push her up against the wall. Hell, if Junior weren't there, I think I would have made good use of his bed.

What the fuck is she doing to me?

"I'd be more than happy to show you how charming I can be, Ellie," I whispered.

Startling me, she flinched and took a big step back, holding her hand up against my chest. That mischievous twinkle in her eyes was gone.

"I need to go. I've got to go and check on a

delivery," she said to no one in particular. "I'll come and see you tomorrow, Junior, if that's okay?" she said, looking at my kid brother who looked just as confused as I felt. He nodded in reply. "Nice to see you again, Mr. Slater," she said, not quite looking at me.

Just like that, she dismissed whatever the hell had happened just moments before and legged it out the door, not once looking back in my direction.

"What the fuck happened there?" Junior said, snapping me out of my thoughts. The kid was too blunt for his own good.

"Just playing around, kid," I replied, still looking at the vacant doorway. Still completely unsure about what just played out in a hospital room in front of my brother. *Did I really just hit on her?* I didn't hit on women; they hit on me and served their purpose when I needed to release the tension.

"If you say so," he replied, obviously not buying my answer.

"So what did you talk about?" I asked, changing the subject. I admit I was curious too. She'd done her job. Junior was no longer her responsibility, so why did she visit? Why did I care?

"Nothin' much. First I thought she was family services. Then I figured no social worker would look like a hot biker chick. I think she genuinely just wanted to know how I was doing."

"Just watch what you say. You got that, kid? I've managed to keep family services away for the time being, so I don't want her stirring up any shit."

He nodded. "I don't think we have anything to

worry about. She was cool. We just chatted shit, you know?"

Ellie had made an impression on Junior. Little did she know the kid didn't trust easily, especially when it came to women. I couldn't blame him, not when you had a mother like ours. I could count on one hand the amount of women he'd comfortably have a conversation with. Saint's and Tiny's ol' ladies were family. They'd watched him grow up and were like sisters. But the clubs whores? He might see them regularly, but he didn't trust them. He knew to steer well clear. He knew what you saw is what you got—an easy fuck and a STD if you weren't careful.

Ellie was beautiful, but I doubted this was the reason he'd let down his guard so easily. They spoke to each other like they'd known each other for years, not hours. Junior bonding with her spoke volumes of her character, and for some unbeknownst reason, it gently tugged at my heart. Whether I liked it or not, in such a short time, she'd managed to work her way under my skin.

Chapter Nine

ELLIE

"So when is she due?" I asked the sonographer as Jake squeezed my hand.

"Let's see. Going from your dates and this scan, I would say your daughter is due August tenth."

Today was August tenth, and despite the memory of my twenty-week scan, I actually felt better than I thought I would. The temptation to have a drink was still there, but as each day passed, life became easier. I'd visited Junior a couple more times, grateful not to have bumped into Kyle again.

I was introduced to Tiny, the guy who had Junior on the back of his bike when they pulled into the ambulance bay. The guy was huge and kind of intimidating to look at, but just spending a few minutes with him had me agreeing with Estelle. *Teddy bears.*

I was pleased to hear Junior was being discharged today. I wondered whether Kyle would be the one to come and get him. Just thinking about how my body reacted to him still had me going weak at the knees, but then the memory of me abruptly stepping away shoved me straight back into reality. He was playing with me, and I'd acted like an idiot. I mean, why on earth would someone like him be interested in someone like me? I was nothing. A blip in the shadows, with so much baggage I could weigh down a plane.

I buckled up my boots, grabbed my leather jacket, and headed to my bedroom to pick up the most important part of my outfit. My helmet. As planned, Jake's black Ducati Monster 821 was parked outside my apartment when I got home from work two days ago. It was the last of the things I wanted shipped over from England, and it had taken a bloody long time to arrive.

Helmet in hand, I stepped outside and zipped up my jacket. The temperatures might have been soaring, but there was no way I was getting on the bike without the protection of my leathers and helmet. I'd seen the result of too many accidents to ever justify riding without them. Jake had taught me to ride, and as much as I loved sitting behind him, it was nothing compared to the freedom and rush from riding alone. Today of all days, I wanted to experience that freedom. The rush that confirms against the odds, I'm still alive.

I straddled the bike and fastened my helmet. Touching where the tip of Lyla Rose's angel wing tattoo would be, I said a silent prayer and kick-started the engine. The roar and the smell of exhaust fumes were intoxicating. It was like a drug.

My ride out had taken me to the English Bay. It amazed me how a place so beautiful and tranquil could be only a quick drive away from the hustle and bustle of the city. I found a secluded part of the beach and rolled my bike to a stop. I took off my helmet and shook my hair free. A giggle escaped my lips at my lame imitation of one of those dodgy hair commercials. I stripped off my jacket, threw it over the bike, and wandered over to a nearby rock pool. After taking a seat, I stared up at the bright-blue cloudless sky and listened as the waves gently lapped against the shore, the sun's heat warm against my skin.

"I miss you," I whispered into the light breeze. A flutter of black wings caught my attention from the corner of my eye. I turned fully to be greeted by a crow standing on a rock, staring at me intently. I stared back at the beautiful bird.

"Hello there," I said, watching as it tilted its head, still carefully watching me. "You are beautiful, aren't you?" It hopped closer, but I remained perfectly still, not wanting to chase it away. It tilted its head to the other side and let out a squawk. The blue tint in the black of its feathers glistened in the sun as it expanded its wings and took flight. It wasn't like I was superstitious or anything, but a sense of uneasiness settled in my stomach. *The crow—an omen for change.*

I spent the next hour watching children play in the sand and holidaymakers swim in the crystal-clear waters, trying not to think of anything but relaxing and getting through the rest of the day without any drama. I went for a quick wander along the beach to clear my head before getting back on my bike and heading toward North Vancouver, where I rode at a leisurely pace and drank in the tranquil mountainous scenery. I was living thousands of miles away from my family, in a completely different country, yet I'd never felt more at home.

The traffic on the way back to the apartment was horrendous. Cars backed up as far as the eye could see, but thankfully, I could zip through the middle on my bike. I slowed down my approach as flashes of blue lights ahead caught my attention. Goose bumps surfaced under the fabric of my clothes, my unease bubbling in the pit of my stomach, but I sped up and headed toward the scene.

Bile rose up my throat as soon as I saw the truck jack-knifed across the road and something that should have looked like a car sticking out from under the trailer. The need to vomit was relentless, but I pushed it down, got off the bike, and removed my helmet. Flashbacks of the accident, *my* accident, played in the forefront of my mind like a movie rolling in slow motion. Distant sobs, the sound of a saw cutting through metal, and fire officers and ambulance crew shouting demands at each other echoed around the suppressed air. I was reliving my own personal nightmare, except this time I was the bystander, looking on as the tragic scene unfolded before my eyes. Swallowing hard, I straightened my jacket and ran to the nearest member of the ambulance crew. This time I would be able to help.

The driver of the truck had died of a heart attack at the wheel. According to the police officers on scene, it looked like he'd tried with all his might to avoid hitting oncoming traffic, but unfortunately, as soon as his heart stopped beating, all control was lost and the lorry jack-knifed, completely taking out the oncoming vehicle. I have no idea how, but the young mother driving the car and her three-year-old daughter survived with minimal injuries. I wasn't religious, but I thanked whoever was looking out for them. I knew only too well the outcome could have been a lot different. Adrenaline still pumped through my veins, and I felt as edgy as hell as the ambulance finally pulled away. I said my farewells to the remaining police officers and got back on my bike.

Now dark, I headed toward home, but as I rode along an almost deserted highway, the neon signs of a bar had me pulling into the car park like a moth drawn to a flame. A line of Harleys bordered the edge of the car park, near the entrance. Maybe alarm bells should have kicked in at this point, or maybe I just ignored them. I needed to clean up anyway, didn't I? *Who am I kidding?*

I parked my bike and, without a moment's hesitation, walked confidently through the door. Heads turned and the punters went quiet. I felt like I was in one of those dodgy western movies and half expected people to clear their tables just before shots started firing, but thankfully, everyone returned to their chatter, ignoring the girl with blood on her hands. I saw the sign for the toilets and quickly walked in that direction.

Kicking open the door and shutting it firmly behind me, I made my way to the mirror and stared at myself between the cracks. I looked a mess. No wonder everyone stared as I walked in. I had blood smeared down my right cheek and my hair was matted. I looked down at my bloody hands. I turned on the tap and scrubbed the blood off my face and hands until my skin was raw. I then attempted to finger-comb my hair. It was the best I could do considering the circumstances. Head held high, I walked out of the toilets and headed to the bar. Sobriety be damned, I needed a drink.

"What's a pretty little thing like you doin' in a place like this?"

I raised an eyebrow, a witty comeback on the tip of my tongue, but I thought better of it. The guy might have been older than my dad, but he was bigger than a house, and I didn't feel up to the challenge.

"Tequila, please," I asked, choosing to ignore his comment.

He grabbed a shot glass from under the bar and clutched a bottle of tequila. As soon as he finished pouring, I slammed some money on the bar and downed the shot, smacking my lips together and savouring the familiar burn as the soft liquid lined my throat and warmed my belly.

"Another."

He refilled my glass, and I downed that too.

"Go easy on those, kid. It's not a safe place for

you to be, and it's better for you to have a clear head."

Looking at him more closely, I realised he was genuinely looking out for me. He had a kindness in his eyes that contradicted his overall appearance. I didn't have to be a genius to know he was probably the proud owner of one of those Harleys outside. The clothes, tats, and beard screamed biker, not that it was a bad thing, but in this neck of the woods, I was warned to be careful.

"What's your name?" I asked as I raised my glass to signal for another.

"Slade." He once again refilled my glass, eyeing me curiously.

"Well, Slade, I'm a big girl, and all I'm after is a quick, quiet drink. It's been a long day. What do you say? One more for the road!" In one flick of the wrist, I drank the shot down and slammed the empty glass back on the bar, welcoming the buzz as the alcohol worked through my system.

Several shots later...

"Oh! Oh! Oh! I bloody love this song!" I squealed as Seether's "Remedy" blared out of the speakers of the dimly lit bar. I jumped, or should I say fell, from my stool and had my own little party. Much to the annoyance of the male population of the bar (mainly bikers) and the satisfaction of the whores trying (not very hard) to fornicate with them, Slade made sure I was safe from wandering hands. He wasn't as scary as he looked, or at least he wasn't to me. The glares he gave anyone who dared approach would have me cowering behind the nearest table.

The song finished, and still feeling the effects of

the tequila, I crawled back onto my stool. I would have to call Cassie to come and get me and pick up my bike in the morning. *Shit!* I winced when I realised she wasn't going to be most pleased about having to bail me out once again. I pulled my phone from my pocket.

"Shit," I hissed. Slade was there in an instant. "Phone's dead," I said, still looking at the blank screen, hoping it was miraculously going to revive.

"There's one out back. You can use that." He nodded in the same direction as the toilets. "How'd you get here anyhow?" he asked.

I kicked my booted feet up on the bar, nearly falling backwards in the process, and held up my leather jacket. "I flew!"

"Just 'cause you're wearing the gear doesn't mean you rolled up here on a bike." He laughed at my pissed-off expression. "Okay, you came by bike. I'll take care of it for you when your friend gets here to pick you up. Okay?"

"Thanks, Slade. You are my new BFF." I grinned like the drunken fool I was, and he shook his head, his chest shaking in a silent chuckle. I looked toward the direction of the phone and silently cried. I was pretty certain my jelly legs weren't going to support me long enough to get to the other side of the room. The front door was much closer. "I'll get a bit of fresh air first."

Slade nodded and headed toward a familiar hulk of a man at the other end of the bar. My drunk mind tried to place him. *Tiny?* I giggled. If it were really him, there was nothing "tiny" about him... unless... I shuffled off my stool and headed toward the door, feeling eyes watch me all the way.

"Oh God." The fresh air hit me, and I lost the ability to stand. It was a feeling I was once all too familiar with. My legs crumbled beneath me and I landed heavily on the concrete floor. "Fuck. That's going to bruise," I said to thin air. I tried to sit myself back up, but suddenly overcome by nausea, I decided to lie back down on the cool ground. I just wanted to close my eyes… just for a second. The coolness of the concrete was strangely comforting. I would lie down for a little bit. Just until the urge to puke up my stomach contents passed.

The roar of approaching engines wasn't even enough to have me open my eyes. The engines shut off, and I could hear the sound of approaching footsteps, but I was past caring. Whoever it was could just fuck off and leave me to die in a pool of my own vomit. Besides, it was what I deserved. Jake, Cassie, dear old Mum, even Lyla Rose would be so disappointed in me. I'd fallen off the wagon *again*.

"What the fuck!" The familiar sound of his voice had my eyes snapping open and me sitting up quickly, but unfortunately, my body had other ideas. I didn't even get the chance to focus on the face in front of me before I fell back down and succumbed to the darkness.

Chapter Ten

ELLIE

Jake reached over and placed his palm on my swollen belly, his grin stretched from ear to ear. I grabbed his hand and gave it a gentle squeeze.

"We're taking you to see the horses in the new forest, baby girl," he said, speaking to our unborn daughter, Lyla Rose.

"And the cows with those big nasty horns," I added. We both laughed, remembering our early morning visitor during a camping trip the year before. He placed his hand back on the steering wheel of our new Range Rover. Now that I was carrying precious cargo, the Monster stayed in the garage.

We drove in comfortable silence, my eyes becoming heavier as I watched the world go by from the passenger *window. I was lost in the thoughts of my new life when Jake slammed on the brakes and the seatbelt tightened across my shoulders and stomach, locking me in place. He turned the wheel, but the steering locked, and as if in slow motion, we cruised toward the side of the artic lorry jack-knifed across the road. I screamed...*

I woke from my nightmare still screaming, and as usual, I was alone. A T-shirt I didn't recognise clung to my damp skin, and then a pain so intense ripped through my skull, causing me curl up clutching my head and close my eyes. When the sharp pain receded, I was left with a constant ache, but I opened my eyes, mainly because I had no idea where I was. I pulled my knees along with the black satin sheets from the king-sized bed up to my chin as I looked around the room for my clothes. I glimpsed the sun shining through a gap between dark curtains, but without seeing a clock, I couldn't tell what time it was. I felt sick to my stomach thinking about my obvious sleepover.

Well done, Ellie. You've outdone yourself this time.

The room itself was large and bleak, with dark walls and minimal furnishings. A large sound system sat in the corner between two cabinets piled high with CDs. I spotted a pile of towels and my clothes folded neatly on a chair next to a door, which I assumed to be the bathroom.

Conscious that I was in an unfamiliar room, I tried to recap the events of the day before. I remembered the beach, the crow, my scenic ride, and then the accident on the way home. I then remembered the overwhelming draw to the neon lights of the bar, chatting with Slade, and several shots of tequila. The night then became kind of vague after that.

I crawled out of bed, head pounding, and slowly walked to the bathroom. I grabbed my clothes from the chair, deciding to leave the towels. I would shower when I got home. My immediate concern was leaving quickly and, with any luck, quietly. Unfortunately, my body had other ideas as bile rose up my throat and my walk turned into a jog. Only just making it, I hugged the loo and threw up what was left of my stomach lining, like always, making enough noise to wake the dead. More flashes of the evening appeared, and I groaned loudly. If memory served me right, I'd already made friends with this toilet during the night and someone had graciously held back my hair. It was the memory of who was holding back my hair that had me cradling the loo once more. If only purging my stomach contents could erase memories too.

"Oh. My. God," I whispered as the rest of the night unfolded.

I remembered dancing solo, Slade glaring at anyone who dared speak to me, my phone dying, and then heading outside for a breath of fresh air. I remembered lying on the floor outside the bar as I struggled to keep my eyes open and those strong hands picking me up and carrying me inside before I successfully passed out. I wasn't sure how long I was out, but memories of me being sick as he held back my hair and allowed me to sob against his warm, solid chest swirled around my foggy brain. Every now and then, he would gently stroke his hand up and down my back to comfort me, and I would cry harder.

Oh my God, I had been a mess. Yet he stayed and looked after me. The intimidating, tattooed hulk of a man who'd been a feature of many of my recent dreams had kept me safe and looked after me. I should have been jumping up and down for joy, but I'd never felt so ashamed of myself.

I stripped off the T-shirt, not wishing to remember how I got it on in the first place, and threw on my own clothes. They were crumbled but didn't look too bad. At least I hadn't puked on them. I looked in the mirror and cringed at the sight before me. I'd certainly looked better. My mascara had left nice snail trails down my pale cheeks and my eyes were red and bloodshot. My hair was so matted finger-combing wasn't going to be successful, so I pulled it into a messy bun—messy being a major understatement. I was grateful I never left home without a hair band secured around my wrist. Filling the sink with warm water, I quickly washed my face.

I left the bathroom and found my boots under the bed. Hurrying to put them on, I stumbled and nearly face-planted the floor. *Should I drive?* Maybe I was still drunk. I probably shouldn't have even contemplated getting on my bike, but apart from the headache, I really did feel fine, and to be honest, I didn't have much choice.

Quiet voices and movement behind the bedroom door had me freezing in place. *So much for escaping unnoticed.* Like a deer caught in headlights, I stared at the door and didn't move a muscle. I hadn't realised I was even holding my breath until Junior walked in with a glass of water and what I assumed to be two little white pills.

"Hey, you're awake," he said, stating the obvious. "Headache?"

I nodded and he handed me the water and aspirin like it was an everyday occurrence for me to be standing in front of him like a statue. I popped them both on my tongue and swallowed them down with a large gulp of water. He sat on the chair, moving the towels to the floor. I still stood in the middle of the room, watching him like a hawk.

"So… last night you were pretty wasted."

"Yeah." I looked everywhere but his face and then settled on a spot on the floor. Finding the courage, I looked at him and was surprised to see nothing but a friendly face. "How are you doing?" I asked, finally taking a seat on the edge of the bed.

"Stiff and stomach hurts like a bitch, but I'm good," he replied. His expression changed as he stared at me intently. He looked like he wanted to say something but didn't quite know how.

The silence was awkward, but I'd been in worse situations. Last night, for instance. I dismissed it, not really wanting to know what he was thinking. I had a feeling knowing would only make me feel worse, not better.

"I'm glad you're doing okay. You look well at least. So do you live here?" I asked, curiosity getting the better of me. I couldn't escape unnoticed anymore, so I figured I might as well get some answers.

"Nah. Just stayed here last night because somethin' kinda came up." He smirked, and I blushed.

"Me."

"Don't worry, Ellie. You're not the first pissed-up bitch I've ever seen and pretty sure you ain't gonna be the last."

"Oi, watch your mouth," I snapped. Who did he think he was calling me a bitch!

He held up his hands in surrender. "Whoa, Ellie. Was just stating a fact."

I crossed my arms across my chest and looked every bit the child I was behaving like. "Is this Kyle's room?"

"Yeah, but don't worry. He slept in Saint's room with me 'cause we couldn't go back to the house with you being here." I couldn't recall sleeping with Kyle, but I was silently grateful Junior had answered my unspoken question. "Trix, Tiny's ol' lady, helped dress you. She thought you might be more comfortable in just a tee."

"Great," I said, embarrassed. "It's been a long time since someone's mother has changed me."

He laughed like I'd said something incredibly funny.

"What!"

"Trix ain't Tiny's mother," he said between belts of laughter. "You better never let her hear you call her that! She'd lay you the fuck out."

"You said 'old lady.' Where I come from, my 'old man' is my father, so I guessed it would have the same meaning." I huffed. I wasn't used to having such chirpy company when I had a hangover. It seemed I was extra grouchy.

"Sorry, Ellie. Where I come from, 'old lady' means she's his missus."

Realisation dawned on me and I felt like a fool. I mean, I'd read enough MC novels and, of course, there was always *Sons of Anarchy*.

"Right." Not the best of comebacks I must admit, but my head still hurt and this wasn't helping me with the awkward conversation I was having with a teenager. Granted, a teenager I could normally have a decent conversation with, but a teenager all the same.

I got up from the bed and zipped up my jacket. "I'd better go. Cassie will be worried," I said as I reached the door. With a smirk on his face, Junior watched me from the chair he was still sitting on. "Thanks, Junior. Sorry about last night. You look after yourself, okay. Make sure you keep out of trouble. I don't want to have to pull any more bullets out of you."

"I'll be fine, Ellie. Don't worry about me. I'll be seeing you soon, preferably not at the hospital," he said, still smirking.

"Sure." I returned his smile. "Can you please say thanks to Kyle for me too for… you know?"

"That's all right, Ellie. You can tell him yourself. He's just outside."

"Oh. Okay. Outside where?" I replied cautiously.

"Out front. He's putting your bike on Saint's truck."

Chapter Eleven

KYLE

I heard her before I saw her, and smiled.

"GET MY FUCKING BIKE OFF OF THAT TRUCK NOW!" she screamed. I continued to fasten the chain without looking at her. "Now, Kyle," she said, much quieter this time but with just as much venom behind her words.

I glanced over my shoulder and grinned wider. She looked as cute as hell standing there with her hands on her hips, glaring daggers at me. Her hair was a mess, her eyes red and shot to pieces, but she was the most fucking beautiful thing I'd ever seen.

"I'm driving you home." I tugged the chain to make sure the bike was secure. Putting on my game face, I sauntered over to where she stood with as much arrogance as I could muster, wondering if she would back down or shoot me down like a spitfire. I was guessing she'd do the latter and smiled when her eyes narrowed and her hand started waving animatedly in front of her face.

"Like hell you are! Who the fuck do you think you are, touching my bike and mouthing off your orders?"

I stopped in front of her, but not close enough to invade her personal space. Her face was red with anger and the way her hand flew all over the place while she fisted the other, I figured it was better to keep some distance.

"I'm only going to say this one more time, Kyle, so make sure you listen to me carefully." She stepped forward confidently, getting in my personal space. Hell, I just wanted to pull her in and taste her. "GET MY FUCKING BIKE OFF THE BACK OF THAT TRUCK BEFORE I RIP YOUR FUCKING BALLS OFF!" she screamed.

The way she'd just spoken to me... I'd killed people for less, but instead of losing my shit, I laughed. Damn, she had everyone laughing. Trix was laughing so hard she was clutching onto Tiny to keep from pissing herself. Bear even smiled, and he was normally a moody son of a bitch. I hadn't realised it, but our little discussion had attracted a crowd.

What the hell is she doing to me?

I felt it better to ignore them. They were already looking at me like I was appearing in some sort of freak show. Yes, I was smiling. The crazy bitch in front of me had that effect on me.

"Not happening, angel. Now get that ass of yours in the truck," I said, walking back toward the driver's side. She didn't budge. "I mean it, Ellie. Get in the fuckin' truck," I said, losing my smile. Apparently, even with her, I only had so much patience.

"No."

I stopped in my tracks and faced her, impatience evident in my face. She straightened a little, some of her confidence evaporating. Legs parted, she stood with her feet firmly planted on the ground and her arms tightly folded across her chest. It was a pure act of defiance, and the blood rushed from my brain to my dick. Her challenge was majorly turning me on. Already battling the bulge appearing in my pants, I raked in my bottom lip with my teeth and let out a hissed breath. As she stood there smouldering in her own rage, I was instantly drawn to her tits as she involuntarily pushed them together, nearly toppling them out of her tank. *Fuck.* After dropping her home, I seriously needed to get back and take care of what was stirring down below. Without another second's thought, I marched toward her, grabbed her by the waist, and threw her over my shoulder, enjoying a bit too much the way she sounded as she screamed out my name.

"PUT ME THE FUCK DOWN, YOU SHITHEAD!" she shouted while kicking and hitting me in the back. I tightened my grip and walked faster to the truck without saying a word. Once I had the passenger door opened, I chucked her inside and slammed it shut.

The bitch was driving me crazy in more ways

than one. She had me laughing, smiling, and driving her home, for fuck's sake! Since seeing her at the hospital, she was all I thought about, and when Tiny phoned to say she was at the club, drunk off her ass, I knew I had to get there. I knew what went down at the club, and there was no way any of those dirty fuckers were going to lay a single hand on her.

Tiny and Slade agreed to watch over her until I arrived. Seeing her practically passed out on the ground pissed me off. She was so gone anyone could have taken advantage of her. How could she be so stupid? What the hell was she doing getting wasted at the club anyhow?

I scooped her up and took her straight to my room. *My* room. I laid her on my bed, then shrugged off her boots and jacket. There was a new bike in the parking lot, and I guessed it was hers. It was a powerful bike, and fuck me, the thought of her gripping hold of that machine between her thighs made me hard.

I watched as she tossed and turned under my sheets, wondering what she was dreaming about to cause the small beads of sweat on her forehead. The next thing I knew, she woke up screaming before running to the toilet to puke up her guts as I held back her hair. Me, holding back some bitch's hair. *What the hell?*

In between the puking, she cried hard. My heart ached as she sobbed relentlessly and spoke about her late husband Jake. I didn't think she intended to tell me anything, but as she cried, she poured out her heart and soul. Not everything she said made sense, but I guessed she must have helped out at the accident I'd heard about earlier. Slade mentioned she'd walked in with blood on her hands and face, but he thought nothing of it at the time. That's the thing with the club. Fucked-up things like that are a daily occurrence, so it wouldn't have sparked any real interest.

As I held her in my arms, without revealing too much flesh, I gently pulled down her straps so I could look at the tattoo across her shoulder blades. I saw Jake's name inscribed in one wing and the name Lyla Rose inscribed in the other. I didn't know who Lyla Rose was, but I guessed she was another person she'd loved and lost.

When she finally calmed down, I got Trix to help her get changed. Then, for about an hour, I watched her sleep. The unfamiliar need to protect her surged through me, right down to the marrow of my bones. She looked so peaceful lying there in my bed. She looked like a fucking angel. I squeezed my eyes closed, trying to shut out the foreign emotions I was experiencing. This wasn't me. I didn't do this kind of shit. People were scared of me because I showed *no* emotion, and now I was smiling like a kid getting a shiny new bike and laughing at lame jokes.

I jumped up and headed back to the bar without glancing back. I wanted a drink and I needed to get laid. The first came easy. The second did not. All I could think about was the beautiful mess of a girl sprawled out in my bed.

I shifted uncomfortably in my seat of the truck as I remembered the night before.

In complete silence, we headed downtown. She refused to tell me where she lived, so I grabbed her purse and found her driver's license. She didn't protest. She'd stuck her feet on the dashboard and looked out the passenger window, looking completely vacant. Never having driven a girl home before—because, let's face it, I've always been a selfish dick—I felt completely lost as to what to say or do. Her feisty attitude was long gone, replaced by one of abandonment. It made me nervous.

"You going to be okay?" I asked, breaking the silence.

"Uh?" She blinked and looked at me like she'd forgotten I was there.

"Are you going to be okay? Is there anyone at home?"

"I live with my friend Cassie. She should be home."

Knowing she wouldn't be alone made me feel slightly better, but I still couldn't shake the feeling of wanting to look after her.

"Thanks for the lift, but I could have gotten home by myself, you know," she said just above a whisper.

"Doubt it. You're probably still over the limit." That was the truth. Slade had told me she'd practically downed a whole bottle of tequila. Considering how small she was, I was surprised she even managed to get outside before passing out. "So why such a big bike?" I asked, genuinely interested and changing the subject. I got the feeling she didn't want to rehash the events that led to her sitting beside me as I drove her home.

"It's just a bike," she replied, returning her attention to the world as it passed by the passenger window, ending the conversation and subsequently putting an end to my curiosity. For now.

When we pulled up outside her apartment, she jumped out of the truck before I'd even turned off the engine. As I stepped out of the truck, a busty blond ran out of the apartment. Nearly knocking her off her feet, she pulled Ellie into a tight hug before stepping away. Her face went from relief to anger in a second flat. The blonde eyed me suspiciously before ripping a strip off her friend.

"What the fuck, Els? I've been worried sick. Where the hell have you been? I nearly filed a missing persons. Shit, I nearly even called your bloody parents; I was that worried," she scolded. She looked back at me. "Sorry, but who the fuck are you?"

Ellie held her hand up protectively. That single gesture warmed my normally cold heart. "Cassie, leave him alone. This is Kyle. He… he, ah… he looked after me," Ellie stuttered.

"Oh, I bet he did," Cassie replied, still staring daggers at me.

"No, Cas. You've got it wrong. It wasn't like that." Her cheeks went red as she tried to explain. "I had a bit to drink." She continued, looking uncomfortable.

Cassie closed her eyes and sighed. When she opened them, her expression had changed from annoyance to sympathy, and she pulled Ellie in for another hug. This time she cradled her with such care you'd think she was hugging a child.

"I'm sorry, Els. I thought you were doing okay," she whispered, just loud enough for me to hear.

Leaving them to talk, I walked around to the back of the truck and unchained the bike. After rolling it down the ramp and parking it on the side of the road, I handed Ellie her keys. When she looked at me, I could see moisture glistening in her eyes. When she blinked, a single tear escaped and slowly rolled down her cheek. Without realising what I was doing, I wiped it away with my thumb.

"See you around, angel." I got back in the truck and drove away, wondering what the fuck just happened.

Chapter Twelve

ELLIE

Both in onesies and curled up on the sofa, we tucked into our single tubs of ice cream. I told Cassie what I could remember from the night before, and she went from happy to sad to pissed to sad to emotional to pissed and then to happy again without a moment's hesitation. She wasn't best pleased I'd hit the bottle again but didn't question why. That was one of the reasons we were best friends. She never needed to ask the questions; she already understood. She got emotional when I told her how Kyle had looked after me while I puked and cried into his chest. She was a bit too happy about this piece of information, probably dreaming up the possibilities of Kyle and me.

"So," she said. A small smile played on her lips and she struggled to keep it at bay.

"Spit it out, Cas." I laughed.

"Kyle. He's kinda hot." At least she was predictable.

"Really? Didn't notice." I lied. Of course I'd noticed. It was hard not to notice his bulging muscles flex as he hauled my bike off the truck. It was hard not to notice his beautiful brown eyes as they looked so intensely into mine and how he wouldn't take no for an answer about taking me home. No one had given a crap about my wellbeing in a long time.

I noticed everything about Kyle Slater. When he chucked me over his shoulder like a caveman and threw me in the truck, the only thing stopping me from jumping straight back out again was the probability my legs would have crumbled beneath me. I squeezed them together just thinking about it. And then there was the moment the world disappeared around me when his strong, calloused hands gently wiped away the stray tear I didn't even know I'd let fall.

I looked at Cas, who just grinned like an idiot. She'd seen more in those few minutes than I was comfortable with.

"You know, Els, Jake would have wanted you to be happy," she said, reducing her huge grin to a small hesitant smile.

"I know. It's just hard. I don't want to forget him. I don't want to forget Lyla Rose." I fought back the threatening tears once again. For someone who hardly ever cried, it seemed to be the only thing I did lately.

"You won't ever forget them, hun. You'll love them forever, but..." She took a moment. "They're gone. You're still here and you need to live again, Els. At the moment, you're just existing. Learning to love again won't be easy, but what's a life without love?"

I looked at my beautiful friend. I mean truly looked at her. She was naturally blond, catwalk model tall, with a figure some women would pay good money to own. She was gorgeous on the outside, but despite all the shit she'd gone through in her own life, the beauty she held within outshone her external beauty like a beacon. She lived life and she loved. A lot. No matter what crap was thrown her way, she still came up fighting and shining like the fucking star she was. She was a fighter. I wasn't, but maybe, just maybe, she was right. I think deep down I knew she was, but the thought of moving on scared the shit out of me. I wasn't sure I was ready.

"So. How're things going with Adam?" I asked, changing the subject.

Her smile lit up the room.

"Adam who?" She laughed. I sighed. She deserved to find her Jake, and maybe I did deserve to live a little too.

KYLE

Slade leaned against the bar when I walked in, chatting with Trix and Sadie. The place was otherwise empty. Not totally unusual for the middle of the afternoon, but even so, something seemed off. The big fella was my dad's best mate and the oldest member of the crew. Now he and his ol' lady Big Mamma deemed themselves "too old for this shit" and took a step from the clubs' "activities." He was happy to man the bar, the one that was open to the public, and Big Mamma, well, she was just happy to play mom to any poor soul who didn't have anyone who gave a shit.

"The boy's back home," Slade said, referring to Junior. Trix and Sadie just eyed me cautiously.

"Everyone else out back?" I questioned, meaning the club's private quarters, which played office, home, and general grounds for the Angels of Death MC.

"Yeah. Saint sent the girls out here." I knew what that meant. We had company. I popped my neck and fingers and headed out back where Red, Bear, and a few of the other brothers were eagerly awaiting me. No sign of Saint and Tiny, which meant they were already in the shed.

The scream I heard coming from the shack confirmed my suspicions. Question was, who was it that deserved the beating being dished out by my VP Saint? The sound of metal against flesh pierced through the air, causing me to smile.

"WHO THE FUCK ARE YOU!" Tiny roared. Okay, not Saint. I kicked open the wooden door, making the poor fucker chained to the chair nearly shit his pants.

Saint nodded as he stood calmly against a wall. Tiny towered over the kid, because that's all he was— a kid not much older than Junior, with a chain hanging loosely from his hand.

"What we got here?" I asked, walking over to the knife rack.

"Kid was snooping around last night at the bar. Slade thought nothing of it, but then we found him this morning, trying to get into the club. No mark. Said he would only speak to you," Saint informed me as I pulled down my favourite knife.

His face was a mess—one eye completely closed, his lip bloody, and chain marks crisscrossing his naked torso. There was no rival tattoo and nothing that screamed threat, but even in his bloody and beat-up state, he oozed arrogance. No tat didn't necessarily mean he wasn't part of a rival MC. I mean, look at Junior. Apart from the cross tattooed on his arm in memory of our father, he looked like a regular kid but was undoubtedly one of us.

I knelt before him and lazily dragged my blade against his neck, watching his Adam's apple bob up and down as he visibly gulped. *Not so arrogant now.*

"I know who shot Junior," he croaked. "But I need your word you'll hear me out."

"Go on," I said.

"It's not who you think… It wasn't the Irish." The Irish were a rival MC, also known as the Murphys. They were the ones responsible for killing my dad, which was ironically settled by calling a truce. Or so I thought.

"And how do you know that?" I said, resting the blade against his pulse.

"'Cause we weren't even here." He winced as the blade pierced his skin. He said *we*. "We were at a wake. I know you plan revenge, but it wasn't us. We have a truce and prez had no plans to break it," he rushed out.

"Why should we believe you?" asked Saint.

"They got one of ours too. We now have a common enemy and we learned something we thought you might want to know." He gulped nervously as I pushed the blade against his skin, leaving an indent, but not drawing blood. "They plan on doing something to the bitch you were seen with this morning."

This time it was me who flinched as I grasped the handle of the blade a little too tightly. He must have been referring to Ellie. I shouldn't care, but when I was with her, my thoughts and actions were hardly normal. The thought of her being hurt and being involved in this shit turned my stomach.

After getting more information from the kid, we let him go, but not without a warning. The truce would remain, but only if it was confirmed he was telling the truth. We would meet on neutral grounds should we need to, but if he or his club fucked us over, there would be war.

I headed toward my bedroom. To the room where she'd just spent the night in my bed. The bed was still unmade and her scent still lingered in the air. *Fuck.* I'd never let a bitch sleep in my bed. *Never again.*

Who was I trying to kid? She was mine. She was mine the moment I saw her, packing my kid brother's bullet wound in the middle of a hospital waiting room. She just didn't know it yet.

Chapter Thirteen

ELLIE

Three days had passed since my drunken night at the club, and no matter how much I tried, I couldn't stop thinking about Kyle. I also couldn't stop thinking about what Cassie had said. I was going to try to start living again, albeit one day at a time. I'd just finished a busy night shift but was too hyped up to go home. Sleep wouldn't have come easy to me anyway, so I jumped on my bike and headed downtown to the shop I'd been toying with entering.

The bell chimed as I walked into the tattoo parlour. An Asian girl with a full tattooed sleeve of bright exotic flowers down her right arm, face full of metal, and bright-blue short spiked hair looked up to greet me. She eyed me from head to toe whilst chewing on her lip ring before breaking into a grin.

"Virgin, right?" she asked, shocking me.

"Pardon me?" I looked down at my skinny jeans, boots, and then to my naked arms. I had left my jacket and helmet on the bike. I was just wearing a burgundy vest, but still, my outfit didn't scream virginal to me.

"First tattoo? You don't really look the sort. I dunno. You look too… cute," she said, waving her hand at me. This time I just laughed.

"No. That cherry's already been popped." I pulled back my long black hair and turned around. My top was low enough at the back so she could see my angel wings. She jumped down from the stool she was sitting on, and I silently celebrated the fact I'd finally met someone shorter than me. Who wasn't a child, of course.

"That's fuckin' smart. Funny, they have angels tattooed across their backs too." I smiled but raised an eyebrow in question. "Local MC," she answered. "The Angels of Death, except they don't just have the wings. So what you gettin' done now?" I reached into my jeans and pulled out a piece of paper. She took it out of my hand, looked at it, and grinned again. "Fuckin' A."

An hour later, I walked out of the tattoo parlour and I couldn't have been happier. As I approached my bike, I noticed a couple guys hovering around it, so I slowed down. There was something about them that made my skin crawl. I'd seen enough guys like this at the hospital. Their clothes, the way they talked all screamed gang member, but it was unusual to spot them in this neck of the woods, especially at this time of day.

"Hey there, pretty lady," one of the guys said. I could see under the hood of his jacket that he looked Hispanic. A gold tooth shone in the sun when he spoke. "Nice ride."

"It is," I said, trying to remain calm. "Now please move away. I need to leave."

"Now that's not gonna happen, *angel*," the other guy said, emphasising the word angel. He was shorter but stockier. He was white, and his nose looked like it had been smashed across his face a few times and he had cauliflower ears, reminding me of some rugby players back home. He wasn't the most attractive person I'd ever seen.

I went to step back, but Ugly adjusted his sweats, revealing a gun, successfully putting the fear of God into me. Not a single person stopped to help; they just walked on by even though the colour had completely drained from my face and I was obviously distressed.

"What do you want?" I asked, my voice breaking now. I'd started to shake but would not give them the satisfaction of seeing me scared.

Goldie nodded to the direction of a parked, blacked-out van on the other side of the road. "We're just gonna go for a ride, pretty lady." A familiar sound of roaring engines approached. "Now," he said more urgently, but I didn't move.

"ELLIE!"

Never in my life had I been so glad to hear someone shout my name. I could hear Tiny over the sound of his Harley as he and two others pulled alongside my bike. I didn't even question how he knew where I was. I was just grateful they'd arrived when they did. Surely nothing would happen now.

Goldie and Ugly looked at each other, communicating silently. Whatever they decided, it was enough to have them walking to the van.

"Another time, angel," Ugly said just as he slid open the door, but not before he swiped a finger across his neck, revealing a mouth full of missing teeth when he smiled.

I grabbed hold of my bike before I fell.

"Thank you," I said to Tiny and then the others. "I think you just saved my arse."

"Yeah, I think we did. Prez wants to speak to you," he said.

"Prez?"

"Yeah. Kyle. He wants you to come to the club."

"Ah, no. Sorry, I need to go home to sleep. I've just done a night shift and I nearly got kidnapped. Or something. I just want to go home. I need to rest and tend to this," I said, waving my newly bandaged wrist in his direction. I had absolutely no intention in going. "Maybe some other time," I said, shrugging on my jacket and grabbing my helmet from my handlebars.

"You ain't got no choice, bitch."

I flinched and swung 'round to glare at the biker with the reddest hair I'd ever seen, styled in a mohawk. He was skinny, but you could still tell he worked out. He had little in the way of ink but obviously liked his piercings. He had a run of scars lining his inner arm, but it was the sight of the metal bars running through the flesh of his right forearm that made me feel squeamish. I was pretty certain he would set metal detectors off in an airport.

"He's right, Ellie," Tiny said, shooting daggers at mohawk guy with his eyes. At least he said it with a little more compassion. "He wants you to check up on Junior, and he really won't take no for an answer."

I sighed. Truth or lie, he knew Junior would be my weakness. "That's a shit move. You know that, right?" He grinned, knowing I would be following them after all. "Fine," I said, forcing a smile.

"Good. You gonna be okay following us?" I nodded. He smiled and any animosity I'd previously felt drained away. "You'll, um... you'll just have to ignore Red. He can be a bit twitchy," he said, nodding at mohawk guy. "Oh, and this is Bear," he said, nodding at the silent blond hottie on the third bike.

I didn't realise I was gawking until Tiny cleared his throat and chuckled. *Paulie's Bear.* I had no idea why Paulie was so intent on chasing James. He might not have had a patch on Kyle, but this guy was hot.

The roar of an engine snapped me back to attention and pushed away my thoughts.

"Come on, then. Lead the way," I said before lowering my helmet.

Chapter Fourteen

KYLE

"She ain't gonna like it, Kyle. There is no way you're gonna get her to stay at the house or the club. You saw how she went bat shit crazy when you stuck her bike on the truck," Junior said, stretched across the sofa, playing with his bandage.

Big Mamma had taken good care of him at our house while I was dealing with business, but the wound was looking a bit inflamed. I'd told Tiny to use the Junior card if she didn't look like she was going to come willingly. It's not like I was lying. I was pissed his wound looked like it was getting infected but grateful it would be a good enough excuse for her to come. There was no way she would refuse if she knew she was coming to help the kid out.

"She ain't got much choice," I replied, pointing my finger in the direction of his stomach.

"Yeah right. Don't think she's not gonna see through that lame excuse either. She ain't fuckin' stupid and neither am I."

I smacked him around the back of the head and he laughed.

"Hey, prez, need me to help you unwind?" Krystal sauntered over in her porno heels, wearing little for the imagination. Her long blond hair trailed over her tanned shoulders, resting on her tits, which were barely covered by the black lace top she wore. Her skirt was so short you could probably figure out what she ate for breakfast. A few weeks ago, I would have had her pushed up against a wall, not giving a shit who saw us as she swallowed my dick. Now the thought didn't even cross my mind.

"Fuck off, Krystal. Not today."

She slowly walked around me, lazily running her fingers along the waistband of my jeans.

"Come on, prez, let me help you unwind. You didn't mind the other night," she purred.

Little did she know even though she did help me *unwind*, my thoughts weren't with her one iota. Sprawled across my desk with her ass held firmly in my hands as I pounded into her from behind, all I could think about was black silky hair balled in my fists and those big aquamarine eyes.

I pushed her away and glared until she got the message and sauntered back across the room. She had a new target in sight. Saint. Hell, the whore had a death wish.

"Get the fuck away from my man, you dirty slut." Sadie walked through the doors of the club, baby Saige strapped across her chest, looking severely pissed off. Krystal held her hands up in surrender, smirking. Sadie would happily wipe it clean off her face if she got too close.

"Hey, my gorgeous girls." Saint placed a gentle kiss on his daughter's head and then proceeded to stick his tongue down his ol' lady's throat with absolutely no shame. Getting the message, Krystal made her way back out front to the bar.

"When she getting here, then? It'll be nice to have some female company who isn't trying to get into Saint's pants," Sadie said, running her fingers through her now ruffled light-brown hair as she looked toward the door Krystal just left through. Her face was flushed and her lips were swollen after nearly being eaten alive. *No shame.*

"Only got eyes for you, babe," Saint said, freeing Saige from the baby harness and cradling her in his arms like she was the most delicate prized possession on earth. Who would have thought before he laid eyes on Sadie, he was as ruthless and cold hearted as me. Don't get me wrong, he could still be an evil son of a bitch if the need arose, and I pitied any poor fucker who threatened his family.

The door slammed open and in walked Trix. "Y'all miss me!" she hollered as she made a beeline for the baby. Big, blond, and bubbly—Tiny couldn't resist her charm the first day she strolled into the bar. Her personality was as big as her heart, and she had that in abundance. Women at the club were plentiful, but they were mainly whores—plastic and false with absolutely no dignity. Looking for a good time and eager to please. Perfect for the emotionless fuck and release of pent-up energy. Trix, Sadie, and Big Mamma were the only ol' ladies at the club.

Although Sadie had just said she was looking forward to more company, I knew she was really here to check out whether Ellie would be a threat. Her insecurities still baffled me. Saint would cut off his own dick rather than look at another woman.

Trix had already met Ellie, not that Ellie would remember it. She was keen to meet a sober Ellie, and I would guess she also wanted some answers to dampen her curiosity. That night she never asked once about the drunken girl she helped dress before helping her into my bed. For that she had my utmost respect and I was truly grateful. Mind you, even if she had asked, I wouldn't have been able to answer. I was still trying to figure that out myself.

"They're here." Junior jumped up from the sofa as the familiar sound of Tiny's, Bear's, and Red's bikes pulled up outside. A new bike pulled in moments after. My hands became clammy and my heart raced.

"Fuck me. I never thought I'd see the day." Saint walked up beside me and slapped me on the shoulder. "She's got you by the balls already, brother. Welcome to my world." He chuckled under his breath. A chorus of giggles came from Trix and Sadie behind him. Hell, even Saige let out a little noise.

Not wishing to tell him he wasn't far from the truth, I kept my face neutral. "Fuck you, brother," I replied, looking over to Junior, who mirrored the smirk on Saint's face. *Shit.* I was royally fucked.

Red quite literally bounced off the walls when he walked into the club. He was twitchy as hell, probably looking for his next fix. Normally, another cut to add to his ever-expanding display of scars. The guy had issues. He was the only person I knew who would go into a fight with the sole intention of getting hurt. I was a bit dubious about sending him for Ellie, but despite his obvious faults, he was loyal and wouldn't let any harm come to her even if it killed him. If anything, he would step into the line of fire, hoping it would.

Bear strolled in next and quietly sat down on the sofa Junior previously occupied. As usual, he looked every bit the brooding model he could be and never said anything to anyone.

Where was Ellie? A few moments later, Tiny walked in with Ellie by his side. They were laughing, and the sound of her voice had my heart hammering against the inside of my chest and my fingers itching to touch her soft skin.

Tiny walked straight over to Trix, and like Saint with Sadie, devoured her. With no baby in the way, their display of public affection made Saint and Sadie's kiss look like a PG-rated movie.

Ellie was left standing at the door with her mouth hanging wide. She looked fucking adorable. She visibly stiffened when she saw I was watching her and then looked everywhere but me. I wasn't sure how I wanted her to react, but her dismissal of me felt like a kick to the gut. I knew she wasn't like one of the club's whores—she had more dignity and class than that—but hell, I was at least expecting a hello. A smile would have been nice. As soon as she spotted Junior, the smile I was hoping to receive broke across her face, and once again, my kid brother looked like the cat who got the cream.

"Hey, Junior. How are you?" she asked in her sexy English accent. She pulled him into a quick hug, and of course, he reciprocated. "Let's have a look at your wound. Tiny said you needed me to have a look at it."

"Yeah. It's kinda red and itchy," he said, still smiling and looking at me over the top of her head, rubbing his proximity to Ellie in my face. Mind you, I would have been smiling too if I'd just been squashed up against Ellie's perfect chest.

Junior sat himself down on the edge of the sofa, and Ellie positioned herself right in front of him. Call me a sick bastard, but all I could think about was the fact that her head was level with his dick, and okay, she might have been playing nurse, but her hands were on him. Jealousy consumed me, and for the first time in my life, I wanted to kick the fuck out of my little brother because he was too close to my bitch. *Mine.* The word resonated through my skull like an echo.

She pulled up his top carefully and looked over his wound. She sighed as she gently brushed it with her fingers.

"Shit, Junior, it looks infected. I think you need antibiotics. Can you get booked in to see a doctor?" she asked while still inspecting it. "I can clean it up and dress it again, but I think you need to get that checked. If you don't, you could end up back in the hospital." She looked at him with concern shining through her eyes.

Desperate to get her alone, I pulled her up by the elbow and spun her toward me. "Fine. I'll take him tomorrow, but right now, we need to talk."

She tried to resist, but before she could say anything, I tugged her arm and practically dragged her to my room.

Chapter Fifteen

ELLIE

Less than twenty-four hours ago, I was working a night shift, and I made the decision that when I left work, my life would change… for the better. An elderly couple walked through the doors to the emergency department, and for the first time ever, I told my story. To a complete stranger. As Betty held the hand of her dying husband of sixty years, she told me hers. She'd met Albert when she was sixteen and had fallen in love, but after leaving school, he left for the army and subsequently left her behind. Four years later, fate played its hand and she met him again. When she was a nurse in the very hospital where she was now saying good-bye to him. *Fate.*

She asked me if I was married. I explained fate

wasn't so kind to me and took my husband and daughter away from me. She looked at me with sympathy in her eyes and with her other hand, grabbed hold of mine.

"Oh, sweetheart," she said. "I can't imagine to have love and lost at such a young age. Albert is my life." She stopped and wiped away a tear. "Or at least he was. I know he won't be walking out of here with me."

My eyes filled with tears, and she just squeezed my hand tighter.

"Don't cry for me, sweetheart. Albert wouldn't want you to shed any tears. We've had a good life. Sure, we had our bad times, but that just made us stronger. For as long as I live, I will remember all those times fondly. You know, you'll always remember your Jake and your Lyla Rose. Whether you decide to move on or not, they will forever be in your memories. In your heart. Albert told me when he passed, he wanted me to continue living. Not sure what the old sod expects me to do as I'm a bit past going out and partying." We both laughed.

"But here's the thing. I will do as he wishes because I love him. I will see my children, my grandchildren, and maybe even their kids grow up. It will be hard without him, but I won't give up. Now I obviously didn't know your Jake, but I suspect he was a little like my Albert. He wouldn't want you to shed any more tears, my dear. He would want you to be happy. To move on. To live. It may be an old cliché, but time really is a healer." She gave me a hug, and I left the room for her to say good-bye.

Albert died thirty minutes later, and I was left pondering over her words.

Now I stood in the bedroom of the president of the Angels of Death MC. I'd just been told that a new gang had moved to the area and were attempting to take over their patch. At first, they thought a rival MC had broken their truce and was responsible for shooting Junior. It turned out the new gang hit them first and they were at the wake of their fallen club member. The new gang wasn't an MC—not sure why this titbit of information was essential, but I kept quiet and let Kyle talk.

Apparently, they were just a bunch of amateur drug dealers trying to make it big. I must admit I laughed when he said that. Maybe it was just nerves. I mean the whole thing sounded like a poor action movie. I quickly shut up when he told me it was no laughing matter and all threats, no matter where they came from, should be taken seriously. He said it with such sincerity I just nodded, clearly not knowing what to say.

According to Kyle, they had someone checking out the club's bar the night I got wasted and then, spotting me with him the next day, guessed I was his "old lady." The whole situation was seriously fucked up, and I was living a real life nightmare once again.

I looked down at my wrist and ran my finger over the bandage covering my new tattoo. When I got it this morning, I'd intended to go home, sleep, and then wake up with a new outlook on life. This was certainly not what I had in mind.

Kyle stood staring at me, his chocolate-brown

eyes boring holes into my soul.

"No." He let out an exasperated sigh. "I will come and check on Junior as I have done so today, but I am going home, Kyle. I can't stay with you. I appreciate your looking out for me, but I don't even really know you, and let's face it, I really don't think I fit into your lifestyle." There was absolutely no way he was getting me to stay.

"Did you not hear anything I just told you? For fuck sake, Ellie, I'm not asking you to move in. It's for three days tops while we get this shit sorted."

"Oh, I heard you, but it's just ridiculous. Like I said, I don't know you. I don't know this life, and to be honest, I don't want it. I honestly thought this shit only happened in the movies. Besides, I have spent too long hiding away from the shit that has happened in my life. It's time I grew up and dealt with it like an adult." *And without alcohol.* "Okay, maybe I don't know how all this works, but surely they'll just leave me alone once they realise they made a mistake," I said calmly. Considering what Kyle had just told me, I was surprised how calm I actually was. I think maybe I was in shock. Shouldn't I have freaked out by now?

"That's fuckin' stupid and you know it. They shot Junior—a kid. Have you forgotten you were going to be shoved into the back of a truck only a couple hours ago? What do you think they were going to do, Ellie? Take you for a drive and chat about the weather? We can protect you here." The look he gave me was so fiercely protective it nearly knocked me off my feet. "I can protect you," he almost whispered.

Still trying to figure out why he was looking at me like that, I nearly missed what he said. Those four words finally made it through my ear canal and registered with my brain a few minutes later.

"Why?" I was met with silence. From the little information I knew about Kyle Slater, I knew I should have been scared of this man in front of me. He was intimidating, he was rude, and there was good reason he was prez. Yet right now, he looked vulnerable, and I was struggling to understand it. "Why do you even care? You don't even know me."

In just two long strides, he was standing before me. My eyes stared into his solid chest as he towered over me. I wasn't confident enough to look at his face. I didn't want to see his expression, the judgement in his eyes. I gulped as I felt the warmth of his breath against the skin of my exposed neck. Goose bumps appeared along my skin, causing me to rub my hands along my arms in an attempt to get rid of them.

"I know you more than you think. I know you drink to forget or to numb your pain." I closed my eyes, trying to stop the tears from falling. "I know you ride a motorcycle too powerful for you because you don't just enjoy the freedom, you enjoy the danger of it. The ride is exhilarating. It's like a drug." He stepped closer. He was so close my breasts brushed just under his chest and my head almost rested in the crevice of his armpit. "It's the same reason you came here today and maybe the other night.

"Okay, the other night you didn't know where you were, but today you knew exactly where you were heading. Sure, you probably would have come and checked on Junior because you have a big fucking heart, but deep down you know I'm not exactly what you would call a good guy. God knows why, but you have a self-destruct button and you're ready to blow. Why do I care? Ain't got a fucking clue. For whatever reason, angel, you've gotten under my skin and fate has landed you on my doorstep whether you like it or not. So get your fucking head out of your ass and check into reality. Life's a bitch, and as there is no one else in this fucking mess who can protect you, I will."

I gently placed my hands on his chest and finally looked up at his face. I could feel his erratic heartbeat against the solid wall of his ribcage. A single tear rolled down my cheek, and like the other day, he gently wiped it away with his thumb. We were standing so close. I could feel his every breath and sense every small movement he made. His hands flexed at his sides as if he didn't know what else to do with them.

"I don't need protecting, Kyle. I can look after myself." *I have all my life.*

"I don't doubt that, but in this instance, you don't have much fucking choice. I'm not leaving you alone."

"I'm not alone. I have Cassie," I replied.

"That's not what I meant." He let out an aggravated growl and grabbed both my hands, holding them against his chest. He leaned down and gently brushed a kiss to my knuckles. "I need to ask you something," he said, walking me over to the edge of his bed. Sitting down, he let go of one of my hands but still held on tightly to the other. "How long ago did Jake die?"

"Pardon?" I said, stunned. Out of all the questions he could ask, I wasn't expecting that.

"The other night when you were drunk, you told me about Jake. Not everything, but enough for me to know you may be strong, but you are not capable of handling this. You're still hurting and it's breaking you up inside. Anything could have happened when you got wasted. If you were somewhere else, do you really think you would have made it home okay? You could have been beaten, raped, murdered. If it weren't for Tiny recognising you, it could have even happened in my club." I gulped nervously. "Not going to lie, some of the company I keep is questionable, and now you have a mark on your head. You're a fucking target. What happens next time you get drunk? Sure, you have Cassie, but she can't be there all the time."

"No, she can't be, but trust me when I tell you I'm better off on my own. I've never needed anyone to protect me in the past and I sure don't need anyone now. I've survived so far without any help."

"You sure about that? What about Jake? He was your husband; he must have protected you. If I recall from your drunken conversation, he found you puking your guts up somewhere too. Same shit could have happened to you then, just as it could have happened the other day." He countered. "Then there's Cassie. The way she looked at you when she realised why I'd brought you home told me it wasn't the first time. Sorry to be blunt, angel, but you're doing a fucking shit job of looking after yourself."

"That's not the same," I lied.

"Fine. Whatever. So what was he like?" His expression was unreadable, and I couldn't help feeling a little afraid. He was intimidating when angry, and I guessed this was only a patch on what really lay underneath. Sensing my apprehension, his features softened and he offered a smile. He squeezed the hand he was holding, offering reassurance, and I relaxed in return.

We sat side by side, our knees slightly touching, as I told him he was right about Jake. He found me drunk and puking my guts up and he spent our first night together holding back my hair too. I told him how my parents hated Jake with a passion and that's why we eloped to Gretna Green to get married. I told him how Jake saved me from the brink of self-destruction because he was right; I did drink to forget, and when I met Jake four years ago, I was at my worst. My parents, or more so my mother, were overbearing, controlling, and selfish. I sought solace in the bottom of a bottle frequently until Jake turned up like a knight in shining armour, effectively stopping me from killing myself slowly.

Hearing the anger in my voice as I mentioned my parents shocked me. I hadn't realised how much I resented them, and I never realised how much Jake truly protected me until I said it out loud. *Clever bastard, he knew I would eventually see the truth.*

Kyle just listened intently, only smiling when he realised I'd figured out I needed protecting after all.

It was like I'd come down with an intense case of verbal diarrhoea as I continued to open up about Jake.

Finally speaking about him was freeing in a way I never thought possible. I told Kyle about how my love for bikes started when I started to watch Jake race and how he taught me how to ride. I told him he was right about loving the freedom, but I secretly loved the thrill more. I poured out my heart while he sat back and continued to listen patiently. Who would have thought talking to Kyle would be better than any therapy session I had with Dr. Cole?

"Just one more question. Who's Lyla Rose?"

I had managed to avoid talking about her. For some reason, I found it harder to accept her death. Was it because I felt guilty? Because I never got the chance to be her mother? Or was it because I would forever hear my mother telling me how she loved her more?

I'd held off the tears, but as soon as he mentioned her name, the dam broke. I stood up and got some tissue from the bathroom before he once again pulled me against his warm chest and let me cry. He stroked my hair and held me until my sobs stopped and I could cry no more. Pulling myself together, I looked at him through bloodshot eyes and continued my story, the pressure in my chest lessening with each word.

"I was in the accident that killed Jake, and I was pregnant. Lyla Rose was delivered by emergency C-section. I was in a bad way, and the decision was made that her chances of survival were better if she were born prematurely, but she didn't make it. I never got to meet her, hold her." I choked back another sob, and Kyle gently pressed a kiss to my forehead. I melted farther into his strong arms.

"Shh, now. You don't need to say anymore."

"Thank you," I whispered.

"What for?" he asked.

"For listening. You know, for such a scary-looking guy, you're easy to talk to." I laughed and he playfully pushed my shoulders.

"Just don't tell anyone. They'd never let that shit lie," he said. I missed his warmth instantly as he stood up. I rubbed my hand absently over my bare arms. "So let me have a proper look at that tattoo."

"Which one?" I asked, wiping the excess tears from my face. I knew he'd seen both.

"The angel wings."

I nodded and pulled my straps down slowly before turning around. I felt his presence immediately behind me, causing me to suck in a deep breath. I shivered as he gently traced the outline with his fingers. Releasing my breath, I closed my eyes, savouring his touch. I hadn't been touched like that since Jake. *Jake.* I abruptly stepped away and pulled my straps up, confusion lacing my thoughts. *Jake was gone.*

"It's beautiful," he said, not commenting on my sudden behaviour. "What about the other one?" he said, looking down at my wrist.

"This... well, it's too soon to take the bandage off," I said, suddenly feeling slightly overwhelmed. "So what about your tats?" I asked, shifting the conversation away from me.

I quickly averted my eyes when he shed his top unabashed, revealing his full sleeve down his left arm.

He then turned around, obviously keen to show me the dark angel nearly covering his entire back, her wingspan spreading across the entirety of his shoulder blades. *Like mine.* I moved closer to get a better look and found myself tracing the outline of the wings with my fingertips. He shivered under my touch, making me feel powerful and encouraging me to continue.

"The lady at the tattoo parlour said you guys all had this," I said.

"Yeah, if we have the room. Tiny was already tatted up, so you'll notice if he ever takes his top off in front of you that his is across his chest and ribs."

I walked 'round him slowly until I was facing him once again. A large Celtic cross stood on its own at the top of his right arm. "What about his one? Junior has one like this too, doesn't he?"

"He does. It's in memory of our dad."

I felt awful. I had unloaded all my baggage onto him, but not once did I ever question him about his life. His family.

As if sensing my change in mood, he held me gently by the arms. "You don't need to worry about me, angel. Death has always been part of my life." I offered a weak smile. "So the cross will eventually make up another sleeve, but not got 'round to deciding what I want yet," he said, keeping the conversation light.

"I love this one," I said as I returned to running my fingers along his skin. This time it was to trace the outline of the phoenix that dominated the upper part of his left arm.

"The phoenix I got when I was sixteen, when my mother walked out on us. It means resurrection."

"I know," I replied huskily. The intimacy of the moment had my mouth going dry and stomach in knots. This had started out to be innocent curiosity, but as I explored his body, the tension between us became electrifying. My fingers followed a natural path along the flames that started just above the Celtic band around his wrist and thinned out as they reached his upper arm where the phoenix then took centre stage. My fingers traced the flames that surrounded the phoenix until they reached their final resting place just above his heart.

He put his hand above mine and held it in place. I watched his eyes as he stared at my lips, causing the knots in my stomach to erupt into butterflies. I licked them subconsciously. Was he going to kiss me? Did I want him to? He leaned down and delicately placed a kiss along the side of my mouth. The disappointment I felt when he pulled away told me yes.

A loud bang on his door made me jump out of my skin and blush like a fool. Not that we were doing anything to interrupt, but I felt like we were doing something wrong. I adjusted my clothing and ran my fingers through my hair while Kyle quickly shrugged his top back on. He opened the door to Junior, who walked in wearing a stony expression on his face.

Chapter Sixteen

KYLE

I can honestly say I have never felt a connection like that with anyone in my life. As she traced her delicate fingers along my skin, I felt every sensation. At one point, I shivered. I actually fucking shivered. She was getting me so worked up I had trouble concentrating on not doing anything stupid. Like kissing her. I was desperate for a taste of those perfect plump lips, but considering we hadn't long ago been talking about her dead husband, it didn't feel right. So I made do with just lightly touching my lips against the side of her mouth, and even then, I felt like I was taking advantage. *What the hell is she doing to me?*

Up until now, the only conversations I'd ever had

with women outside family (including Big Mamma, Trix, and Sadie) had just been bedroom talk. Hell, the only things I ever wanted to do with women until now were purely sexual. I'd never felt the need to kiss a woman so strongly before, especially the innocent little pecks that offered more comfort and affection than anything else. When she told me about her baby, I swear my fucking heart shattered to pieces. Not knowing what to say, I just kissed her forehead. When she'd talked about her parents, all I wanted to do was jump on a plane to England and hunt down the bastards.

Okay, she never said anything to make me think they'd been physically abusive, but sometimes, emotional abuse could be worse. Cuts and bruises can heal, but when someone repeatedly belittles you or tells you how worthless you are, you start to believe them, and it doesn't matter how many times people tell you otherwise. She was broken long before she met Jake, and yes, he helped fix her, but something in her behaviour and her recent drinking had me believing he hadn't quite knocked down all those walls she'd so carefully erected. Even though she cried, laughed, or got angry, she displayed each emotion carefully, constantly assessing my reactions. It was as if she were subconsciously worried how I would react to what she was saying.

She expects to be rejected. She expects to be put down.

There was a lot more to this beautifully broken girl than met the eye, and I was determined to find out everything about her. I was determined to help break down those walls. There was no denying the chemistry between us, but the connection we seemed to share felt like it ran at a much deeper level. As she melted perfectly into my side, I realised it was like she was made for me. Hell, we even had almost matching tattoos.

As much as I'd enjoyed talking with Ellie, and her intimate touch, I was grateful for Junior's interruption. At the end of the day, there's only so much a horny guy can take, and I was a fraction too close to thinking with my dick rather than my brain. Her scent, the softness of her skin, the silkiness of her hair, and those gorgeous aquamarine eyes had me itching to touch every inch of her body.

My first glance at Junior's expression had me falling back to reality with a thud. He tried to act casual for Ellie's benefit, but like he told me once, she wasn't stupid. By the way the colour drained from her face, she'd sensed something was wrong. It was his eyes that gave him away. They were too cold, too calm. It was like looking in a mirror. Every time I saw that expression on his face, I felt guilty and responsible for giving him this life. Sure, I probably couldn't have prevented it, but I should have at least tried. He was brighter than most and could go far, but he'd already been tainted by life at the club. Graduating wasn't top of his priorities now; getting the club's cut was.

Dear old Mom took off when Junior was five. I was sixteen and had already made a name for myself. She wasn't the most caring of mothers. That was clear from the start. From as early as I could remember, she informed me daily that I was an accident—a broken rubber after a night full of drunken sex. She wasn't one of the club's whores, but she wasn't exactly ol' lady material either. He'd gone away on business, and she was a singer my dad met once in a bar. Being a good man and despite being the current prez of the Angels of Death MC, he made her his ol' lady because he was going to "do things right by his kid."

She didn't argue. In fact, she made a good life for herself, reaping the benefits of the club's rewards. She was very convincing at playing the part of a good mom. Dad never suspected once. Not in the beginning anyway. Behind closed doors, she would remind me how I ruined her life, made her fat, stopped her from pursuing her career as a singer. I was a worthless piece of shit who was going to end up like his good-for-nothing father. Everyone had been oblivious to the dark-haired, brown-eyed beauty who hid behind fake smiles and sunny demeanour.

So when she fell pregnant with Junior, shit really hit the fan. She wanted an abortion, but Dad told her she wasn't going to get rid of his kid. I was eleven years old and remember hiding under my bed as they screamed at each other. I listened as my mother hissed that she wished I'd never been born. The sounds of furniture and glass breaking had me shrinking farther under my bed. I was so scared I dug my nails into the palms of my hands until I drew blood. The deafening sound of flesh on flesh, bone on bone echoed from underneath the floorboards, and everything went silent. Moments later, a door slammed, and I crept downstairs to find my mother sobbing, sitting with her back against a wall, clutching her jaw while blood dripped through her fingers. I quietly walked over to see if she was okay, but as I leaned down to give her a hug, she firmly shoved me away. I landed on my ass with a thud, my hands narrowly missing a piece of glass embedded in the carpet.

"This is all your fucking fault, you piece of shit," she said through blood-stained teeth as she stood and walked away, leaving me alone and helpless.

But rather than break me, it made me harder. After that day, I spent every possible minute at the club with my dad or with Big Mamma. My mother had Junior, but she was purely an incubator. She showed even less love for him than she did for me. From the moment he was born, I looked after him with the help of Big Mamma. Of course, Dad did his bit, but he was often away or caught up in club business. In those days, there was no truce between us and rival MCs.

By the time I was thirteen, I could ride a bike, shoot a gun, throw a knife, and of course, change diapers and look after a baby. The incubator turned into a drunk, until one day she up and left, never to be seen again. Rumour had it she followed her dreams of becoming a singer after all. Some said Dad had her disposed of, but even though he hit her that one time, I knew he'd never hit her or any other woman again. And he just didn't have it in him to kill the mother of his boys, no matter how much he wished her dead. Of course, all this shit meant Junior was submerged into club life long before I was and already had a good taste of it.

"Hey, Els. Trix and Sadie are desperate to meet you," he said. She looked at me and offered a weak smile before heading out the door.

"What's up?" I asked, crossing my arms across my chest.

"Saint's getting the others ready. Tiny, me, and Slade will stay here. The Irish have requested a meet at Carter's place. Their VP's ol' lady got her throat slit about an hour ago by the two guys who were speaking to Ellie earlier. At least they matched the description Tiny gave us."

Shit. They obviously struck out with Ellie, so this bitch was the next best thing. Ellie could raise hell, but she wasn't going anywhere.

"Go to the house. Make sure you all stay together," I ordered as I shrugged on my cut and stuck my gun down the back of my pants and strapped my favourite knife to my ankle.

Junior sped out of my room, shouting out my demands. I walked out just a moment later.

"No way, Junior. I told Kyle I wasn't staying here." Ellie had adopted the position I'd grown to love. Arms crossed firmly across her chest, determination set in her face.

"You won't be here. You'll be at the house with me, Tiny, Trix, Sadie, and the baby. Slade and Big Mamma will be there too." Junior was trying to placate Ellie, to no avail.

I thought I'd give him a minute before I stepped in and laid down the law. I needed to use my brain and treat this whole situation right before there was absolutely no chance she would agree to stay. Her eyes blazed with anger, but I realised early on this was normally a mask to hide what was really bubbling underneath. Not that she would ever admit it, but she was scared. And all I wanted to do was hold her in my arms and tell her everything would be okay, but I couldn't. There were no guarantees in life, and as much as my body and mind screamed to protect her, I could make no promises. I could only promise I would move heaven and earth trying, and I would do this the only way I knew how. My expression turned cold and my body tensed, ready to meet her stubborn determination with my own.

"Get your fucking shit together, Ellie, and follow the others on your bike."

She looked like she was going to say something probably very unladylike but thought better of it. Instead, she shouldered past Junior until she was standing right in front of me, a challenge evident in her eyes.

"I've told you before, Kyle, and it's about time you fucking listened to me. You do *not* get to tell me what to do. I haven't slept for nearly twenty-four hours. I am fucking tired and now a tad pissed off. I'm going home. To *my* home. Right. Now."

"No chance." I held my finger to her lips before she protested further. She went to shove me away, but I was quicker and grabbed hold of her hands, keeping them out in front of her. "First of all, do not try and shove me again. You won't like the consequences. Secondly, the guys who found you earlier probably had you followed, so I'd guess they know where you live. Those two guys? They just slit some bitch's throat."

She relaxed her hands, my last statement obviously hitting home.

I let her hands drop to her sides. "They don't know where my house is, so you'll be safe there with the others. I won't be there, but Tiny, Slade, and Junior will be able to keep you safe in my absence. You have to trust me. If I didn't think it was safe at my house, I wouldn't be sending you there, especially with Sadie taking Saige."

She closed her eyes and muttered something under her breath. When she reopened them, as much as it pained me to see, I was grateful to find defeat there. I felt like a dick, but I kept my face hard and unyielding. I'd never intended for her to feel like she had no choice, but for her own safety, I had no choice but to take it away from her. She'd spent her life being controlled, and now I was no better than her parents.

There's no other way.

"Fine. I'll go, but I need to make a stop before I get to your house." This time she was the one who held a finger to my lips before I could protest. "If they know where I live, then Cas isn't safe, and I'd die before I put her in trouble. So she needs to come with us too. If I go, she goes, but she won't get on a bike, so she'll have to go in the truck with Sadie and Trix."

"Hey, sugar, my ride's with Tiny." Trix interrupted.

"Sorry to be rude, but I really don't give a shit," she snapped.

Trix just shrugged it off and held up her hands in

mock surrender. I bit back a smile.

"She's definitely a keeper, prez." Tiny laughed from alongside her. Trix shoved him playfully in the arm. The pair was behaving like we had all the time in the world. Even Junior had a shit-eating grin on his face. It was getting harder by the second to keep my own smile at bay. She really had no idea how she affected people. Especially me.

"Okay, so let's go get your girl and get the hell out of here," Sadie said, kicking open the front door.

What choice did I have? Ellie said she would die before her friend ended up in trouble, and I believed every fucking word.

Everyone grabbed what they needed and followed Sadie out the door. All except Ellie and me. She looked like she was pitching for an argument, but I had no intention of adding fuel to her fire. I let my guard drop and reached down to tuck a stray strand of hair behind her ear. I loved how she almost melted at my touch and was desperate for more. I ran my fingers down her soft cheek and revelled in the tiny noise she made when she sucked in a breath. She looked up at me, warmth now replacing the earlier anger and frustration in her eyes. In the short time I'd known Ellie, I'd learned to read her emotions through her eyes. It was like reading a book. I'd seen anger, frustration, fear, sadness, and even a hint of happiness, but right now, I saw trust. I was starting to break down the walls she'd carefully erected, and hell, the happiness I felt in doing so made me feel good inside. Without even knowing it, Ellie was thawing out the heart I never even realised I had. Until her.

"You may have to be there for a few days. Not sure how long this will take," I said, cupping her chin in the palm of my hand, tilting up her head to look at me properly.

She kept her eyes steady, but already I could see her defences rising back up. The warmth from only moments ago evaporated right before my eyes. Now she was looking at me like she was trying to put together a puzzle and was missing the final piece. The happiness I'd felt was short lived, and I would give my right arm to have that feeling back again.

"No. I have work and so does Cas. We're both at work the day after tomorrow," she said, dipping her head.

I sighed in frustration. She was going to continue fighting me.

"Quit being so stubborn, Ellie. You're not at home now, princess." Wrong thing to say.

She knocked my arm away, her eyes turning cold, but the fire behind them had been ignited again. I held her by the shoulders, but she continued to try and move away, so I grabbed her by the sides of her head and made her look at me again.

"How many fucking times do I have to tell you you're in danger? Do you have to be dead before you finally get the message?"

"Fuck you, Kyle."

Control. Snapped.

I let out a deep, rumbling growl before pulling her face toward me. I smashed my lips down on hers with so much force we lost balance, nearly stumbling over the side of the sofa. I devoured her mouth like a starving man, and she returned my kiss with equal hunger. Regaining my footing, I pushed her backward until her back was flush against the wall, our lips only breaking contact in short, sharp bursts. One of her small, delicate hands curled around my neck, pulling me closer, while the other made a journey up my chest. My hands found her backside, and I lifted her until her short legs were wrapped tightly around my waist. My tongue sought access farther into her sweet-tasting mouth. She opened wider, wrapping her tongue around mine. It was hot, frenzied, and messy, and if I didn't slow down, there was no way I would be able to restrain myself. I turned my attention to running kisses along her jaw and neck. She tilted her head to one side, giving me better access, and I groaned in approval. She let out a small moan of pleasure, and it took everything I had to keep my control and not rip off her clothes.

She's not like the other girls.

I raised one of my hands from her ass and settled it on the soft, warm flesh just above the waistband of her jeans. She didn't so much as flinch, and my hands were desperate to farther explore. She arched her back, shoving her tits into my chest, and my pants felt like they'd shrunk three sizes. Unable to resist, I ran my fingers up along the length of her spine, marvelling in the softness of her skin. She trembled in my hands, pausing our kiss to savour every inch of my touch. The look on her face was euphoric, and I was completely captivated by her raw beauty. Never in my life had I seen something so stunning. The selfish bastard in me craved more. I wanted to know what she would look like when I finally tipped her over the edge, but something inside my head told me to slow down.

I stopped at the edge of her lace bra and tentatively ran my thumb along the edge of the soft fabric. She let out a little gasp and froze in my arms before her petite hands delved under my tee and not so gently explored every part of my abdomen and chest. I took this as permission to explore farther and gently cupped one of her breasts, rubbing a thumb over her nipple. I could feel it harden under my touch and smiled when she let out a small whimper.

Such a sensitive little thing. She was completely at my mercy.

A loud bang on the front door had us breaking away from each other and me swearing profusely under my breath.

She slid herself down my body and stumbled when her feet met the floor. She was flushed and breathless, and I fucking loved being the one responsible for it. I caught her by the waist and held her longer than necessary, still craving to touch her any way I could. I fought the grin threatening to explode across my face but soon became concerned when I realised Ellie wasn't smiling. In fact, she wasn't doing anything apart from looking at me like she was trying to piece together a puzzle again. Had I read the signals wrong? I didn't think I had. She'd seemed more than willing, but I couldn't shake that feeling that maybe I'd gone too fast. I stared at her intently and watched as a small smile appeared on her angelic face, and my grin broke free. She dipped her head forward, trying to avoid my eyes as if embarrassed, and I chuckled, grateful to see some life seeping back into those gorgeous aquamarines.

Someone started banging on the door again, causing Ellie to jump and subsequently snuffing out that spark and the smile. I didn't know where the Ellie I was with just seconds ago went, but she wasn't there now. I watched as she adjusted her clothes and ran her fingers roughly through her hair, all the while the cogs evidently turning ferociously inside that complicated head of hers.

I wondered what she was thinking. It wasn't like this was unexpected. It was inevitable it was going to happen at some point. Every time we were together, the chemistry was explosive, but maybe it was too much too soon. She definitely wasn't like any other girl I'd ever been with. Despite the way she moved her hands and the way her tongue masterfully played with mine, I'd put money on her having only ever been with Jake. Her reactions were too pure and unpractised. Not that I was complaining. Those tiny gasps and whimpers stirred a reaction in me I'd never felt before, and as much as it scared me, I liked it. I liked it maybe too much. This was why, despite whatever argument I attempted to put together in my head, her reaction had me feeling like I'd just been kicked in the gut.

Chapter Seventeen

ELLIE

Kyle's house was nothing like I imagined it would be. It was a good-sized three-bedroom detached house in the suburbs. I wondered what the neighbours must have thought when we pulled into the large driveway on our bikes, Sadie in the truck. You could see the curtains twitching a mile away. A big black lady greeted us at the door with a welcoming smile. She pulled Sadie into a hug and cooed over Saige before moving on to the others, until finally getting to Cassie and me. I guessed she was the infamous Big Mamma Junior had told me so much about. Cassie beamed as Big Mamma pulled her into a hug too. I thought my friend would have kicked up a fuss about coming with me, but she came willingly and actually seemed excited—though maybe a bit too excited if you asked me. It made me think she was doing some running of her own. When Big Mamma's eyes finally found me, I was taken aback by the love I saw shining through them. How could this complete stranger look at me like that? She sort of looked at me how I would imagine a normal mother would look at her daughter. It made me nervous and had me fidgeting uncomfortably.

"Hey there, sweetheart. You must be Ellie." She grabbed hold of my hand and squeezed it fondly. Maybe my expression gave me away, but it was as if she sensed a hug would make me feel uneasy. "I've heard so much about you from young Junior. I'm so pleased to finally meet you." Her smile was warm and friendly, helping me relax a little.

I hadn't realised I'd been so tense until I could physically feel the pressure lighten from my neck and shoulders. I offered a weak smile in return and followed her into the house while she kept hold of my hand.

The front door led straight into a large, spacious open-planned lounge with a spiral staircase leading upstairs. Toward the back of the room, double doors led into what I assumed to be the kitchen. There was a large window overlooking the front garden, soft-cream feminine drapes hung on either side. The floor was laminate, but a huge cream Persian rug covered the floor central to two large coffee-coloured sofas and matching recliner. There was an open fireplace along the remaining side of the rug and the biggest TV I'd ever seen mounted on the wall above the mantel. The dining area of the open-planned room was home to a large oak table and matching seats. A fresh vase of blood-red roses decorated its centre. I wondered whether they'd been left by Kyle or whether Big Mamma had added the feminine touch to make me feel better. Something told me they were Big Mamma's touch. Flowers didn't strike me as being Kyle's style, but I couldn't help but daydream about who had left them and the reason behind why they were there. *Do I want Kyle buying me flowers?* The little party of butterflies erupting in my stomach at the thought gave me the answer I was looking for.

Once I'd been given a small tour of the place, I made my excuses and went to bed for a few hours. Big Mamma showed me to Kyle's room. Unlike his room at the club, this was bright and spacious. Going by what I'd seen already, I had a feeling she had a huge influence on the decoration throughout. There was a feminine feel to his room, similar to the rooms downstairs. I could easily see myself living in a place like this, eating family meals at the table, barbecues in the back garden, kids riding their bikes up and down the long drive. It was a home fit for a family.

Family.

I pushed away the thoughts quickly. It wasn't like I was moving in, and there was no chance of me having my own family anytime soon. *Nope, I'm on my own.*

I kicked off my shoes and sat on the edge of Kyle's bed, wondering how the hell I ended up there in the first place, and then my thoughts drifted to what happened before we left. That kiss was still at the forefront of my mind. *What was I thinking?* That kiss, if you could call it that because it certainly went above and beyond, had me weak at the knees and completely succumbing to his every touch. I was putty in his hands, and if it hadn't have been for that knock at the door, I didn't know if I would have been strong enough to stop.

Never in my life had someone made me feel like that. As much as I hated to admit it, not even Jake. It was those emotions Kyle had induced that had me thinking about my late husband, setting my emotions at war against each other once again. How was I supposed to move on when every time I thought about or spent time with Kyle, I was overcome by guilt? How could I tell Kyle I was thinking about Jake immediately after one of the best kisses I'd had in my life? Like the coward I am, I settled on leaving him stranded so I could deal with the internal battle alone. I thought I would handle it better this way, but glimpsing the dejected look on his face before I walked out that door ripped my soul in two.

The temptation to have a drink was strong, but thankfully, I was too tired to care. Trying not to overthink the significance of me sleeping in Kyle's bed, I pulled off my jeans and slid between the soft satin sheets. As soon as my head hit the pillow, I was gone.

I slept for three hours and felt marginally better for it. Dreams of the accident, Jake, and Kyle made for a restless slumber, so unfortunately, I still carried bags under my eyes the size of shopping trolleys. After jumping in the shower and changing into clean clothes, I made my way back downstairs to join in with the raucous laughter I could hear coming from the lounge. I was happy to see Cassie had been welcomed into the crowd. Not that I expected any different; she was hard not to like. For as long as I'd known her, she'd always been the life and soul of a party, and from hearing the tail end of one of her stories, I knew she wasn't pulling any punches.

Junior, Tiny, and Slade were in the kitchen playing cards. They all greeted me with smiles when I grabbed a Coke from the fridge. I left without saying much, not wanting to interrupt their game, and I didn't want to draw attention to my obvious shock. The whole scene would have all looked very normal if it weren't for the shotgun lying on the side counter and the other guns I could see in the waistbands of Tiny's and Slade's jeans. When I headed back into the lounge, Sadie had Saige tucked in her arm, sound asleep, on the sofa. Saige was absolutely gorgeous and her tiny features on her snow-white face reminded me of a porcelain doll. I didn't realise I was staring at her until Cassie gently took me by the arm and sat me next to her on the opposite sofa. Trix sat next to Sadie with her feet tucked under her bottom, and Big Mamma sat in the recliner, knitting what looked to be pastel-pink booties. That feeling of longing stirred deep inside my gut and had me resting my hand on my nonexistent baby bump, until I realised what I was doing. A huge belt of laughter from Trix had me looking at the TV. They were watching *22 Jump Street,* but not even Channing Tatum could distract me from my thoughts of Lyla.

The evening was a blur of conversations, and for

the first time in a long time, I sat back with a glass of wine without feeling the need to finish the bottle. *Okay, lie.* Maybe it was because of my conflicted feelings for Kyle, maybe it was because I was sleeping in his bed in his gorgeous family home, or maybe it was because I was in the company of a baby girl, but my thoughts and emotions were all over the place. I was more than tempted to drain the bottle, along with a couple more, but Cassie and the girls watched as I took every sip. Apparently, I wasn't going to be drowning my sorrows with them on guard. Thankfully, I had Trix, who succeeded where Channing Tatum couldn't. She was an absolute legend, and the stories she shared about her and Tiny had me in hysterics. I hadn't laughed like that in ages, and it felt good to finally let myself go. If Tiny could hear us and was at anytime embarrassed, he didn't show it. Apparently, he was nicknamed Tiny because nothing about him was. Absolutely NOTHING. I blushed profusely, making the others laugh at my supposed innocence. *If only they knew.*

Sadie told us about how she met Saint on one of their business trips, and it was love at first sight. Or should I say fight? She was lucky he could father children after she took her knee to his groin when he grabbed her arse. She was a girl after my own heart. We all then gushed when she told us about their beach wedding and laughed when she told us about Kyle's attempt at a best man's speech.

Big Mamma told us a few stories too, mostly involving a fun-loving Junior and a "little shit" called Kyle—her words, not mine.

Cassie joined in by announcing she now had her eye on James from the hospital and would quite happily give Paulie a run for her money. Jiggling her best assets, she proclaimed she was ALL woman after all, and Paulie was still a mere girl. We laughed until we had tears in our eyes when she told us how she managed to get him alone in a store cupboard, but the janitor interrupted before she even managed to get his shirt off. James didn't stand a chance, the poor man.

They didn't ask many questions about my past, and for that I was thankful, but they couldn't contain themselves when it came to wanting to know more about Kyle and me. I sure as hell wasn't going to tell them how just before we headed to his house, he had me pushed up against a wall while he devoured me with his hot, wet mouth and set my body on fire with the slightest touch. My body remembered the sensations, and I fought back a flush. It was probably purely sexual, but there was absolutely no denying it. I was totally and utterly attracted to Kyle Slater. But rather than be excited about this revelation, it scared the shit out of me. What if it could lead to more? Was I ready to move on? Was I ready to let someone else see the real me? The one that was fragile and broken. Apart from Cassie, the only other person I'd ever let in was Jake, and when he died, it left me in pieces. Could I go through loving again only to have it taken away?

Cassie sensed my change in mood and tried directing the conversation back to Sadie, but unfortunately, she wasn't having any of it.

"You know, Ellie, I have no idea how you've

done it, girl, but you've got him hook, line, and sinker. Do you know how many girls have tried to tame the *slayer* and not even come close?" Sadie said, waving her hands around excitedly. She cursed under her breath when Saige stirred.

"I've never seen him look at anyone like he does you. Actually, I've never really seen him crack a smile at a woman until you. Hell, you've even got him laughing, and that's a fucking miracle. Don't get me wrong. I love the prez to pieces, but God is he an angry, mixed-up, miserable shit. The guys don't know whether to be worried or grateful. When he was holding back your hair the other night… when you were so elegantly chucking your guts up… Fuck me, it was the sweetest damned thing I've ever seen," Trix added. She had such a way with words. Considering the topic and I was the main focus, I laughed, ignoring the blush rising up my cheeks and the bloody butterflies in my stomach that made another appearance.

"So why did you call him the slayer?" I asked, picking up on Sadie's comment earlier. I wasn't sure if I really wanted to know the answer, but curiosity got the better of me.

"Because he's good at killing people." I hadn't even heard Junior walk in behind me. "You've probably already worked out he isn't just prez 'cause he was Dad's son." He looked at me, concern etched into his handsome young face, trying to gauge my reaction. Was I shocked by his answer? *Yes.* Did the answer matter? I was surprised when I internally answered, *No.*

"It's not as bad as it sounds, though." *Seriously?* "It's mainly business. He would never hurt a woman or anyone who didn't deserve it." I could feel eyes from every direction burn into my soul. It had me squirming in my seat.

"Oh. Okay. Just wondered," I said, lifting my legs into the lotus position. Not the wisest of decisions. My hip was knackered from the accident, and this was putting more strain on the joint than necessary, but it was the only thing I could think of to stop me from fidgeting. "So do you have a nickname? Wonder Boy? Lady Killer?" I joked.

The atmosphere became lighter when they all realised I wasn't running for the door, and we were back to being comfortable with each other again. Junior sat on the arm of the sofa and beamed, revealing perfectly straight, white teeth and two little dimples I'd never noticed before.

"Junior is my nickname," he replied, kicking a booted foot up onto a coffee table I'd barely noticed before. "It got confusing with both me and Kyle at the club, so Dad just called me Junior and it kinda stuck. My real name is Seth."

"Well, hello, Seth," I said, holding out my hand. "My real name is Eleanor." Junior smirked and shook my hand, looking at me like I'd just been let loose from the funny farm. "I fucking hate it 'cause it's the same as my mother's." I winked, and the whole room erupted into spontaneous laughter.

Tiny and Slade joined us in the living room, where we all continued to chat until the early hours of the morning.

Chapter Eighteen

ELLIE

The guys had slept in the lounge, each taking a turn to, I assume, keep watch for the bad guys. I still struggled to get my head around the surreal situation. My mother would have a fit if she found out, or at least she would have a field day informing the neighbours about her unruly daughter who could still do no right. Trix and Sadie shared Junior's room, and Cassie slept in the guest room. Slade and Big Mamma lived in the house next door, so she had gone back home to sleep in her own bed. We hadn't heard from Kyle or the others to let us know what was happening or if they were okay. Apparently, this was quite normal. I don't know how Trix and Sadie stood it. The waiting. The unknown.

I snuggled under the cream satin sheets of Kyle's bed, pulling them up under my nose to inhale his lingering scent. I wondered when he last slept in this room. Junior and Big Mamma told me he'd never brought anyone home to his house, and I couldn't help the happiness I felt knowing even though he wasn't beside me, I was the first woman to have ever slept in this bed. *Hopefully the last.*

An anxious knot formed in my stomach when I realised just how much the idea of anyone else sharing his bed disturbed me. I wasn't fond of the green-eyed monster that stirred underneath my skin, but I knew it was there. It had reared its ugly head on several occasions when I first started dating Jake. Needless to say, I often ended up pissed off and drunk if I caught him talking to another girl. Despite constant reassurances, I found it hard to understand why he was interested in me. Why would he want me when no one else did? The poor man deserved a medal for persevering and not giving up on me. My insecurities were always deep rooted. Would Kyle stick around or would he run at the first sign of trouble?

Movement outside my door had me glancing at the clock. It was 10:00 a.m. To be honest, with a baby in the house, I was surprised I wasn't awake sooner. There was a small knock on the door and it creaked open. I expected to see Cassie, but it was Sadie who popped her head around the door, with Saige swaddled across her chest.

"Hey, do you mind if I come in?"

"No, it's fine. What's wrong?" I asked.

"Nothing. I just wanted to see if you were okay. I

know it's hard when they go away," she said, as if reading my mind from earlier. "I hate not knowing if Saint's okay. If he's going to come home to me and our daughter." As if on cue, Saige gurgled. "Do you want to hold her?"

I fumbled awkwardly with the sheets. *Do I want to hold her?* "No, it's okay. She's happy where she is," I replied, suddenly feeling awkward. In truth, I might have become a mother, but I'd never held a baby. The thought stabbed me right through the chest, and I choked back an impending sob.

"I'm sorry," she said quietly, watching my reaction carefully. "She didn't want to say anything, but Cassie... She told us about Jake and Lyla Rose. We kinda forced it out of her when you were asleep. We were curious about why you seem so lost sometimes. Why you drunk yourself into oblivion that night at the club. She didn't say much, just that —"

I held up my hand to stop her from going on. I didn't need to hear her say it.

"It's fine. I'm kind of pleased you know, especially as it seems we're going to be spending more time with each other." She looked relieved, but I could still see the sadness palpable in her eyes.

"Kyle will sort everything, you know. Despite what we said last night about how he got his name, he's a good guy. He pretty much raised Junior and he's turned out to be a good kid. Everyone respects Kyle, and not just because he can be scary as shit. He always makes good on his word. He promised to sort it out so you can go back to your life, and he will."

"Thanks, that means a lot," I replied. There was truth in her words and they were strangely comforting.

She went to stand but hesitated. She bit down on her lip and sighed. "He might kind of break this promise, though."

What?

Sensing my inner turmoil, she reached out and placed her hand on my arm reassuringly. "Something tells me you won't be heading back to your old life. Not completely anyway. What Trix and I were saying last night, we weren't making fun. We meant every word. He's different around you. People either look up to him or tread on eggshells around him, scared of how he might react. Before his mum left, despite how she treated him, he always managed to laugh and have fun, but when he took on the responsibility of looking after Junior, he lost part of himself. Determined to look after his little brother and give him the best in life, he closed himself off and forgot to live his own life along the way. It made him bitter and sometimes scary as hell."

"Trust me, I've seen him scary," I rebuked, letting the rest of what she said sink in. *Was he really different with me?*

"Nah, honey, trust *m e* . You've seen him frustrated, maybe a little bit angry, but you haven't seen him lose his shit." She smiled before her expression turned serious. "Now, you need to have a think about what I've just said. It's obvious you and Kyle both like each other. The question is what are you going to do about it? I like you, Ellie, but if you're not ready, you need to stay away. He may look tough on the outside, but someone like you has the potential to break Kyle's heart." She got up and left the room without saying another word, leaving me speechless.

Cassie and I had phoned work and requested leave due to a family emergency. We weren't exactly lying. We were family, and the situation was somewhat an emergency, just not in the normal sense of the word. Thankfully, they were understanding, because two more days passed without any word.

Chapter Nineteen

ELLIE

The routine was always the same. We got up, ate, chatted, ate, chatted some more, watched a film, then yes, you guessed it… ate some more. We then went to bed and woke up to repeat the day as it was before. Except this day was different. I woke up feeling refreshed and lighter than I'd felt in a very long time. It was simple. The time away had given me a chance to think, to compartmentalise the shit and make the decision to actually do what I'd intended the day I got my second tattoo. I was going to do everything in my power to lower my mental walls brick by brick and move on.

The distant roar of motorbikes had me joining Slade at the window, where he'd been standing guard all morning. I dismissed his amused expression, not interested in what he was thinking. I was desperate to see Kyle and experience those soft lips on mine once more. I wasn't in the mood for Slade's smugness, even if it was all meant in good spirits. I tried to look calm and collected, but apparently, I wasn't pulling it off effectively. Slade's expression was obviously infectious, as I glimpsed the same smartarse look on Junior's face in his reflection in the window.

Sadie soon joined me at the window and held my hand in hers. Her face and body language told me she was just as anxious to see Saint. It was strange to receive such an affectionate gesture from a stranger. Sure, we'd spent a lot of time together the past couple days and shared a few intimate stories, but it wasn't like we were the best of friends. Despite my initial reservations, her hand in mine was comforting. I squeezed it gently in return, enjoying the momentary kinship and secretly hoping this newfound friendship would become more.

I peered at Junior watching the door, just as anxious. I motioned for him to come over and placed a hand on his shoulder when he approached willingly. He offered a small smile in return, which I reciprocated with my own. The unfamiliar feeling of belonging warmed my heart, and I longed for more. Standing waiting for Kyle to return felt right and suddenly, everything became clear. All the wars I'd fought in my head seemed meaningless when I realised, although these people came from a completely different walk of life, they accepted me for who I was and I'd never felt more at home.

As the rumble became louder, Sadie squeezed my hand and Slade's expression went from amused to grim. My stomach clenched. Something was wrong. I should have heard it before; the bikes weren't cruising home. There was urgency in the way the engines reverberated down the suburban roads. The air became deathly still as we all held our breath, waiting for whatever came around that final corner.

The first bike came into view and Sadie sobbed her relief. It was Saint. She let go of my hand and ran to the door, but Slade stopped her by the elbow and shouted for Big Mamma to get everyone out of the living room. Sadie looked torn between the front door and her daughter. Big Mamma, who I didn't even know was there, picked up a screaming Saige and ushered Sadie, Trix, and Cassie to the kitchen, but I wasn't going anywhere. For whatever reason, my feet were firmly rooted to the spot. Junior attempted to make me leave, but I shrugged his hand from my elbow.

Saint pulled into the driveway and almost jumped from his bike before it came to a complete stop. The other bikes came into view and rode toward the house at speed, their formation taking up both lanes. One, two, three… six. There was a bike missing. It was then that I also noticed the figure slumped behind Bear. It was Kyle. I looked to the skies and silently screamed at whoever was listening. *Why?* I must have been such a bad person in a former life for this shit to be happening to me again. The resolve I'd found just a moment ago evaporated like steam rising from an iced-over lake.

The door nearly flew off its hinges as Saint stormed in. Sadie ran from the kitchen and jumped into his arms. He squeezed her tight and snuggled his face into her neck. It was a brief encounter but visibly eased some of the tension that had been radiating from his body when he first arrived. He pushed her back toward the kitchen and she reluctantly walked away. She quickly looked at me, fear evident in her eyes. You didn't need to be a genius to work out what was going on in her head; it was written across her face. The bikes soared into the driveway. The silence was deafening when they all cut their engines, but it was soon replaced by angry shouts and heavy footsteps as they ran toward the house.

"Ellie, you should go into the kitchen with the others." It was Saint. I shook my head and shut down any impending thoughts. It was time to go to work. Junior and Tiny had run outside. Slade stood silent, holding open the front door.

"Clear the table and get me a first aid kit," I ordered. He didn't move, but as soon as Tiny and Bear dragged a barely conscious Kyle through the front door, he quickly turned on his heel. An uneasy Junior followed closely behind, worry unmistakably etched into his young face. It was like déjà vu, except this time, the roles had been reversed and we weren't at the hospital.

"Cassie!" I shouted as Saint cleared the dining table, sending those gorgeous blood-red roses flying across the floor. He helped Tiny and Bear lay Kyle on the surface.

Cassie came through the door, took one look at

Kyle, and nodded, strength and determination set in her face. I thanked my lucky stars she was there. The room was becoming crowded as the crew filed in behind me. I shot them all a warning glare, which they all chose to ignore.

"Back the fuck off!" Saint shouted, and they all jumped at his command.

Junior came running into the room with a first aid kit and a bottle of vodka. *Antiseptic.* The kid had obviously been in a situation like this before. I saw the neck wound the moment Kyle was dragged in, but there was so much blood I wasn't certain it was the only bullet hole I would find. Not bothering to grab the scissors from the first aid kit, I ripped off his shirt at the seams. Saint, Junior, Tiny, and Slade watched on as Cassie grabbed all the essentials and started cleaning the neck wound. Kyle let out a hiss as the alcohol touched his open skin, temporarily rousing him from unconsciousness.

"Kyle, it's Ellie. It's going to hurt like hell, but we need to clean you up so I can see what we're dealing with. Okay?" I said calmly. He groaned in reply. "What the hell happened?" I screamed. Saint went to reply, but I held up my hand. "Save it," I snapped. "Hang in there," I whispered for Kyle's ears only. *Please.*

As Cassie and I cleaned the wounds, I sighed in relief as I realised the neck wound, although deep, would be easily fixed with stitches. Obviously not being in a hospital with suitable medical supplies, I had to make do with the needle and thread Big Mamma later supplied. I scanned my eyes down from his naked torso to his waist, this time to check for damage rather than admire the view. On inspection, I could see he'd been shot in the shoulder. Cassie and I rolled him forward and once again sighed in relief. *Went straight through.* Although it was cause for a lot of blood loss, it didn't look like it had nicked anything vital. It was the bullet wound in his chest that had my heart racing and stomach tied in knots. If he'd been a smaller man, he would surely be dead.

"Breathe, Ellie. You can do this." Cassie rubbed my arm in reassurance and attempted a smile. She was concerned too but gave me the strength I needed to continue. She washed out the wound with the vodka and wiped away the excess blood. She poured some into a cup and doused some tweezers. I retrieved them with a steady hand.

I'm not sure how long it took to fix up Kyle, but I was both mentally and physically exhausted. Cassie was the same. We'd managed to pull the bullet out of his chest with surprising ease. It had embedded itself into muscle, just a fraction away from his lung. He was one lucky bastard. We cleaned up the wounds again before making use of that needle and more thread. It seemed a convenient moment to laugh at the chosen colour. *Pink.* We tied off the last bandage and collapsed on the floor. Kyle would be fine but would be sleeping awhile. He'd passed out from loss of blood and probably pain. I was a little more than anxious for him to open those intense brown eyes, but all I could do was wait with the others.

Chapter Twenty

KYLE

The pain in my neck was excruciating but nothing like the pain ripping across my chest to my shoulder. My body sank farther into the mattress as I tried to move. I was grateful to be in my own bed rather than a hospital. They ask too many questions, and besides, I had my very own nurse. Didn't I?

I rolled rather ungracefully off the bed, trying not to put any unnecessary pressure on the side I was shot. *Shot*. Never in my life did I think they would pull that off. Everything was in control until gunshots from the shadows had me hitting the deck as I was shot in quick succession in my shoulder and chest. The final bullet sliced through the side of my neck. Red managed to take the fucker out, but not before taking a bullet in the arm himself. I could have sworn the sadistic shit had a smile on his face on impact. I smiled at the memory and winced as I turned toward the footsteps approaching the door.

The door creaked open and Sadie popped her head around the corner. Not that I wasn't grateful for her visit, but I was kind of disappointed it wasn't Ellie.

"Shit, Kyle. Get the hell back into bed."

"No can do. Need to check on the guys."

"Saint sent everyone back to the club. He said everything had been dealt with and it was safe to return. It was getting a bit crowded down there, if you know what I mean. There's only me, Saint, Junior, and Ellie left," she said, fussing over me like a mother hen.

"She still here, then?" I asked. From the coy look on her face, I guessed she knew who I was referring to.

"Yeah, she's still here. She had you sprawled across that dining room table and worked on you like a pro," she said, grinning from ear to ear. There was something seriously wrong with the way my body, or at least a part of it, reacted to that comment. *Sprawled across the dining room table...*

"Yeah, I know." I might have been out of it, but I did remember her delft, delicate hands running across my chest. If it hadn't have hurt like a motherfucker, I would have cherished every touch.

"You like her, don't you?" she asked, sitting next to me on the bed.

"What's not to like?" I replied vaguely.

"Yeah, she's great, but we both know that's not what I meant." I felt like I was in high school again.

"How's Red?" I questioned, changing the subject. Sadie might be Saint's ol' lady, but I wasn't comfortable discussing my private life with her right now.

"He's good. Everyone was so wrapped up with your sorry ass they forgot he'd been shot too. Not that you would've known it. I'm sure that guy gives a whole new meaning to high pain threshold. He couldn't keep the smile off his face when Cassie was stitching him up. He is totally fucked up in the head."

"Ain't we all?" I challenged. "So Ellie didn't fix him up, then?" I desperately wanted her to say no. I knew Cassie could do it, so I didn't feel like too much of a jerk for not wanting her fixing him up too. My possessiveness surprised me.

"Nah. She kind of zoned out after she finished up with you. Cassie was cool, though. It was just a scratch really, so she had him fixed up in no time. Now he's gone off on a high with the others to do whatever he does to help him relax," she answered. I went to stand, and Sadie grabbed me by the elbow to support me. "So is it over now?"

"Yeah, we're fine until the next lot of assholes want to take a shot at us."

"That's good. I know I should be used to it, but I've got a kid now. I don't want her to grow up without her dad. You know?"

Yes, I did know. That's the reason I was in shitloads of pain right now. I had Saint as far back as I could get him without royally pissing him off. I didn't want to be responsible for that little girl not having a father.

"Don't you dare, Ellie!" Cassie's screams drifted through the floorboards and had us both heading out of the bedroom quickly.

"I need to get the fuck out of here, Cas. I can't do this!" Ellie screamed back. The sound of the front door slamming had me running down the stairs, despite the pain shooting through my body with every step I took. I made it downstairs in time to hear Ellie's bike roar to life and hot leg it down the road.

"Fuck!" Cassie shouted. From what I knew of Cassie, she was bubbly and outgoing. It was unusual to see her lose her shit with her best friend.

"What's going on?" I asked.

Cassie ran her fingers through her blond hair as she tried to regain some of her composure. People told me I was scary, but I would put money on them fancying their chances with me rather than her right now.

"She's running again," she replied without looking at me.

"What do you mean?" I snapped. That possessive streak had come to life again and all I wanted was to have Ellie back where I could see her. "Saint!" I shouted. He ran out of the kitchen with Junior hot on his heels. "Need to use your bike."

"No," Cassie snapped. I raised an eyebrow, aggravated. "Don't fucking look at me like that. Look, sorry, I didn't mean to snap. She's just pissed me off." She huffed out a breath. "She just needs time to think and get her head straight. You coming home the way you did kind of stirred up some shit in her head."

"So you expect me to just sit here and wait until she comes back?" I asked.

"Yes. She needs some time, but no offense, I doubt she'll come back here. She'll go home when she's ready." She frowned as she thought of something else, and it took everything I had not to shake it out of her.

Junior rested his hand on my shoulder and steered me in the direction of the sofa, probably to stop me from falling over. Or punching something.

"Come on, bro. She'll be fine," he said, but I could tell he was lying. He even knew that was far from the truth.

The next two hours were the worst of my life. Who would have thought I could get this worked up over a woman?

Cassie paced the living room anxiously before declaring she was going to head back home and wait for her there. She made sure she gave me her and Ellie's number before leaving. Sadie, Saint, and Junior watched me like a hawk, probably expecting me to erupt at any minute. I didn't blame them, because I did literally think I would burst out of my skin. I dug out my phone and dialled Ellie's number first. The sound of Metallica's "Enter the Sandman" had me walking to the dining room table.

Shit. Ellie must have dropped her phone when she was looking after me. I picked up her phone and it rang again. It was Cassie. I answered but didn't get the chance to say anything before she started shouting shit through the phone.

"Whoa, Cassie. It's me. Ellie must have dropped her phone."

She cursed under her breath.

"I'm heading out to look for her. You really should be resting up, but if you want to look for her too, we need to start looking in the bars."

Fuck.

Chapter Twenty-One

ELLIE

I spent a good couple of hours riding aimlessly, trying to figure out what the hell was going on in my head. I was doing okay. Even when Kyle came back, semi-conscious with blood pouring from his body, I'd accepted that shit just happens. I set to work like it was any other day, and then I watched him sleep. After Saint and Tiny helped move him upstairs to his bed, I sat and watched as his chest moved up and down with each steady breath. He looked so peaceful considering what he'd just been through. I wanted to crawl beside him and snuggle into his side, desperate to touch him. To feel his warmth.

I don't know what it was about this gorgeous man. He represented everything I was advised to avoid. Everything I told myself to avoid. He was arrogant, dangerous; he had *killed* people. Yet despite the occasional glimpse into his dark side, all he'd ever shown me was kindness. He made me feel safe. *He could have died.* Realisation hit me like a slap to the face. I already knew I'd grown to care for this man more than I should. More than I ever thought I was capable of again, but then that thought struck me down to the core.

He could have died.

I swallowed down the bile that had risen up the back of my throat and fought the compulsion to run, but it was too strong. I needed to get out. The bedroom walls were caving in around me and I couldn't breathe. I ran down the stairs, nearly taking Cassie out at the bottom. The look on her face told me she knew what I was going to do, yet she tried to stop me anyway. Grabbing my jacket, helmet, and keys, I headed for the door. Cassie screamed at me to stop, but I couldn't. I needed to run. Losing Jake and Lyla Rose nearly killed me. I wasn't strong enough to go through that shit again.

It felt good zipping in and out of traffic and driving at full throttle along the desolate roads I discovered on my first ride out. The beautiful scenery helped ease my mind a little, but I couldn't find peace no matter how many mountain ranges and lakes I took in. They'd always helped calm my wandering thoughts, but not this time. I decided to head home, hoping no one would be there to greet me.

I chucked my keys next to the letter along with my helmet. I went to dig out my phone from my back pocket and cursed when I realised it wasn't there. *Oh well.* I headed toward my bedroom, unzipping my jacket as I walked. As I opened my door, I shrugged off my jacket and threw it on my bed. I then stripped off my boots and jeans and grabbed a clean towel from the closet. I was in desperate need of a shower.

I turned on the spray and let it run for a few minutes before stepping inside. I gingerly slipped in and closed my eyes as I stuck my head directly under the full blast of the water. I felt some more of the tension leave my body as the heat pummelled my skin. I washed my long black hair, shaved, and then smothered myself in lavender-scented body wash, hoping it would calm my nerves. *It wasn't working.* After rinsing off all the bubbles, I turned off the shower, grabbed the towel, and stepped out onto the soft bath mat.

Staring at myself in the mirror, I noticed how old I was starting to look. Deep purple bags under my eyes highlighted I hadn't slept properly for a while, even though I'd slept like a log the past couple of nights. My lips were marked from excessive chewing, probably from the last couple hours. It was a bad habit I was scolded for constantly as a child. I loosely dried myself and wrapped the towel around my body. I grabbed a smaller towel and wrapped it around my head before heading back to my bedroom to get changed. The apartment was still silent.

Now fully dressed in another pair of skinny jeans and a red cotton blouse, I sank into the sofa and switched on the television. Nothing grabbed my attention as I flicked through the channels. My nerves were shot to pieces and there was an all-out war going on in my head. I jumped up and grabbed my keys from the side cabinet. I needed to numb the pain.

I found myself sitting alone in a pub ten minutes from the hospital. It wasn't one I normally went to, not that I'd visited many bars lately, but it was one of the only places that didn't look packed. When I went in and noticed the old-timers holding up the bar, I guessed that was the reason.

"What can I get ya, darlin'?" I looked up and was greeted by big, blue smiling eyes. The barmaid looked to be in her fifties, and aside from me, was probably the youngest in the dimly lit pub. Silver streaks ran through her chestnut-brown hair, which hung in loose curls over her shoulders. Her rather large chest was trying to climb out of her too-small top as she wiped down the bar.

"Just a Coke please." *Really?*

"You sure, darlin'? You look like you could do with somethin' stronger."

And the prize goes to…

"Yeah, add a shot of vodka to it please."

The barmaid winked and grabbed the bottle. God, I was weak.

Three vodka and cokes later, I was still perched at the bar, alone. No one bothered me, and I was grateful the old-timers left me in peace. A group had gathered in one corner and were playing a rather raucous game of dominoes. Another old boy sat alone at another table, reading the paper, and just a few seats away from me sat a slightly younger gentleman but still at least twenty years my senior, chatting up

Dee, the barmaid.

Dee had tried to talk to me on a few occasions, probably trying to save me from myself. She seemed the type—friendly, caring… motherly. At least I guess that's what being motherly was like. It's not like I'd experienced much of it growing up. Eventually, she gave up when she realised I wasn't going to break down and do something stupid. Over the years, I'd mastered the art of drinking. Yes, sometimes it resulted in me being sick and too drunk to stand straight, but really, three vodka and cokes had very little effect. It was just enough to take the edge off. One more would start to numb the pain. I raised my empty glass, and Dee walked over, this time with a frown on her face, but she didn't ask questions as she refilled my glass.

Why shouldn't I be entitled to have a drink anyway? Two years ago, I was happily married to the love of my life, and we were expecting a baby. Really, life couldn't have been better. Now, I was a widow before I'd even hit thirty. I'd lost my daughter. I'd moved thousands of miles away from home to get away from my overbearing family and start a new life, had gotten myself caught up with a local MC, and found myself seriously attracted to their "prez." A man I had no business having feelings for, whether it be innocent or purely sexual.

It's hardly surprising though. He was like a living and breathing god, and I hadn't been with a man since Jake, so I was bound to be frustrated. I am human after all. The fact that he'd shown interest made the attraction stronger, but why had he shown any interest at all?

Men like Jake only like girls who are easy, so my guess, Ellie, is you offer it to anyone willing. Let's face it. You're hardly going to win any awards in the beauty stakes. My mother's words hung heavily on my shoulders.

I downed my drink and held up my glass for another, but this time I asked for the vodka neat.

Stop eating, cut yourself, hide away until you rot for all I care. You are weak. The words she said to me when I was fifteen years old. A year after she…

No, I would not think of that now.

In one fluid motion, I knocked back the clear liquid and winced as the heat warmed the back of my throat. My mother's taunts became louder and louder until I couldn't bear it anymore. *Just one more drink.* I squeezed my eyes shut, hoping they would disappear, but the memories still plagued me.

Don't bother getting too attached to anyone when you're away. They'll leave you too when they realise how damaged you are. You'll eventually come crawling home, expecting me to pick up the pieces. The last words my mother said before I left for Vancouver burned into my skull.

A chill ran across my back as the door opened behind me, but I didn't look up. It was probably another old boy wanting to join the game or escape his wife for an hour or so. Dee's frown increased as she looked from me to the door and back to me again. Her frown turned into a small smile.

"Well, he ain't here for me, sweetheart," she said as she winked and handed me my drink. I turned around and my heart sank to my stomach. Kyle stood filling the doorway, a series of emotions washing across his beautiful brown eyes. I was definitely buzzed now, but there was no mistaking what I saw. At first, I saw anger, then frustration. I think I even saw concern, but above all, I saw disappointment. It was a look I was familiar with after all. I'd been gifted with it most of my life.

Chapter Twenty-Two

KYLE

I was beyond pissed. I had circled the area on my bike for what seemed like hours before receiving a text from Cassie saying her bike was at the apartment, but she wasn't there. It was time to search the bars. Problem with that was it's a big neighbourhood and there were plenty of them to search. I texted Saint and Junior, who willingly agreed to search the opposite side of town.

The Tavern was last on my list, and I prayed if she was going to be drinking herself into oblivion, this would be the place. It was an old-timer's bar, and she would be safe. Plus, Dee used to be a regular at the club in her youth, and from what I could remember, she was a diamond who would throttle any fucker who tried to take advantage of a vulnerable female. Imagine my relief when I saw her small, delicate body perched at the bar when I walked in. Dee saw me and frowned before giving me a small smile and alerting Ellie to my arrival.

Her haunted look did something strange to my insides. I tried to push aside any feelings of anger before I walked toward her. I tried to hide my disappointment at her drinking again, but the defeated look she gave me confirmed not only had she seen too much in my face, but she was already disappointed in herself. I felt completely helpless not knowing what to say or how to help her. When I sat down, she didn't even flinch. Instead, she waved her empty glass at Dee, signalling for another. Without Ellie seeing, I caught Dee's attention and shook my head no. There was no way she was taking another sip.

I might not have known what to do to make her feel better, take away whatever it was that was causing her pain, but I wasn't going to see her drink away her life in front of me. I had first-hand experience of what alcohol could do to people. Not only could it destroy the person doing the drinking, but it could destroy the lives of those around them. Family, friend or complete stranger, at the end of the day, they too had to survive the aftermath. The problem was it didn't matter if I, Cassie, or a doctor told her not to drink, because she was the one who had to acknowledge the fact she had a problem. She was the one who had overall control of what she chose to do with her body. She was the one who had to fight the temptation and say *no.*

We sat in silence, staring ahead at nothing in particular. That feeling of helplessness continued to gnaw at my bones. Normally, I knew what to say and pretty much always got what I wanted, but right now, I was lost for words. Her glazed look told me she was buzzed from the alcohol, but there was no light behind the windows of her eyes. She had completely withdrawn into herself, and I found myself desperate for the feisty Ellie to return. But hell if I didn't know how to bring her back. The life had been completely zapped out of her, and the worst thing was I didn't know why. I looked down at her wrist and saw the tattoo she'd recently gotten. A single black feather started at the wrist and went up the inside length of her arm; the tip of the feather broke into several little blackbirds. There was a hint of blue in the detail. It was stunning. Like her.

"Freedom?"

She looked at me, confused, not understanding my question. I nodded at the tattoo, and she subconsciously ran her delicate fingers across it. The skin surrounding the tattoo was still slightly inflamed. Had she been applying the cream? Why did it even matter to me? *Because you care.*

"Something like that," she replied, returning her attention to behind the bar. I waited patiently for her to continue. "It's silly really."

"If it means something to you, then it's not silly, angel." *Angel.* The nickname I'd given her rolled off my tongue like it was something I'd been calling her all my life.

"You remember when you found me at the club?"

"Not going to be able to forget that in a while, sweetheart." She looked hot as hell as she blushed and the redness continued to rise up her normally pale cheeks. It reminded me of when I had her up against the wall, my hands running through her silky black hair, trailing the skin just above the waistband of her jeans, the feeling of her thighs tightly wrapped around my waist as she hungrily devoured my mouth like she was starving…

"Suppose not," she said, snapping me from my thoughts. I readjusted myself on the stool, conscious of the fact that if she looked down and saw the prominent bulge in my pants, she would work out exactly where my mind had drifted off to.

"That day I went for a ride out to English Bay. I was thinking about Lyla Rose. It was a difficult day, but I didn't want to end up in a place like this," she said, waving her hand around the bar. "Turns out it didn't matter anyway." She sighed.

Without thinking, I laced my fingers through hers and gave her hand a reassuring squeeze.

"I was sitting watching the holidaymakers, and a single crow perched beside me. I watched it for a while, fascinated by its beauty, the way the blue in the black of its feathers glistened in the sun. I also couldn't help thinking about the significance of it sitting there, especially because of the way I was feeling. I was feeling so… low. Some say the crow is an omen for death, which at the time seemed fitting because I stumbled across that accident on my way back to the apartment. The accident reminded me so much of my own it was too much. That's how and why I ended up in the club. You know, that great big neon light you have flashing outside was like a bloody homing beacon.

"Anyway, some say the crow is also an omen for change. I didn't realise it at the time, but when I woke up in your bed the next day, my life really had changed, because it brought you back into it, and even though the thought was scary—and maybe I sound like the drink is talking—but I felt some sort of connection with you. It took a conversation with an old lady called Betty to make me see things a little clearer, and I made the decision I would try and embrace the changes in my life, so I got the tattoo."

I wasn't sure who the hell Betty was and quite where she fit into the scheme of things, but I wasn't going to question it. Her reasoning behind the tattoo seemed logical enough, and it's not like I had any right to comment. The upper part of my body was becoming my own personal mural of art.

"So what changed?" I asked.

"Everything and nothing." She sighed heavily, and those lightless eyes glistened as they pooled with unshed tears. She swiped at her face defiantly. Almost like she was ashamed to cry. Ashamed to show a chink in her well-established armour. "You should leave me be, Kyle. Just let me sort shit out in my own way. I'll be okay in the end. Always am. It kind of comes part and parcel of being brought up by parents like mine. I've had no choice but learn to be okay. Contrary to what Cas might think, I'm too broken to be fixed, so there's no point in even trying. I don't deal with things well, as you already know," she said, pushing her empty glass across the bar. "I'll always be broken, but I'll always be okay," she whispered, probably hoping I didn't hear.

"Come on. Let's get you home." I nodded at Dee and gently held on to Ellie's elbow as I helped her off the stool. Her knees buckled slightly, but I held on to her waist to keep her steady. Her breathing hitched, either because she nearly fell on her ass or because she too felt that spark the moment I touched her. Whether I was responsible or not, it felt good to get some sort of reaction from her, even if it were small, because maybe then there was still hope. Hope that Ellie was only temporarily out of commission and that light void from her eyes could be ignited again.

I climbed onto my bike and offered her a helmet. She took it grudgingly and stared at the seat behind me while she processed whatever she was thinking about. I guessed it had something to do with Jake, but I didn't push her for answers. I felt certain she would come to the right decision. She eventually swung her leg over the bike and slid down the seat so she was sitting snuggly behind me. She wrapped her small hands around my waist loosely and waited patiently for me to bring my Harley to life. Admittedly, this wasn't how I pictured getting my ol' lady to sit behind me on my bike for the first time, but hell if the warmth from between her thighs didn't feel good as she nestled closer into my body.

My ol' lady? I dismissed the thought, putting it down to a mental slip of the tongue, and pulled her arms around my waist tighter, grateful she didn't resist. Whether it was by choice or the alcohol, she rested her head against my back. The gentle pressure that appeared in my chest when I realised how much she was putting her trust in me took me by surprise, but I pushed it away as quick as it arrived. Not that it mattered though, because there was no denying the fact I felt like the luckiest son of a bitch alive.

"Thanks for finding her, Kyle." Cassie stood expectantly at the door and stepped aside, allowing us through. Without words, she took Ellie from me and guided her to what I assumed to be her bedroom, leaving me standing in their living room. I don't know what I expected, but I thought a place two professional women shared would be immaculate. Don't get me wrong; it wasn't dirty or anything, but the place was chaos. Considering I knew how Ellie liked control, this surprised me. DVDs, CDs, and books were piled everywhere, the bin was overflowing, and even though it was highly inappropriate to laugh right now, I couldn't help but chuckle at the amount of empty ice cream cartons in there. They were obviously both a big fan of chocolate.

Cassie cleared her throat from behind me. "Uh, don't mind the mess. We're not home much to tidy it." She grinned, knowing I wasn't fooled by her comments, and chucked a soda at me. "Sorry, not been shopping lately so that's all we have to drink."

I caught it one-handed and waited for it to settle

before opening it.

"She'll feel like shit in the morning, but she'll be fine. It's not like she hasn't nursed a hangover before."

She slid over the side of the ratty sofa, falling neatly into its corner, and grabbed a cushion, gripping hold of it like it was her only lifeline. There wasn't a spare seat considering the seat other than the sofa had a pile of clothes stacked high on it. Not wanting to sit directly next to Cassie, I chose a position on the floor with my back leaned up against the wall.

"Trust me. She'll work through it in her own time. It's not for me to really share, but I think I know what's triggered this episode. Question is, are you going to be hanging around to help her through it?" she asked.

The question caught me off guard, but I was surprised the answer was relatively easy. "Yes," I answered truthfully, and Cassie sighed in relief.

A smile lit up her pretty face. I could certainly see why men would find her attractive. She was undoubtedly a stunner, her Scandinavian heritage obvious from her blond hair and blue eyes, but in my eyes, she didn't have a patch on Ellie. Cassie knew she was gorgeous and knew how to work it for her own advantage, whereas Ellie was totally oblivious to how she affected people. She was petite and filled out in all the right places, but appearances didn't matter with her. All she had to do was flash a smile or laugh and you could single her out in a crowd.

"Good, because if you're serious about sticking around, you're going to have to be patient." She eyed me for a second. "And put up with shit."

"I put up with shit on a daily basis," I replied.

"Sure you do, but this will be different. This will be emotional shit. You won't be able to solve it by shooting her or smacking her in the face." *Ouch!* "And by the way, if you even consider either, I will castrate you myself."

"What do you take me for?" I asked, pissed off she could think such a thing. I was a lot of things, but a woman beater wasn't one of them.

"You know, Sadie and Trix said how different you were with her, and I honestly thought they were talking crap. I'd heard all these stories about you. Not from Ellie I might add. People talk at the hospital. The patients, the staff. They don't paint a good picture, so when Ellie started talking about you, I had mixed feelings about you and her. She's already been through so much, so at first, I was worried about what effect you would have on her, but then over the past few weeks, I've started glimpsing the old Ellie again. The one I met when we were kids, before… well, before some shit happened. The happy, carefree Ellie I knew from when she was with Jake was slowly coming back to life." She finally took a breath.

"So I figured I'd keep my mouth shut and see how it all panned out. Okay, I wasn't expecting the past few days, but I don't think I would change them. In a seriously mixed-up way, I think all this drama has done her some good."

I looked at her, confused by her statement, but didn't argue. She knew Ellie better than anyone after all.

"I guess I mean all this drama has made her open

her eyes. The problem is she's struggling with what she sees and what it means." She stopped and looked at me like she was trying to see into my soul.

"Still listening." I challenged.

"You know, I still had doubts about you up until about…" She looked at her watch. "An hour ago, but seeing the way you looked at her earlier, I reckon I might have been a bit rash with my first opinions."

"Thanks. I think."

"I also saw she means more to you than maybe you even realise."

Chapter Twenty-Three

ELLIE

"So how are you doing today, Ellie?" Dr. Radrie asked as I entered his office.

As usual, it was spotlessly clean and everything was lined up neatly along the straight lines of his desk. When I first entered his office, I thought it unusual for a psychiatrist to be so tidy, but I'd since discovered even consultants in the field had their problems too, and his was OCD. Granted, I could hardly say I had OCD. My home was as messy as my life, but somehow knowing this man, this doctor, had his own problems and managed to get past them put me at ease with trusting him with my own state of mind. Unlike a lot of people in his position, he could draw from his own life experiences and actually help.

It had been three weeks since I emerged from hibernating in my room for four days. Thankfully, work had approved some last-minute leave. Otherwise, I would have most definitely lost my job. There was no way I would have been able to get through the day when just getting out of bed was too much effort. My body felt like a lead weight as I struggled with the exhaustion. When I sank into a depressive state, sleep only really came in the early hours of the morning, and even then I would only get a few hours. Thoughts, emotions, ideas, memories all ran wild and my mind became a rollercoaster.

When things got hard, I liked to drink, but when things got hard *and* confusing, I locked myself away. I became depressed as I mulled over my thoughts and struggled with the overwhelming barrage of emotions that consumed me until I felt like I could crawl out of my own skin. I closed myself off to the world until I felt I could move on. It wasn't something I did often, but I'd obviously done it often enough for Cassie to turn into a mother hen. If it weren't for her though, I wouldn't have eaten or gotten out of bed. Of course I would get up to use bathroom, but admittedly, taking a shower wasn't top of my list when all I wanted to do was curl up in a ball and disappear.

Cassie turning into a mother hen made me love her even more, not that I'd ever tell her. I think she'd always had an inkling about what went on in my mind during these episodes, but even she didn't know the full extent of my damaged soul. My thoughts became so dark, I would often think about hurting myself or running away. Literally packing my bags, changing my name, and starting from scratch. Basically disappearing off the face of this earth. Thoughts of ending it all with a combination of booze and pills weren't uncommon either, but thankfully, they remained just that—thoughts. When I'd learned of Jake's and Lyla Rose's deaths, those thoughts were the most pronounced of them all.

Four days was actually a record. These spells of mine had been known to last up to two weeks, if not longer, so imagine Cassie's surprise when after only four days I left my bedroom, got showered, and dressed before she'd even surfaced from bed. To be honest, I probably didn't even need to hide away this long. I might have gone about things the wrong way, but I realised at the end of the day, no one had died. I didn't have overbearing parents trying to control my life. I actually had nothing to be depressed about. I was waging an unnecessary war in my head because I was unable to let go of the past and deal with the problem like a sensible adult, choosing to forget my problems by drinking myself to death slowly.

The last time I thought alcohol was the answer to all my prayers, Jake stepped in and took over where Cassie failed. Not through any fault of her own, she just couldn't get through to me the way he did. It didn't happen overnight, but eventually, Jake pulled me out of the gutter and helped me take back control of my life. The problem was he wasn't around now. It was down to me to pick up the pieces. It was time for me to pull myself together and take another step forward, away from my past.

Fate played its hand on my first day back at

work. I tried not to get too attached to patients, but sometimes someone came in who I instantly connect with and I found myself going above and beyond to make sure they got the best care possible. An hour into my shift, I found myself connecting to Beth, a young girl who was admitted for attempting to take her own life by overdose. At only twenty, she'd decided life wasn't worth living after a bad breakup with her long-term boyfriend. It's not like she was the first attempted suicide I'd tended to, because she wasn't and certainly wouldn't be the last. Maybe it was timing or simply the way I was feeling about things in my own life, but we connected because I understood. I understood sometimes, no matter what's happening in your life, life just doesn't seem enough. A bad relationship, family problems, stress at work, or just general everyday living—if all you can feel is despair, the dark thoughts become all-consuming. So when Dr. Radrie walked through that door to see Beth, I accepted fate's hand and requested an appointment. For me.

"I'm good. Have been writing everything down as you suggested. It's just a bit scary seeing it in black and white," I admitted, finally answering his question.

"Why's that?" he asked, entwining his fingers and placing them in front of him on his desk.

This was only my fourth session, but I'd already picked up this was something he would do to stop himself from straightening objects on his desk. I looked at the clock on the wall and began my silent countdown.

"It makes things more real. It made me realise my

mother's constant insults, the way she kept putting me down, the controlling, the guilt trips, etcetera, basically all boiled down to emotional abuse. I suppose I'd always known this, but seeing it written down, remembering it all… It's hard, you know?" *Two minutes.*

"So how have you been dealing with it?"

I knew what he was asking. He was wondering whether I'd paid a trip to the bar or nearby off-licence recently, but truthfully, laying off the drink had been surprisingly easy. Cassie breathing down my neck every spare minute might have had something to do with that, though. I actually came to work for a rest.

And then there was Kyle.

"I've not had a drink since that time in the bar, and I'm fine. I do think about it though, occasionally." *A lot.* "Like when I think about Jake and Lyla Rose or when I remember stuff," I answered. Thankfully, after our four previous sessions, Dr. Radrie knew what "stuff" I referred to.

"That's good to hear, Ellie. Writing down your thoughts will become easier and, sure, it may open a can of worms, but I think in time you will realise nothing that happened in your childhood was your fault. Despite your self-beliefs, you are a good person. People quite often bully others because they feel threatened themselves. Transference."

Five minutes. Dr. Radrie relaxed his fingers and started straightening the pens on his desk like a man possessed. I don't know why I did the countdown, possibly to distract me from the conversation or for my own amusement, but it worked every time.

Despite the topic, I couldn't stop the corners of my lips turning up slightly.

"Being only a child, you wouldn't have fought back, making it easier for her to continue with the abuse, and naturally, all you would have wanted was her love and approval." He continued.

The corners of my lips now dropped back into a straight line. My temporary respite from the shit going on in my head took a backseat. "I'm not a child anymore."

"Very true, but because you've suffered abuse since a child, it's more deeply rooted. You have almost become conditioned to believe the worst about yourself because you don't know any different. You shy away when someone shows you any form of affection because you weren't shown how to love. Have you ever asked yourself why you feel uncomfortable if someone you don't know well hugs you? It's not because you're weird. It's purely because you don't understand it."

I nodded, agreeing with his analogy. *But...* "I let Jake and Cas hug me."

"I said 'almost.' Besides, even you said yourself it took a while for you to feel comfortable with Cassie and Jake hugging you."

"True, but what about sex. You know I'm not a virgin, right?" I asked, trying not to blush as I lightened the tone.

"Sex doesn't necessarily mean love and affection, Ellie. For some people, it's purely lust and human nature's way to relieve some tension." His old, knowing eyes burned into my soul. "So how have things progressed with Kyle?"

I gave up fighting the blush. There was no stopping the heat rising up my cheeks.

Suddenly, a speck on the floor seemed far more interesting. I knew he would ask; I just didn't know how to answer. "Good, I guess," I said, trying to avoid eye contact. From the corner of my eye, I saw him raise a bushy grey eyebrow at me and smirk. His silver hair and receding hairline made him look older than his fifty years, but his eyes were kind and just. "We've spent some time together and we've talked a little, but I don't know. I'm hardly his type anyway, so it doesn't matter. Besides, I don't think I'm ready to move on."

"You sure about that?"

Am I?

"Of course. Why would he be interested in me? I'm all kinds of broken, I'm hardly his usual catwalk model blonde, and seriously, he's the complete opposite to Jake. And he's a bloody criminal for God's sake." *He's also hot, intense, kind, and makes my skin tingle every time we breathe the same air.* Who was I trying to kid?

"Why would he not be interested in a smart, funny, pretty young thing like you? What exactly is his type anyway? Do you even know or are you guessing and just putting yourself down again? Do people even really have types? Do you have a type, Ellie? Think about it. You have only ever been with Jake, so how do you really know who you'd be attracted to?"

Valid point.

"I really think we need to work on that image you have of yourself. Despite what your mother has led you to believe, you are a beautiful person, and I'm not just talking on the outside. With regards to Kyle's lifestyle…" He said "lifestyle" in air quotes, causing me to break out a rare smile. "What makes you think he's not broken too? Not being funny, but to live as he does, he's got to have some of his own problems. Also…" He looked down at his desk sheepishly. It was another endearing quality I noticed he had when he was going to say something possibly deemed as unprofessional. "Just because he is who he is doesn't necessarily make him a bad person."

This time I laughed. "Did I just hear you right? It almost sounded like you were condoning a relationship with a known criminal."

"All I'm saying is he's more than capable of loving you the way you deserve to be loved, if not more so. From what I know, some of these gangs or MCs or whatever… they're closer than family."

The relationships between Tiny, Trix, Saint, Sadie, Junior, and the others flashed across my mind. Of course I knew he was right. They were closer than any family I'd ever known, not that I had much to go on. My best friend grew up in care, I didn't have a lot of other friends, and I couldn't really compare a good family to my own.

"You also said you didn't feel like you were ready to move on. Why?"

"It feels like I'm trying to replace Jake. It's too soon."

"Maybe it is; maybe it's not. Some people grieve

for years; some move on a lot sooner, but ask yourself this: are you happy to live the rest of your life alone? How soon is too soon? One month, ten years? Ask yourself what Jake would want for you."

"He would want me to be happy. He only ever wanted me to be happy," I said quietly.

"Exactly, and if I'm honest with you... Yes, I do believe you feel guilty about moving on. It's only natural to feel this way when losing someone you love, but I also think you're using Jake's death as an excuse to stop you from moving on because you don't feel like you deserve to. Just like you use Jake and other 'triggers,' as you call them, to go out on a binge."

Tears threatened as I realised how close to the truth he was. He smiled, but it wasn't arrogant; it was comforting and reassuring, but it didn't stop me from looking at the clock, eager for the session to come to an end.

"Here's what I want you to do. Along with your current journal, I want you to write down at least three positive things every day. Whether it be about something good you've done at work or simply the way people make you feel," he said.

I nodded, understanding all too clear who he was referring to as "people."

"Okay," I replied simply and stood up to leave.

Dr. Radrie stopped me just as I reached for the door handle.

"Ellie. I also want you to do something else, if not for me, for yourself." I waited expectantly for him to continue. "Stop hiding." I went to reply, but he raised his hand to stop me again. "I mean it. Think about it at least."

"I will," I replied honestly and smiled. I was shocked at how the smile came so naturally. It wasn't forced this time. It was probably the first genuine smile I'd smiled in ages.

I'd gone to see Dr. Radrie straight from a long shift, so I needed to make a quick stop in the locker room to get changed. I'd walked to work and planned on walking back home through Stanley Park. A walk I'd come to love over the past few weeks. The sun was shining, showing summer was still holding on by a thread even though subtle signs of autumn approaching showed by the yellowing and falling leaves. I was still smiling as I swung the door open at the bottom of the stairwell into the emergency department and wound my way through the maze of corridors between bays and trauma rooms.

As much as it scared me, I would try and do as Dr. Radrie said. I would try and stop hiding, and I would try and be a little bit more optimistic about my future.

My focus only being on getting to the locker room so I could quickly get changed and walk home, I'd completely zoned out. I was walking in a daydream and was totally oblivious to my surroundings. Quickly walking past the final bay, I didn't see the solid wall of muscle I was about to run into. I quite literally flew backward, the wind knocked out of me. Gasping for air, I stumbled on my feet, but before my backside made friends with the ground, I was caught by strong, familiar hands.

"Whoa. What's the rush?" The deep sound of his voice rumbled through my body, causing and explosion of butterflies to erupt in my stomach and tingles to shoot up my spine. Catching my breath, I finally found the courage to look up. I was greeted by those intense, gorgeous brown eyes that had now made several appearances in my dreams.

Excited. Happy. Alive. The first three words I would be writing in my journal.

Chapter Twenty-Four

ELLIE

It was official. I'd become one of those guys. The guy who goes out of his way for the attention of a woman. For three whole weeks I was the sounding board, the shoulder to cry on, and not once had I attempted to get in her pants, because something told me I needed to give her space to work out the shit going on in her head. And I'd loved every minute of it. The guys gave me shit about it. Sadie, Trix, and even Big Mamma gave me shit about it. Hell, I gave myself shit about it, but truthfully, I couldn't care less. I now knew what Saint and Tiny meant when they tried explaining what it was like when they first laid eyes on their girls. I was completely whipped, and that was before I'd managed to get her naked and in my bed.

The sad truth was it wasn't about sex with Ellie. It was so much more than that. For sure, she was the reason my dick had become reacquainted with my right hand, but during the past three weeks, I'd gotten a glimpse of the girl Cassie told me about. I saw what was behind the foul mouth and feisty attitude, and I liked it. A lot. As suspected, there was much more to Ellie than met the eye. She was funny, she was smart, and she was beyond beautiful, inside and out. Yep, I'd become one of those poor, pathetic guys, and I really couldn't give a flying fuck.

I phoned Cassie when I got out of bed this morning, and she told me Ellie had an appointment with her shrink after work. I wanted to see her. I wanted to see if she was okay. She'd walked into work, so it was the perfect excuse to turn up at the hospital and offer her a ride home. Not that we would go straight back to her apartment. I wasn't ready to part with her so early in the day. With the help of the girls, Cassie in particular, I'd made other plans.

I'd intended to wait outside, but patience had never been a strong point of mine. A quick glance at my watch confirmed she was late, and my protective instinct came soaring to the surface. Or was it my newfound neediness? I walked through the entrance of the emergency department and headed toward where I knew her locker room to be. That's when I saw a flash of silky black hair darting between the emergency bays. She had a fuck-off big grin on her face and the sight tugged at my heart. *Beautiful.* Although it was starting to come out more regularly, I hadn't seen her smile like that in a while. I found myself standing alone in the middle of a corridor, wearing a fuck-off big grin of my own. *Idiot.*

I started to follow her and even shouted her name, but it fell on deaf ears. Why was she rushing? She was so focused walking down the corridor she was completely unaware of what was going on around her. I sped up to catch her, taking my own shortcut between curtained-off bays, resulting in a few screams from patients and nurses. I heard her quick footsteps as I approached the final bay and then, *wham...* she collided with my chest. On instinct, I grabbed her by the shoulders before she landed on her ass.

A blush heated her face as she caught her breath and righted herself, but she didn't look up. I asked her what the rush was, and her blush deepened when she realised who she'd just face-planted. She looked at me through her lashes before finally looking up properly and meeting my stare. Her pink, luscious, and very kissable lips turned up slightly at the corners, and being the sap I'd now become, my heart skipped a beat at the sight. She brushed her sweet little tongue over those perfect lips, and I was completely undone. I was desperate for a taste, but her giggle completely crushed my thoughts of having my way with that mouth of hers in front of everyone in the middle of a hospital corridor, because... well, she giggled. I'd seen her smile, I'd heard her laugh, but that giggle... It was like music to my fucking ears.

"Just keen to get home. That's all," she replied huskily in her sexy English accent. She was staring at my face so intently, I couldn't find my voice. Her eyes moved to my mouth and she ran that tongue over her lips again, and it took everything I had not to grab her face and pull it to my own. She could feel it too. The raw chemistry that simmered between us like highly charged electricity.

"You got your bike?" I finally asked, my voice hoarse and laced with desire, not sounding like my own. Had it gone up an octave?

"No, I walked in. It's so lovely out there today I thought I'd take advantage of it before winter sets in." I knew what her answer would be and just about heard her, but my focus had returned to those lips, her jawline, her exposed neck… shoulder blade. *Damn.*

"What are you doing here?" she asked. Had she realised my head had just wandered back to the gutter? She looked completely innocent, but there was a spark of mischief in her eyes and something else. Lust?

"Thought I could give you a lift home, but first, I have a surprise."

She raised an eyebrow and smirked. "Well, well, Mr. Slater. The fact you've even thought of a surprise for me is surprise enough. I never would have thought a guy like you would even know how to surprise a woman," she quipped mockingly, tapping a single finger of my chest. In challenge? "Like me."

Perfect. My angel was playing with me and something strange and unfamiliar stirred inside.

She brushed past me, walking away with a gentle sway of her hips. I watched for a few seconds before jogging after her. She stopped and looked at me shyly when I caught up with her. She looked so damn cute as she tried to work out what she was doing. I could literally see the cogs turning behind the windows of her eyes.

"Well, Miss Dale, you'd be surprised at how capable I am at satisfying a woman," I said, wondering if she caught my double meaning. The blush rising up her cheeks told me she did. I grabbed hold of her hand and tugged her gently toward the exit while pulling my phone out of my pocket and sending Tiny a quick text to finalise my plans.

She stopped dead in her tracks and held me back. "I kind of need to get dressed first," she said, waving her hands over her hospital scrubs. She pulled away before I could answer and practically skipped toward the locker room.

As we drove into Whistler, I felt her hands tighten around my waist and I could have sworn I heard an excited squeal over the sound of my Harley's engine. I pulled into a parking lot and shut off the engine. I swung my leg over the bike and lifted Ellie, who was frantically trying to remove her helmet, before slowly resting her feet on the ground.

"I've always wanted to come here," she said excitedly. "I've just not had the opportunity to come this far yet." The more excited she got, the more animated her hands became, and I don't think anything in the world would have been able to take the satisfied grin off my face. "I hope the surprise isn't skiing though, 'cause I can't ski for shit and I already spend most of my time at the hospital. I don't want to be there if I don't have to be." She rambled on without stopping to take a breath, making me laugh.

"Relax, angel. No skiing." She let out a relieved breath and then quickly turned to the sound of the approaching bike. "Right on time," I said.

"Is that Tiny?" she asked, raising a hand just above her right eye to shelter her gaze from the sun.

"Yeah. He's got the rest of your surprise," I replied, waving a hand at Tiny as he pulled in alongside us on his bike.

"I thought this was my surprise."

Damn, she was getting more and more adorable by the minute. I took a moment to look at her perfect face and took in a deep breath when I realised I was staring like a creeper. She blushed and dipped her face shyly when she saw me looking at her, nervously tucking a loose strand of hair behind her ear.

"Hey, brother. Thanks for bringing this." Turning my attention back to Tiny, I grabbed the carrier bags from where they'd been secured on the back of his bike.

"No problem. Hey, Ellie. How you doing?" he asked.

She looked up and smiled. "I'm good. How's Trix?"

"She's doing good. She said for me to tell you that you girls should meet up. Maybe get a beer or something."

I wanted to smack the thoughtless fucker in the face, but Ellie beat me to it. Verbally.

"I'd love to meet up with her. Maybe we could avoid bars for the time being, though. You know, considering I have a bit of a problem with alcohol.

Maybe we could just stick with going for a cuppa?"

"Shit, Ellie. I didn't think…" he said. At least he had the decency to look embarrassed.

"No worries, Tiny. I'm just playing with you. I didn't mean to make you uncomfortable," she responded with a wink.

I was so damn proud of her right then I think my heart actually hurt. *A little bit.*

After a few minutes more of light conversation, Tiny nodded and signalled his farewell before taking off back to the club. Ellie looked from me to the bag and then back to me again, confusion etched in her perfect heart-shaped face.

"So what's in the bags?" she asked teasingly, with a small skip in her step.

"This, my sweet angel, is your surprise," I answered, seizing her small hand as I led her to the foot of the mountains.

Chapter Twenty-Five

ELLIE

I liked this side of Kyle. The sweet, caring, and considerate Kyle. Don't get me wrong; I liked the other sides of Kyle too, but this side of him made him seem less of an arsehole and more... human.

He unexpectedly held hold of my hand, a sentiment that had my insides squirming and my cheeks flushing like an overexcited schoolgirl, as we walked through the beautiful resort village of Whistler. I'd desperately wanted to visit Whistler since arriving in Vancouver but had never gotten around to it. Fidgeting with the bottom of my top, tripping over my feet as I attempted to walk in confident steps, and rambling incessantly—you would think I'd never been on a date before. I hoped he thought my excitability was all down to the magical scenery, but I knew different. It was him. It was all him.

The Blackcomb Mountains dominated the crystal-blue skies, as did the alpine meadows. The contrast between the blue of the sky, the green of the large expanse of pine trees, and the white of the snow-capped mountains made a picture postcard look dull in comparison. Whistler was as breathtaking as I thought it would be, but not as breathtaking as the ruggedly handsome man walking alongside me. His plain black T-shirt pulled taut against his well-defined biceps and broad chest and his dark blue jeans hung low on his waist, allowing me a glimpse of those perfect abs when he lifted his arms. His black biker boots and leather cut finished off his outfit to perfection and made him look every bit the bad boy his reputation made him out to be. He hadn't shaved for a couple of days, giving him that sexy five-o' clock shadow I'd grown to love, and my God, did I have the urge to run my fingers along his jawline through the soft dark stubble. The deep scar on his neck from the bullet that could have killed him was still red but strangely added to his appeal, as did the scowl he gave any man, or woman, who dared look in my direction.

It should have been comical or even pissed me off. I wasn't his possession after all, but I loved how his protectiveness made me feel. He made me feel safe. He was also the cause for the heat building right between my thighs and the tingling sensations erupting over my entire body as I thought about running my fingers over the contours of his muscles, through his thick dark hair, and tasting his lips once again. Never in my life did I think I would be turned on by alpha male bullshit, but boy, was I wrong. Maybe Dr. Radrie was right? I had only been with Jake, who was Kyle's complete polar opposite, but really, what did I know? All I knew was as we walked through the village and headed toward the sign posted Valley Trail, he was all I could see through my lust-filled haze.

"I swear, angel, if you keep eye fucking me like that, we're not gonna to make it."

Shit. I knew I was looking, but I didn't realise I was openly undressing him with my eyes. I quickly dropped my gaze to the ground, embarrassed.

He tugged my hand gently, jerking me so I looked back at him. "Don't fucking look away from me, angel. There's never any shame in looking. In fact, I like you looking. You just have to stop looking so damn hot doing it, because there are way too many people around to witness what I want to do to you right now, and I'm not sure if I have the willpower to stop myself."

I blushed shyly, but his words had more impact than he knew. I liked knowing I had this effect on him, and with each word, my confidence grew. His body shook as he chuckled. I playfully shoved him in the arm, trying to contain the grin I was trying to hide. I might have liked his flirting, but I wasn't quite ready for him to know that just yet.

We continued along the Valley Trail for about fifteen minutes before veering down a small path through the forest. Pine trees were officially my new favourite smell. The forest air was fresh and amazing. A vast difference to the smoggy, smoke-filled air back home in England. When we got to the opening at the end, I gasped at the sight before me. We were at the Lost Lake, a secluded glacial lake hidden in the depths of the stunning green forest. And I instantly became lost in the scenery.

"Beautiful," I whispered.

"Very," Kyle replied, but he wasn't looking at the lake.

The scenery then took a backseat when every nerve ending felt like it was on fire as I sensed him coming up behind me. Instant heat rushed through my body as he tugged me toward his chest and encircled my waist with his arms. He tucked his head into the crook of my neck and goose bumps rippled across my skin. We stood for a moment in complete silence, just watching the calmness of the water, and I could feel whatever was left of the walls I'd carefully erected starting to crumble around me.

"So what's your home like?" he asked, the warmth of his breath caressing my neck.

I closed my eyes for a second and savoured the feeling and relaxed farther into his embrace.

"Dull, flat, boring. My home was in a smallish town about an hour from London, in the county of Essex. Don't get me wrong. There are some beautiful parts of the UK. I just didn't live in one of them. The New Forest, Cotswolds, Peak District are nice. Maybe the Lake District could come close to this, but I don't know. It's different here."

"You said your home *was*. Does that mean it's

not anymore?" he questioned.

I thought for a moment before answering. I remembered how I felt when I stayed at his house with Junior and the others.

"No, it's not been home for a long time," I said quietly.

"Come on."

A chill whipped down my back as soon as Kyle stepped away from me. I missed his warmth instantly, but he held out his hand and nodded toward a secluded area, away from other tourists. I took it without hesitation and let him walk me.

He sat on the ground and pulled me down with him, positioning me between his legs. Once again, I welcomed the heat he provided. It wasn't like it was cold or anything, but having his body wrapped around mine made me feel secure. Safe. And I'd be lying if I said I didn't like the contact and intimacy.

Shifting me slightly to the side, he reached in front of me and opened one of the carrier bags. I'd completely forgotten about them, but now my curiosity was piqued. Realising I was anxious to see what was inside, he prolonged revealing its contents. Frustrated, I pushed him playfully in the side, causing him to roll backward, taking me with him. He made no effort to sit back up. Instead, he turned me so I was facing him and lifted me so I was straddling him across his crotch. I didn't need to see the lust in his eyes to know he liked exactly where I was sitting. The hardening of his cock underneath my arse was proof enough.

I fought off the blush that was threatening. *I can*

do this. Feeling brave, I leaned down and gently brushed my lips against the side of his mouth. I'd been dreaming of those gorgeous full lips on mine anyway, so why not take a chance?

"Thank you," I whispered before leaning down and brushing another kiss against the other side. I sat back up and watched as he fought for the control he was holding on to by a fine thread. I moved my hips slowly, and he closed his eyes, his breathing hitched, and his hands gripped my thighs tighter.

"For what?" he replied huskily.

My confidence grew as I saw and felt what my actions were doing to him and spurred me on. I leaned down again, stopping inches away from his face, and braced my hands beside each side of his head. Loose strands of my hair spiralled over my shoulders and gently rested against his cheeks. He went to move them away, but I held his hands down. My breasts hovered just above his chest, and I continued to move my hips slowly. His grip tightened until it was almost painful, but I put on what I hoped was my best seductive smile and continued to move.

"Every—"

Quick as lightning, he moved his hands and grabbed me by the back of my head, roughly running his fingers through my hair and pressing my face to his before I even finished what I was saying. There was no softly-softly; the action was swift, filled with passion and heat. It was more intense than any kiss we'd ever shared, and I wanted more. I met his mouth as forcefully with my own, our tongues hungrily delving deeper into each other's mouths and linking together mercilessly. He released his grip from my head and moved it to my waist but made no attempt to move his hands. I wanted him to move them. I wanted him to touch me.

Breaking our kiss, I brought one of my hands to his shoulder and tightened my grip around his waist with my thighs to give me balance as my other hand made a journey under his T-shirt, across his abs, and travelled farther up to explore the contours of his chest. He stilled and looked me directly in the eye. Finding his answer, he practically growled and pulled me back to his mouth while his hands found the exposed flesh around my waistline. They continued to roam higher and higher until they skimmed the outside of my bra. It felt like ten thousand volts had just exploded through my body. I slowed the kiss and closed my eyes. His thumbs gently rubbed across each nipple, above the light fabric of my bra, and I couldn't contain the whimper escaping my lips.

"Ooooh. Gross."

Oh. My. God. Those two words had me snapping back to reality with a thud and any lustful thoughts evaporating. Kyle's hands abruptly dropped from under my top and rested on top of my thighs, which were still gripping hold of him like a vise. His face was red, but not from being embarrassed. He was desperately trying not to laugh. *Not funny.* Heart racing and still panting, I slowly looked around and was greeted with two very blue and curious eyes.

"Hi," I said to the little blond girl who couldn't have been more than six.

"Hello," she replied with a smile revealing a gap

in the bottom row of her teeth. "What you doing?" she asked, swaying from side to side.

"Trinity!" *Saved by the bell... or at least by her mother.* "Oh, I am so sorry. She just wandered off," said the tall blonde with matching blue eyes.

I felt sorry for her. The poor woman didn't know where to look. She coughed her apologies once again and almost ran off, dragging her poor daughter behind her. I faced Kyle, who looked like he was about to explode his cheeks were so red. It wasn't long before I collapsed on his chest and we were both laughing.

Once we'd pulled ourselves together and adjusted our clothes, I went back to sitting between his legs and watching the lake. I was quiet for a while, still stunned by my attempt to nearly jump his bones in the middle of a very public place. *What was I thinking?*

"So what's in the bag?" I finally asked.

He pulled the bag open, and I burst out laughing when he revealed pre-packed sandwiches, a couple chocolate doughnuts, and a couple cans of Coke. *Such a romantic.* It didn't escape my attention that the other bag remained unopened.

We lay side by side watching the clouds go by until afternoon slowly turned into evening. We spoke about everything and nothing, and sometimes we just lay in comfortable silence. At first we simply held hands, but as the temperature dropped, Kyle pulled me into his side and wrapped me tight in his strong arms, engulfing me with his body heat. Everything was perfect. Kyle was perfect. *Thank you.* I silently looked to the skies and thanked fate for crossing my path with the man responsible for making me smile again. I closed my eyes as he gently stroked my hair, lulling me to sleep.

"Hey, angel. Don't go to sleep on me," he whispered in my ear.

I jerked awake and then shuddered when Kyle's warm breath touched my cool skin.

"Uh?" I said, rubbing my eyes. "Sorry, just tired all of a sudden. It's been a long day." I pulled out my phone and looked at the time. *Shit*. "God, I didn't realise how late it was. We really should head back home."

"Don't worry about that. We don't need to head back until morning. I've booked us a room at the resort." I blinked and must have looked pissed off rather than confused because he held his hands up in surrender, worry etched in his handsome face. I silently laughed at his reaction. He was such a softy and didn't even know it. "Els, it's not like what you're thinking."

"What am I thinking?" I challenged seductively.

Admittedly, I was shocked at first, but now I was actually excited about the thought of spending the night with Kyle, and my inner minx was reawakening. I rolled toward him, flung a leg over his waist, and pulled myself up so I straddled him once again. Before I had the chance to get comfortable, he flipped me over onto my back and pinned my arms down above my head. My small body lay helpless between his strong thighs, under his broad chest and firm grip. He towered over me as he applied just enough pressure so he wouldn't crush me but enough to exert his presence. My entire body hummed with anticipation. There was too much distance between our bodies.

"It's not about sex, angel. Although, don't get me wrong." He licked his lips and his eyes raked over my body in a lust-filled gaze. "After earlier and you just sitting on my fucking cock again, it's kinda the only thing on my mind right this minute."

He dropped his hips lower, and I could feel exactly what was going through his mind. I gulped nervously, and for the first time in a long time, Jake couldn't have been any further from my thoughts.

Chapter Twenty-Six

KYLE

Ellie's firm little ass rubbing against my cock had me awake and very alert in an instant. I tightened my hold around her waist and she let out a contented little moan, but slow steady breaths and the fact her eyes were still closed told me she was sleeping.

I honestly did only intend to sleep with Ellie last night. I'd genuinely just wanted to experience waking up with her in my arms. I never even thought I was capable of thinking about being with a woman in this way. Until her. I had every intention to take things slowly and see how they developed. There was no denying the connection we had, but it was obvious Jake still played a big part in her life. Of course, this was natural. He was her husband, the father of the daughter she lost. It was hard playing second fiddle to a ghost, but I knew, or rather hoped, she would stop fighting the attraction and see what we could have, in time.

Time. Cassie was right, I had come to care for Ellie more than I realised, and even though it scared shit the out of me, I was willing to give her all the time she needed. Turned out she'd apparently had enough time to figure some things out. Not that I was complaining. I gently stroked her arm up and down, causing her to smile in her sleep and push closer against me. The thin layer of her panties was the only barrier between us, and I was a stone's throw away from removing them with my teeth.

I should let her sleep. I adjusted my boxers before they became more uncomfortable and rolled onto my back. Not wanting to wake her, but still wanting to feel her against my skin, I carefully pulled her with me and fit her snuggly under my arm. She let out a contented sigh. I closed my eyes and drifted off to the memories of what happened when we left the Lost Lake.

The hotel room was clean, quaint, and simple. Ellie's eyes almost bulged out of her head when she saw it. She obviously saw more to the overpriced room than I did, but to be honest, I only had eyes for my five-foot-nothing firecracker and of course, the king-size bed. Walking from the lake to the hotel had been somewhat uncomfortable. Thinking of Tiny naked couldn't even reduce the bulge in my pants, but if Ellie noticed, she didn't say anything. She was probably struggling with her own discomfort anyhow, and that thought alone was reason enough for the visual of Tiny's naked ass not doing the trick.

I practically stripped down to my boxers as soon as we walked through the door, then headed toward the bathroom for a cold shower. I stared at my reflection in the mirror, trying to work out what Ellie saw that no one else did. She'd always been at ease in my company. Any discomfort seemed to stem from her own thoughts and insecurities rather than as a result of me. She'd added herself to the handful of people I could be myself around, therefore working her way a little closer into my normally impenetrable heart.

I looked at my new scars. They were healing nicely. Ellie had done a good job. The memories of her delicate little fingers digging inside my chest as she tried to fish out the bullet flashed into my mind. *She's too innocent for this life.* Until that moment, I'd never really thought about how my lifestyle would affect Ellie. I lived in a crazy fucked-up world in which she didn't belong.

My thoughts had always been purely selfish, but I'd always been a selfish asshole. *I'm no good for her.* But she made me happy, made me laugh—something I couldn't recall doing in a long time. She was my light in an otherwise dark world. She was a drug, and I was addicted. Addicted to Ellie. Addicted to suddenly feeling alive. Addicted to feeling wanted. Pushing aside the thoughts, I stepped inside the shower and stuck my head under the full force of the water. Bracing my hands on the tiled wall in front of me, I became further lost in my warring thoughts.

The sound of the door clicking shut had me snapping back to attention. "Ellie?" I questioned. No answer. I looked around and came up with no possible option for a weapon. I balled my fists and hoped I didn't need to use them. A small release of breath had me relaxing my hands and hardening in other places.

Ellie was on the opposite side of the shower curtain. Watching the curtain expectantly, adrenaline rushed through my veins. The anticipation burning through my entire body felt like every nerve ending was aflame, but in a good way.

"Angel, what you doing?"

Another small breath and then long feminine fingers appeared around the side of the curtain. My breathing hitched as it opened slightly and a dainty foot stepped in, followed by a toned calf and then abruptly stopped. *Fuck me.* I considered turning the water to straight cold because I was pretty sure if the rest of her stepped around that curtain, the sight of my cock standing at full attention would have her running. I'd been trying to be good. I didn't want her to think it was just about sex, but hell if my body didn't want to help me out at that moment. Long black locks of hair cascading over a bare shoulder appeared from behind the curtain next, and then her anxious eyes locked with mine.

"Hi," she said, holding the curtain across the rest of her body. She bit her bottom lip as she raked her gaze from head to toe, lingering on my torso before building up enough courage to look farther. She gasped when her eyes landed on my junk, and damn if it didn't take on a mind of its own as it twitched and, if possible, got harder.

"Fuck, angel, you're going to ruin me."

She returned her attention to my face, all traces of anxiety gone. Instead, a wicked gleam sparkled in her eyes. The Ellie I'd had the pleasure in meeting at the Lost Lake was back, and this time there was no chance of interruption.

"Think about what you want, angel, 'cause if you take one more step, there's no fucking going back."

Confidently, she pulled back the curtain and stepped fully into the shower as naked as the day she was born, and then like any male thinking solely with his cock, I pounced, unrelenting.

As I twisted my fingers around her hair I pulled her mouth to mine, ramming my tongue inside so I could devour her. I grabbed her by the ass, lifting her so she could wrap those tiny toned legs around me. She gasped when she felt my hardness between her thighs, spurring me to move my mouth faster against hers before turning my attention to her jawline and her neck. She arched her back, grabbed my shoulders, and tilted her head to allow me better access. She was like fluid in my hands; she responded to every touch, and damn, I wanted to touch… all of her.

I thumbed her nipples, causing her to let out little moans of pleasure. I sank my wet mouth over one of her breasts and sucked. Hard. She bucked against me, and I cursed silently. If she carried on being so fucking responsive, this would be over quickly. I lowered her from my waist and turned her so she had her back to me. One hand continued to caress her breasts while the other travelled south, moving on its own accord. She reached an arm around my neck and tugged my head down, tilting her head to the side again. *She likes her neck being kissed.* She trembled in my arms as my fingers found their destination.

"Fuck, angel, you're so wet."

She only whimpered in reply.

I turned her back around so she faced me, the shower splashed down over our naked bodies, and I watched the droplets of water glisten as they rolled over her breasts. I instinctively ran my tongue along the watery trail, loving how the water tasted against her soft skin. She let out another little whimper, causing the animal inside to rise closer to the surface. I pushed her back against the tiled wall, and she automatically grabbed me by the shoulders to stop herself from falling.

Too rough.

A small smile spread across her now swollen lips and fire burned behind her eyes.

Or not.

She blatantly perused my body, and I felt it right down to my very core. Her desire stole my breath and had me gasping for air. My fingers travelled back south, confirming she was ready for me.

"You sure you want this, angel?" She nodded, biting the side of her bottom lip once again. I leaned down and pulled that lip between my teeth, nipping, sucking gently. "Because I mean it. There's no going back after this."

She moved her hands from my shoulders and ran

then over my pecs slowly. I watched as her hands travelled lower and lower until…

"Fuck, Ellie, I won't be able to hold out much longer if you keep touching me like that." Her eyes sparked mischievously, telling me she knew. "Shit, angel. You're too much," I said as she continued to work me with her hands. Never. In. My. Life. Had something felt so fucking good.

"Need to be inside you. Now," I barely spat out. I picked her up by her ass and she wrapped her legs around me like a vise. As much as I wanted her right there and then, I didn't have a condom, and I wasn't completely stupid. I went to step us out of the shower, but she squeezed me with her thighs. I stopped, the feeling of her wet heat enough to make any sane man pause to consider his next actions carefully. I wouldn't make it to the fucking bedroom.

"I'm on the pill and I've not been with anyone since…" she whispered into my chest. Finding her resolve once again, she started to lap up the water rolling down my pecs, letting it dissolve on her tongue. *Sexy as hell.*

Any semblance of control slipped right out the window. My brain was a lust-filled haze but also full of raw emotion. I became lost in those aquamarine eyes, lost in her smell, that sexy British accent. I became lost in everything that was Ellie. She made me all kinds of crazy. She was still broken, my life was fucked-up, and my head screamed at me that nothing good could come of this. We came from two completely different worlds, but nothing mattered in that moment. Despite how wrong everything seemed, it also felt so incredibly right. I didn't realise I was missing anything in my life until she stumbled into it like a fucking tornado. She completed me. She made me feel. With her screaming out my name, I buried myself deep inside her and finally claimed her as mine.

The vivid memories of last night had me tenting my boxers shamelessly, and I started to think I might not let her sleep much longer. Not being able to even look at another woman over the past few weeks, I had denied myself of sex far too long, and you would think, considering we didn't actually get to sleep until the early hours of the morning, I would be satisfied. It hadn't been a problem before. I would find my release by indulging in a mindless fuck and all would be right in the world again. Not with Ellie. Having sex with Ellie was nothing like I'd ever experienced in my life. It wasn't just physical; we connected in every fucking way.

I closed my eyes and tried to bury the unfamiliar weight building in my chest. It was something like I'd never felt before. It was primitive. Scary. Dangerous. Dangerous because, at that moment, I knew I would do anything in my power for the perfect woman curled up under my arm, even if it meant walking away.

She opened her eyes slowly and then stretched out like a cat, causing me to roll back into her and pull her close. "Morning," she said sleepily.

"Morning, angel. You okay?" I whispered into the side of her neck, wrapping my arms tighter around her waist.

"Yep. You?"

I pushed my hard-on against her ass cheeks, and she giggled. Her fucking giggling was like music to my ears. It was my new favourite sound. "I'm good."

"Feels like it," she replied, slowly rubbing her ass up and down my cock before pulling away abruptly.

"That's not nice, angel," I said, trying to sound angry but coming across like a frustrated teenager. She let out another giggle as she rolled out of the bed, pulling one of the sheets with her.

"I'm not nice, Kyle. Have you not learnt that about me yet?" she teased, smiling when she caught me looking at my shoulder blades. They looked like I had been locked in a cage with a tiger. Remembering the sensation of her digging her nails in and scraping them down my back had me moving out of the bed quicker than lightning. She squealed as I yanked the sheet she was wrapping around her from her body.

"Fuck off, Kyle!" she shouted through fits of laughter as I tugged her back to the bed, the sheet now twisted and being used in a naked game of tug of war.

"I want breakfast. I'm bloody starving," she screamed, tears now rolling down her flushed cheeks. She gave up, letting go of the sheet, sending me rolling back onto the bed. For someone so tiny, she was strong. Without looking back, she ran to the bathroom, trying to cover with her hands the body I'd licked, sucked, and caressed inch by inch only the night before.

"It's nothing I've not seen before, angel, so don't know why you're hiding that hot as hell little body of yours," I shouted after her.

Her head popped around the bathroom door. I expected to see her blush, but instead, the look she gave me had me moving from the bed and heading toward the now empty and open doorway like my life depended on it.

Breakfast.

Chapter Twenty-Seven

ELLIE

Oh. My. God. What the hell happened to me last night? Well, I knew what happened to me. I think the question I should have asked was... *What in God's name got into me?* Although, I knew the answer to that too! Don't get me wrong; sex with Jake was always good, but sex with Kyle was incredible. He had me feeling things and doing things I'd never even thought possible, and my lack of expertise in the area seemed to only fuel his fire. He seemed to get off on my fumbling and inexperience, although he may have been getting off on my keenness to submit to his every touch. Who would have thought I could be so shameless when it came to sex, or was it just sex with Kyle? He looked at me like I was a cherished possession. He also looked like he was a starving man and could devour me in one mouthful. My completely sated body only confirmed I'd been thoroughly serviced and enjoyed every minute of it.

At first, I'd been nervous. That was why I hesitated at the shower curtain before building up enough courage to make that final step. Would he be disgusted with what he saw? I was disgusted on a daily basis but over the years had come to accept my body could be no different. I hated the extra pouch of fat that wouldn't disappear no matter how many sit-ups I did, courtesy of my C-section scar. I hated the scars that marred my left hip and ran down the outside of my thigh. Then there were the others. The ones not even Cassie knew about. All my scars told a story and were a constant reminder. They brought with them memories I longed to forget, but for just that brief moment before I stepped into the shower, I let myself remember.

I remembered Jake and I remembered Lyla Rose. I remembered they were dead. I skittered over the memories of my childhood. I would tackle them another day. I then remembered Cassie, Betty from the hospital, Dr. Radrie, and their comments about moving on. Jake would want me to be happy. He would want me to love again. He would tell me to be strong. Kyle made me happy, and as scary as the thought was, I knew I was falling for the huge, tattooed dangerous man with a heart of pure gold. He made me feel strong.

Fighting my anxiety, I made the decision to take that step into the shower. He didn't even notice my scars. If he did, he looked straight through them. I knew right then that all he could see was me. All of me. My hurt, my pain, my flaws, my conflict, my desire, my love… all the craziness that made my brain tick. He saw me. Only me.

For hours after we came out of the bathroom and made it to the plush king-size bed, we explored each other's bodies. Thoroughly. He traced and kissed every one of my scars without questioning its origin. He wasn't an idiot. He could tell which ones came as a result of the accident and which ones weren't, but he decided to save the questions I'm sure he wanted to ask. For that I was grateful. Finally brushing his fingers along my C-section scar, he looked me in the eyes with such intensity goose bumps rippled across my skin and my stomach did some sort of intense flip-flop. I choked back the tears that threatened once again as he told me never to hide. He told me my scars meant I was a survivor and I should wear them with pride.

Up until recently, I rarely cried. Crying, or showing any form of emotion for that matter, scared the shit out of me. *She* always told me it was a weakness. Finally, I was starting to see she was wrong. When Kyle told me he thought I was beautiful, scars and all, the floodgates opened and years of pent-up emotion rolled down my cheeks in the form of salty tears.

If only he knew.

To cry was liberating, and with each tear that fell, I felt the huge weight slowly lifting from my heavily burdened shoulders. Kyle held me in his arms, his warm, strong, safe arms, until I could cry no more. I looked up into those beautiful brown eyes and drowned in them. There was no pity. There was just compassion and understanding. I told myself I was falling for this man, but who was I trying to kid? It was too late. Without me even realising, he'd come barging into my life and stolen my heart. He kissed away the remainder of my tears, and we fell into a slow and sensuous kiss. Our kisses before had been heated, messy, full of hunger and need. They'd led to hot, fast, and steamy sex. This kiss was different. It was full of raw, unadulterated emotion. A silent communication of how we felt about each other. We didn't need words; each touch spoke volumes.

Rolling me onto my back, Kyle towered above me while we still communicated with a series of kisses and touches. I drank in the bulging muscles on his arms as they flexed to hold up his weight, the ink that painted his tanned skin, and that perfectly sculpted body before returning my gaze to his ruggedly beautiful face. The dark stubble that lined his jaw begged me to run my fingers over it. I never in my life thought I would feel like this again. I never thought I would once again be loved. I would love Jake forever and he would be forever in my heart, but fate had thrown me in the path of this magnificent man, and I thanked the angels above for giving me a second chance at happiness. I once again became lost in the depths of Kyle's eyes as our bodies moulded perfectly together, and for the first time, we made love.

I stepped out of the shower, my body tingling from the thoughts of last night. I'd hoped Kyle would join me, but his phone rang, putting a stop to any thoughts of having my wicked way with him once again. I wrapped the towel around me and started to dry my hair. I could hear him still talking in hushed tones.

Why is he talking so quietly? What doesn't he want me to hear?

My suspicious mind had me pressed against the door and listening, wondering who could have kept him talking for so long. It didn't take long to realise he was speaking to either Saint or Tiny. I exhaled the breath I didn't realise I was holding.

What is he talking about? I silently cursed the anxiety that had unexpectedly started to weasel itself into my head and continued to towel-dry my hair, shoving the unwelcome feelings to the back of my mind with every rub.

No one will ever truly want you, Ellie. I rubbed my hair harder, trying to block out the sound of *her* voice in my head again. It wasn't working. Instead, my stomach churned. I couldn't shake the feeling that something was wrong. I knew in my mind these feelings were irrational, but I couldn't stop myself from thinking the worst, no matter how much I tried otherwise. Thoughts of not being good enough, people leaving me, and all the other anxieties I'd developed over the years came to me as natural as walking.

Hearing that Kyle had ended his conversation, I opened the door and headed back into the bedroom. He looked worried, and that sinking feeling returned with a vengeance. The look on his face told me maybe my anxiety was warranted after all. Something was bothering him, which in turn, bothered me.

"I'm going to be away for about a week on business. Saint just called to let me know we're heading out this afternoon."

"Oh, okay," I replied, not managing to say anything else before my stomach cramped and nausea crippled me. My chest tightened, my breathing becoming erratic. *Breathe.* I used to suffer anxiety attacks when I was a teenager, and like before, the symptoms came from nowhere for no apparent reason, and all of a sudden, I was fighting to take a breath.

The whole paper bag thing? Doesn't work.

"Hey, hey, hey, angel. I'll be fine. Came back last time, didn't I?" he joked.

How can he joke? My chest tightened, my breaths faster, faster until my head became foggy, and I couldn't hear anything over the ringing resonating through my ears.

He gently rubbed my back and encouraged me to slow my breathing, but I could. Not. Catch. My. Breath. Tingling sensations shot down my arms as I struggled to take in enough oxygen. *BREATHE!* I dropped to the floor as my legs started to tingle too. He sank to the floor with me. He was speaking, but I couldn't grasp his words. The pressure in my chest got tighter, the ringing got louder, and the world started to spin. I was sure to black out.

He grabbed my face and forced me to look at him. The pressure on the side of my head snapped me out of my daze, and I focused on the rise and fall of his chest. Turning my attention to his mouth, I concentrated on matching his breaths with my own. *In. Out. In. Out.* My breathing became slower, steadier. The ringing dissipated and my head became clearer, the tingling sensations lessening in my arms and legs. I was starting to gain back my control.

"Fuck, angel. What the hell happened there?" he asked, pulling me into a hug, cradling my head like I was a newborn baby.

"Sorry. Panic… attack," I replied between breaths.

"Yeah, guessed that, but why?" he said into my hair.

"Sorry." I wasn't sure why I was apologising, only that it was another automatic response. I hated having panic attacks. They made me feel weak, and they embarrassed the hell out of me. I hated that loss of control, and I hated people feeling sorry for me. What I hated most of all was not knowing the reason. Why, after all these years, did I have a panic attack now?

"Stop apologising. Why did you panic? All I said was I was going away, and it's not like it's the first time. You know I go away on business, but I'll come back. I'm not leaving you, if that's what you think."

Is that what I thought? *No.* Suddenly, the reason for my panic attack was as clear as day.

"No, it's not that," I replied, now breathing more freely.

Kyle had released my head and was now sitting in front of me, still on the floor. If it weren't for the fact I didn't feel like laughing, I would have found the confusion on his face comical. He really had no idea what he was letting himself in for if he stayed with me.

"The last time you went away, you came back full of fucking bullets," I snapped, finding the backbone I'd temporarily lost during my moment of weakness.

Realisation dawned on his face and he sighed. "That was only the second time it's happened, and considering how many times I've gone away, I'd say my odds are good. Wouldn't you?"

I didn't answer. I didn't know what to say. He made a logical argument after all, and he couldn't help the shit that often invaded my brain.

If Jake and I were ever going to have an argument, my anxieties would be the root of them, but I'd come to learn how to hide these feelings. I would smile at the appropriate moment, laugh when expected to, nod in all the right places. I was a bloody good actress; it was something I'd perfected since childhood, but keeping up pretences was tiring and I didn't want to pretend anymore. If anything were to come of this relationship I had with Kyle, he would have to learn to accept me for who I was. *Who I am.* I told Dr. Radrie I would try and stop hiding and I had already made excellent progress, but I obviously still had a way to go.

"I'm scared," I admitted. "I'm scared you won't come home. I'm fucking scared because I know if you end up dead, you may as well bury me in the ground with you because I can't go through that again. I won't go through that pain again."

"Then walk away now, angel, because this is my life, and no matter how much I care for you, it ain't changing. This is who I am."

You are such a selfish bitch. There *she* was again, taunting me with memories of my past, except this time I couldn't help feeling maybe she was right. I was too wrapped up in wanting Kyle to accept me for who I was. I hadn't even considered his feelings. His life. Everything he represented was what made him who he was. Why would I want him to change when I loved everything about him? *Love.* God, I was such a messed-up bundle of nerves. Realising I'd zoned out for a moment while I battled my inner turmoil, I offered him a shy smile, crawled onto his lap, and answered him with a kiss.

Pulling up alongside the curb outside my apartment, Kyle cut the engine and got off his bike. I remained seated. The drive back had gone too quickly, and it was time to say good-bye. *A week, tops.*

I got off the bike and removed my helmet, handing it to Kyle. He took it from me without saying a word and hung it on the handlebars. I think he was struggling with what to say just as much as I was, which made me feel slightly better. He took hold of my hand and we walked silently toward my front door, where Cassie was waiting for us expectantly.

"Hey, love birds. How was it?" she asked, looking completely smug, until she registered our sombre expressions. "You okay, Els?"

"Fine, Cas. I'll tell you about it in a bit, but can you give us a minute?" I asked.

She shot an evil glare in Kyle's direction. "Tell me you didn't fuck things up," she snarled at Kyle, taking a step toward him, whipping her long blond hair behind her shoulders.

"Cas, back in your cage. It's not like that," I interjected, stepping between them.

Kyle rested his hands on my shoulders and squeezed them gently.

"Okay, I'll just be inside if you need me," she replied, stepping inside, giving Kyle one more *I'll bury you if you hurt her* look. She pushed the door closed, but not so it shut completely. Even now, she was looking after me.

"So." I turned in Kyle's arms so I could face him. "Promise you'll come back in one piece this time?" I said quietly.

He pulled me into his warm chest and I inhaled the smell of fresh air and the leather of his cut. He kissed me lightly on the top of my head, and I melted at the intimacy of his gentle touch.

"For sure. You've got me, angel. Nothing will keep me away now." I listened to his words, but even now I didn't fully believe them.

He cupped my cheeks and pulled my face toward his. At first, his kiss was sweet and gentle, sending now familiar tingles down my spine. I returned his kiss just as gently before opening my mouth wider, inviting him in. As his tongue entered my mouth, it slowly caressed mine as he pushed me into my new favourite position, against the cold solid concrete of wall. I wrapped my legs around his waist and kissed him with everything I had, silently begging him not to go. I wasn't ready for him to leave yet.

His wet mouth trailed down my exposed neck, causing goose bumps to explode across my skin. He worked his way down to my collarbone, sending heat down south, causing him to moan in approval and me to squeeze my legs tighter. His hands searched for the flesh under my top and set upon a journey of exploration. In a tangle of arms and legs, he turned me and we almost fell through the open door to my apartment. And then… Kyle's phone started ringing in his pocket. We broke the kiss and I dropped my feet to the floor, still panting. He abruptly pulled the phone from his pocket, clearly pissed off.

"What the fuck, Saint!" he shouted.

I readjusted my clothing and ran my fingers through my hair, conscious I now probably looked like I'd been dragged through a hedge backward, and I was still standing outside, on my doorstep. They spoke for a bit longer, Kyle giving one-word answers, his mood not getting any cheerier. Finally, he hung up and was back to giving me his full attention. Verbally, anyway. My body screamed at him in silent protest.

"I know. You've got to go," I said, attempting a smile.

Back in the hotel room, after my mini meltdown and the discussion that came after, I slowly came to terms with the fact that he had to go and this was something I had to get used to. It was going to be hard, but I'd been dealt rougher blows in life, so I was sure it was nothing I couldn't handle.

"Yeah. I'll come and see you as soon as I get

back, okay."

I nodded.

He ran a thumb just under my eye and wiped away a stray tear. I hadn't even realised I was crying. *Blasted tears.* I sucked in a breath and abruptly swiped my hands across my face.

"Don't fucking cry, angel," he said, pulling my hands away, probably scared I was going to do some damage.

"I'm sorry," I said automatically.

"What have I said about saying sorry? You have nothing to say sorry for, and it pisses me off you feel the need to keep saying it," he snapped aggressively. I knew the aggression wasn't directly aimed at me, but it made me flinch nonetheless. His face instantly softened, and he leaned down to place a soft kiss on my forehead. My body, still screaming in silent protest from being left tingly and needy, sparked back to life with that innocent touch.

He grinned at me knowingly and it took all I had not to wipe that smug look off his face. Either by kissing him again or punching him, I wasn't sure yet. My head felt like a whirlpool of emotions, and I was struggling to keep them under control. I wanted to be angry, but my blasted brain wanted me to cry. I wanted to be happy, but instead, I felt sad. I hadn't wanted to a drop of alcohol for a while, but right now? Right now, my throat tightened as the need to numb out all feeling controlled my body until my fingers twitched and I was visibly shaking. If he noticed, he chose not to say anything, which was good because I feared if he did, the shell I'd newly encased myself in would crack and I would be left vulnerable and wide open.

"Be safe, Kyle. You promise me you'll come home in one piece, right?" I choked out.

"Right." He placed a chaste kiss on my forehead and walked backward until he reached his bike. "I'll see you soon, angel. Keep that bed warm for when I get back, 'cause I plan on spending a lot of time in it," he shouted, grinning like a fool.

I could feel the heat rise in my cheeks and lowered my head sheepishly. The git still managed to make me blush.

"See you soon," I whispered, but he'd already gone.

Chapter Twenty-Eight

ELLIE

The next four days were torturous, and my overactive imagination had me thinking of many a scenario, each ending with Kyle not coming back and me being left broken and alone. Again. It was also four days of keeping myself busy because there was a huge temptation to visit Dee again at The Tavern, and it wasn't because I wanted to join the old-timers in a friendly game of dominoes. Trix, Sadie, and even Junior had come around a couple times to check up on me. I'm sure they truly intended it to be a friendly visit, but I couldn't help feeling suffocated by their concern. Cas was the most overbearing, and it almost felt like I'd returned home. *Almost*. If she realised I'd compared her to my parents, even fleetingly, she wouldn't react very well and would end up doing something stupid herself. Some days I wondered if she was just as messed up as me, but then maybe that's why we were more like sisters than friends. No, I would stay sober, if not for me, for her.

A knock on the door had me falling on my backside as I tried to squeeze into a pair of skintight jeans. A rush of excitement soared through my body at the thought that Kyle was finally home. Still buttoning my jeans, I opened the door, my expression falling when I realised it wasn't him.

"Hey, nice to see you too!" Sadie said, shoving a squirming Saige into my arms. I tried not to flinch or look too uncomfortable. Easier said than done. Sadie walked in and jumped over the side of the sofa, making herself comfortable.

"You okay?" I asked. It wasn't that she wasn't welcome or necessarily unexpected; she just seemed different. She wasn't her normal laidback self. She seemed a little agitated.

"Yeah. I decided to take Saige out for a drive to get her to sleep and ended up here. You don't mind, do you?" she asked.

I ignored the wave of uneasiness that washed over my body and took a deep breath. Maybe she was just tired and I was imagining how tense Sadie seemed.

"Of course not," I replied, knocking the pile of ironing from the chair in the corner of the living room while balancing Saige precariously on my hip. Sadie watched, amusement in her eyes. I sat and cradled Saige under my arm, feeling a lot more relaxed now that I wasn't standing and holding her.

Without realising, I placed a kiss on the top of her head when she giggled. It felt like the most natural thing to do in the world and she wasn't even mine. Why was affection so hard for my own mother?

I turned her around so I could get a proper look at her cute little face. She had the most unusual grey eyes and a mop of unruly dark hair sticking up all over her head. She was adorable, the perfect combination of both mother and father. A flash of grief hit me as I thought of Lyla Rose. I wondered who she would have looked like. She didn't seem to look like Jake or me in the photos the neonatal unit gave me, but it was hard to see under all the tubes and wires running from her tiny, fragile body. I pushed aside the thoughts and gave Saige a little squeeze, causing her to giggle again, in turn, making me smile and speak to her in a series of goos and gahs, because obviously, babies understand that shit.

"You would have been a good mom," Sadie said when I noticed her looking at me.

"Thanks." I really didn't know what else to say. "So not that it's not good to see you, but are you sure you're okay?"

Sadie sighed, and I knew then my first impressions weren't off. I took a deep, calming breath and mentally counted to ten, just in case a panic attack lurked in the background. I took another deep breath, grateful Sadie seemed to realise what I was doing.

"I got a text from Saint saying they would be away a few days longer." My breath caught, but she was kneeling in front of me in an instant, holding my hand. "But before you go and panic on me, it also said not to worry, as they were all fine."

"Okay," I replied. I picked up my phone and checked for messages. There was none. I was relieved to hear they were all fine, but a small seed of doubt had been planted in my stomach because Kyle hadn't texted or called me himself.

"So why did Kyle not contact me?" I asked quietly.

"Honey, please don't worry about it. To be honest, it's unusual to get a message at all, so please don't worry." She squeezed my hand reassuringly, but doubt gnawed at my bones. Despite her reassurances, Sadie had planted that seed, and it still festered right up until I started my shift at the hospital.

After my late shift, I couldn't wait to get back to my apartment and sink into the realms of the Never-never Land. Sleep hadn't been easy the last few days, and it was starting to take its toll. Cassie was out with a new guy she'd met at work, third one this week, so I would be going home to an empty apartment again. I was looking forward to the silence. As much as I loved her, she was seriously becoming a royal pain in my arse.

"You need a ride?" Paulie said as she joined me outside.

I was glad to be leaving. New patients were entering the hospital in such volumes you would think there was a sale going on inside, but thankfully, being so busy kept any unwelcome thoughts at bay. I'd walked to work and planned on walking home again, but a ride was tempting. All signs of summer were gone now and there was a bitter autumn chill in the air. The cold and damp made my formerly shattered hip and thigh ache, signalling it was more than likely going to rain.

"That would be great actually. Thanks, Paulie."

She looked a bit shocked that I'd accepted her offer. She offered every time she could, and I always turned her down, normally too stubborn to accept help from anyone.

"Hey, it's cold and I don't want to get wet walking home." I laughed.

"Your hip and leg?" I nodded. "That's so creepy how people can tell the weather because their joints hurt. I always thought it was bull until I met you. You're like a walking weather monitor."

I laughed at her analogy. Courtesy of the accident, I seemed to always know when I would need an umbrella.

"At least I have my uses," I said as I followed her to her little car. It was a bright lime-green Ford—very her. Cheerful. I personally would never have spent good money on it, but Paulie was all about making a statement. A black stripe ran down the bonnet, and I could only assume it was to try and make it look sporty. *Or maybe not.* When she opened the door, I was greeted with the sight of a bright-pink fur steering wheel cover and fluffy dice hanging from the mirror, and I had to fight back a laugh.

She pulled up outside my apartment, and I toyed with inviting her in, but my bed was calling and I really was feeling the pain in my joints. She cranked up the volume of her stereo, and I cringed when I realised she was listening to some boy band. I really hadn't taken much notice of the music choice on the way home, but from the looks of her car, I would have expected Eminem rather than One Direction. I remembered having a boy band phase when I was fourteen. I desperately wanted to fit in with the other girls, and at the time, this seemed to be the best way to go, even though I couldn't stand the music. Much to my mother's distaste, I'd always liked rock and heavy metal. My dad had introduced me to Metallica and Maiden when I was a kid. As I grew up, I discovered Korn, Slipknot, and Disturbed. Thankfully, the boy band phase didn't last long. The likes of One Direction simply didn't do it for me.

The car shook, startling me from my thoughts. Peering over at my nutty friend, I shook my head when she started doing some obscene style of dancing in the driver's seat. I opened the passenger door for a quick escape when she started singing "The Story of My Life" at the top her voice. I decided then if anything was going to turn me to drink, the sound of Paulie singing might just be the final straw. Still laughing as she drove off, I hobbled to the front door of my apartment. The pain seemed worse than usual. If what my body was telling me was right, there was one hell of a storm coming.

I shut the door quietly and headed to the bathroom to get some painkillers. I grabbed the packet of codeine I'd stored in the cabinet and spotted my emergency stash of diazepam. I only took them in dire emergencies, as they helped me sleep. I opened the pot and poured a couple of white little pills into the palm of my hand. Getting a glass of water from the kitchen, I knocked the combination of tablets back and grimaced as they started to melt before they even hit the back of my throat. I hated taking pills with water. I usually took them with juice or milk, but the cupboards were empty.

I stripped out of my clothes and changed into some pyjama bottoms and a vest top before crawling into bed. I couldn't even be bothered to wash my teeth. It wouldn't be long before the tablets took effect and I wouldn't even be able to string together a sentence. As soon as my head hit the pillow, I fell into a blissful slumber, and rather than dreaming of eyes as blue as the ocean, I dreamt of eyes as dark as night.

Chapter Twenty-Nine

ELLIE

Ring. Ring. Ring.

"Ouch!" I screamed as I fell onto the floor, landing not so gently on my side, cocooned in sheets.

Ring. Ring. Ring.

In the midst of a sleep-filled haze, it took me a while to comprehend it was my landline phone making that atrocious noise at—I looked at my clock—three in the morning. "Okay!" I shouted, picking myself off the floor and running into the living room. I made a dive for the phone before it stopped ringing.

"Cas, if that's you, you could have phoned by bloody mobile," I shouted breathlessly.

"It's me." The sound of my little brother at the other end had me breaking out in a cold sweat within seconds. My heart rate accelerated and I instantly felt sick. I sank to the floor, clutching the phone to my ear.

"What do you want?" I said sharply, trying to control the panic setting in.

"That's not a nice way to greet your brother, Els," he said, aggravation lacing his tone. "I mean, I've not seen or spoken to you in what…? I don't know. Must be months."

"Six. It's been six months, and cut the shit, Lucas. You chose not to say good-bye. You chose to keep away from me. You suck up to them and don't even give me the fucking time of day, so excuse me if I might be a bit sharp with you. You ring out of the blue at fucking three in the morning."

I was met with silence and an audible sigh. *What? No comeback?*

"Sorry."

Fuck me, did he just apologise?

"Too late for apologies," I snapped.

"I know." I heard him sigh again and then hesitate. It caught me by surprise. My brother was the golden boy. Outspoken, popular, could do no wrong. He didn't sigh. He didn't hesitate. He just took what he wanted, consequences be damned. "I am sorry, Ellie. About everything."

"Whatever. You didn't phone me to apologise, so what do you want?"

"It's Dad."

The nausea increased, and I fought back the threatening bile, my breaths now coming in quick succession. I tried to drown him out and concentrate on not losing control. I thought of Kyle. The way he held on to me at the hotel, the way I used his strength as my own security blanket.

"He's sick. Really sick. He's not got long left to live, Ellie. You need to come home."

No!

"I can't just up and leave," I said slowly, my breathing less erratic now, but my body was so overwhelmed with warring emotions. It trembled so much I felt like I was standing naked in a meat locker. "I have responsibilities here." *And I don't want to see* her.

"Christ, Ellie. It's Dad. Quit being a bitch and come home to your family, or are you too good for us now?"

"Fuck you, Lucas. You do *not* get to tell me what to do. Now or ever. I'm going back to bed, and I'll think about it in the morning." I flinched as I heard him hit or throw something at the other end of the line.

"I know why you don't want to come back, Ellie, but you have to. Dad didn't do anything wrong!" he shouted.

"He didn't exactly fucking help either!" I shouted back.

"I know," he said quieter, calmer. "I know." He almost sounded dejected.

Good, arsehole, that's how I've felt most of my life.

"I'm sorry." His apologising was too much to handle.

"Will you stop saying sorry? What exactly are you apologising for? For ignoring me? For letting me take the blame for you every time you fucked up? For abandoning me?" As my anger intensified, tears started to pool in my eyes. *AGGGHHHHHH! For the love of God, stop CRYING!*

"For everything, but, Ellie, I was just a kid," he argued.

"Don't give me that shit. For a long time, it was you and me against the world, and then everything changed. What happened to us, Lucas?" I cried.

"I remember, Ellie. I remember that night like it was yesterday. That's what fucking happened, and I didn't want it happening to me."

I flinched and sucked in a breath at his words. Those words pierced my skin and stabbed me right through the heart. Absently, I ran my hand across the top of my right outer thigh where the other scars marred my skin.

"You were only seven. You shouldn't remember. You shouldn't have even seen that."

"How can I not remember? How can I not remember the screaming, the sound, all that blood?" He stopped, and I heard him gulp in air. I remained frozen at the other end of the line. The trip down memory lane opened up wounds I thought I'd buried a long time ago. "You came home from the hospital bandaged up like a fucking mummy, Ellie."

"It was just my leg," I replied in a daze, remembering what happened like it was only yesterday.

"I remember thinking, *If she can do that to her, then she can do that to me.* I might have just been seven, but I was old enough to figure it out. She didn't like the way I looked up to you, so I had to stop. Maybe I was selfish or a coward, but for my own benefit, I had to stay away."

My tears dried up a while ago, along with any feeling. I felt numb. I should have said something to comfort him. Any normal sister would, right? I couldn't do it. The resentment I felt toward him and my parents only intensified. Without saying another word, I hung up the phone and headed toward the kitchen.

My head pounded as an onslaught of painful memories hammered through my brain like a violent tornado. *Snap*. The sound of leather meeting leather as she snapped the belt. *Clink*. The sound of the buckle as it dropped through the air. *SMACK!* The sound of the buckle slicing through the bare flesh of my right thigh. *WHACK, SMACK, WHACK!* Over and over again until I was lying in a pool of my own blood. *YOU. EVIL. SELFISH. BITCH!* The words she screamed between every slash of the belt. I lost count of the amount of times she hit me before my father finally stepped in and restrained her.

Father. I use the term loosely, because what father would watch as his daughter gets beaten to a bloody pulp? That day my mother had finally lost it because I dared to voice my own opinion. I was fourteen years old, and when the beating stopped, they left me until I passed out from the pain, and the sad truth was I told the hospital it wasn't her. I told them nothing because I was scared. Scared she would do it again. Scared they would think I deserved it, because I did. Didn't I?

The memory had me shaking like a leaf in the middle of a storm. Every nerve ending felt shot to pieces as the pain, not only in my head, hip, and thigh, consumed the rest of me. *I need it to stop.* Everything hurt so much. The box of codeine still remained on the kitchen worktop where I'd chucked it. Without further thought, I popped out another couple tablets from the packet and rummaged through the fridge and cupboards in search of something to wash them down with, because right now water wouldn't do. Opening the last cupboard, I finally found what I was looking for. I pulled out the bottle that had been hidden behind several tins of food and uncapped it. Not even bothering with a glass, I threw the tablets into my mouth and chased them down, savouring the warmth of the tequila as it rolled down the back of my throat.

Chapter Thirty

KYLE

I roughly rubbed my eyes with the palms of my hands and then ran them through my hair. I'd gone straight to the hospital rather than getting washed up back at the club. The smell of exhaust fumes from the long ride clung to my clothes, as did the reek of cigarette smoke and stale alcohol from the night before. As soon as I got the call from Cassie, I dropped everything I was doing, left Saint in charge, and made the five-hour drive to the hospital. The words "unconscious," "not waking up," "lethal reaction to a combination of diazepam, codeine, and tequila" echoed through my mind the entire journey.

Why?

Cassie tried to convince me she didn't think she

did it on purpose. There weren't enough pills in her system to indicate she'd attempted to take her own life. It was more than likely the bottle of tequila she'd decided to take them with. Apparently, it wasn't uncommon for her to take the painkillers and diazepam when her hip was playing up, but it didn't add up. She was a nurse. She must have known what she was doing. Unless of course she was too buzzed to realise what she was doing. That led to more questions.

Why was she drinking in the first place? She hadn't touched a drop in weeks, her sessions with Dr. Radrie were going well, and when I left her on her doorstep, she seemed absolutely fine. I didn't really do all the soppy shit. It wasn't my style, but I would happily admit our time spent in Whistler was probably one of the best in my life. We might not have said it out loud, but we'd both made decisions to cross that bridge and move forward with our lives.

Junior cleared his throat as he came into the room and sat himself down next to me. The poor kid looked shattered. As soon as he found out Ellie had been rushed to the hospital, he came and hadn't left. That was twelve hours before. In such a short time, Ellie had become like a sister to him, and he was as protective over her as I. This made what I had to do so much harder.

Sitting there listening to the steady beep of the heart monitor, watching her chest slowly rise and fall had me thinking about what it would mean to have her in my life. There was no doubt she made me happy. She made me laugh, pissed me off, calmed me down, made me fucking crazy in a good way, but for reasons I believe had nothing to do with becoming a widow and losing a child at such a young age, she was fragile and still so broken.

When I got that call, I thought I'd lost her. My stomach clenched, I felt nauseous, and I felt my heart literally shatter to pieces. I realised Ellie hadn't just crawled under my skin; she'd embedded herself firmly into my heart. I loved her. That was why I had to leave.

"You're a fucking coward, Kyle," Junior hissed. "I know what you're going to do. It's written all over your face."

"You don't understand," I replied, not meeting the glare he was burning into the side of my head. The kid was pissed, but so was I, and I didn't fancy having a showdown with my brother in the middle of a hospital when the woman I loved lay unconscious an arm's length away.

"Like hell I don't. You forget I know you. You're my brother for fuck's sake, and right now I'm ashamed to be associated with you," he snapped.

"Fuck you, Junior. Look at her," I said, waving my hand at Ellie's prone form, still not looking at him. I was already on tenterhooks. The urge to put my fist through the nearest object was overwhelming, but I couldn't do it. I wouldn't do it because of her. The last thing she needed was for me to lose my shit and possibly put Junior back in the kids' ward. "I was gone for four days. Four fucking days, and she does this to herself. She's not cut out for our life. She can barely manage in her own, and let's face it. Hers is a lot simpler than ours."

"Get over yourself. Do you really think her life is simple? Do you really not know anything about her? Her husband is dead, her daughter is dead, and her family is so fucked up she moved to an entirely different country to get away from them. The only person she had in the world was Cas before she met us. So please tell me how on earth you came to the conclusion her life was simple, because I am dying to hear it." The sarcasm dripping from his voice came in spades.

Knowing he was right, I chose not to reply and just focused on keeping calm. I held on to Ellie's hand and ran my thumb over her knuckles rhythmically, trying to calm the storm raging in my head. In my heart.

"I kept an eye on her while you were away, like I promised I would. So did Cas, Trix, and Sadie, and she was doing fine without you. She might have been sad sometimes, but she was fucking okay. I don't know why she picked up that bottle, but I do know it wasn't because of you. She was holding on to the promise you made her. You know, the one where you promised you would come back to her? Hell, it probably would have been easier if you'd just died. At least then she would know you hadn't just gone back on your promise."

His words cut into me like a knife, and I was struggling to keep the anger at bay.

"It's not like that, and you know it," I snapped, this time twisting and standing so I came toe to toe with Junior.

He stood taller and clenched his fists at his sides. Raising his chin and not once dropping his gaze, he silently told me he would fight for her because in his own way, he loved her too. He would not back down.

"Then tell me. Tell me as your brother," he grated through clenched teeth. I stepped back and sat back down in the chair, running my fingers roughly through my hair before reclaiming Ellie's hand.

"My life. Our life. It's not for her. She's too sweet and innocent. Okay, her life may not be simple, but do you really think she's cut out for ours? Do you think she could cope with me going away on business, dealing with threats from rival MCs, being around alcohol so much, because hell, it's not like we're all going to suddenly become teetotal for her. She may not have been trying to…" I hesitated.

"Kill herself." I winced at my brother's bluntness.

"Yeah, that. She might not been trying to do that, but she's still in here. Attached to those bloody tubes and wires because she drank again, because she couldn't cope, and rather than deal with it, she picked up that bottle."

"You don't know if she's cut out for our life and you'll never know because you're hell intent on not giving her the chance. Surely the choice is hers? She might not want to even be part of it, but for now she needs you, Kyle. She doesn't need you running away."

"I'm not running. I'm protecting her. Staying with me will only end up with her getting hurt. Whether it's because of what we do or if she decides to hit the bottle again. She needs someone who can be there for her, and I can't be there for her all the time.

I don't want to be the one responsible for her drinking herself to death because something happens to me and she can't handle it. She might not be so lucky next time," I replied, my throat constricting.

I could feel tears pool in my eyes. I wiped them angrily and ran my hands through my hair again to try and hide the fact I was just about to cry in front of Junior. *What the fuck?* I hadn't cried since I was a child. I never even cried at my dad's funeral. *What is she doing to me?*

"So you're not thinking about her at all. Not only are you a fucking coward; you're a selfish bastard too," he snapped successfully, nipping that final piece of thread I was clinging to.

"Don't fucking take that tone with me, Junior. Brother or not, I will kick your ass," I hissed.

"Try it, *prez*." He got in my face again.

There was no fear of any threatening waterworks now. I shoved my chair back with such force it bounced off the opposite wall, causing a slight indent in the plaster. Junior stood, legs apart, fists clenched at his sides again, waiting for me to react, and react I did. He might have gotten taller—and maybe when he grew out of his teenage body, he would be a match for me physically—but right now, he didn't stand a chance. My right fist connected with his jaw, and his head snapped back with a sickening crunch. My left fist followed smoothly after, catching him in the side of his face, splitting his lip. He went down hard but scrambled to his feet quickly and ran at me with the speed of a quarterback. His shoulder collided with my waist, taking me down in a tackle his college team would have been proud of.

"KYLE!" Cassie screamed as she ran into the room, pulling Junior off me and putting herself directly between us. The bitch had a death wish.

"You're running away because you're scared." Junior continued, wiping blood from his lip, which was now starting to swell. "This whole thing you're feeling is unfamiliar and it's scaring the shit out of you. I get it. She's like a sister to me, and the fact that I haven't got a fucking clue what to do to help her is eating me up." His eyes glistened with unshed tears as he continued to wipe away the blood, but like me, he wouldn't cry.

"I'm sorry, Junior," I said, meaning it. He let out a bitter laugh. I turned away, unable to look at the damage I'd just done to his face.

"No, you're not. You're a dumb shit who's running scared because he's in love with a woman. Not just any woman. Ellie. The funniest, most caring woman I've ever met, who just so happens to have shitloads of baggage." He looked back as he stood up and walked toward me, but Cassie held on to his elbow, stopping him. He stared me down like the piece of shit I knew I was.

Could he not see this was why I had to leave? I solved problems with my fists or my favourite double-edged knife. I wasn't just concerned about life with the club. I was concerned I was no good for her. She deserved someone better than me.

"You know, you're twenty-eight years old, and I've never in my life seen you smile like you do at her," he said more softly, his anger fading.

"Don't be such a fucking drama queen," I snapped.

"You didn't smile, Kyle. Not properly anyway. You might have moved your lips upward, but your eyes were always cold and lifeless. When you hooked up with a woman, your expression pretty much said, *Fuck me*, and they would oblige because they were whores who just wanted to bag the prez. For them, it was the thrill and the excitement or something they could share with their friends. For you, it was for the release, because let's face it. You weren't that fussy about where you stuck your dick, but when you're with Ellie, you smile with your eyes and they light up like a fucking grenade.

"When you're with her, you're *Kyle*. Not *prez*, not the *slayer*. You're the person I got to see growing up. The one that no one else sees. You love her, Kyle. Don't ruin it because you're too damn stubborn to accept what fate has given you. There's a reason she was waiting in that waiting room that day. It wasn't to save me. It was to save you from dying a lonely old man and for you to save her from whatever hell she's going through."

"He's right, Kyle," Cassie said, surprisingly quiet for her.

"I don't know if I can," I admitted, picking up the chair and moving it back to the side of the bed. I grasped one of Ellie's hands in mine and gently brushed my lips along her knuckles. The beeps sped up, and I could have sworn she smiled in her sleep.

"You're wrong, Kyle. I think you're the only one who can, because trust me. I have tried so bloody hard to help her and she doesn't listen to me," Cassie said, worry etched into her normally happy face. I got the feeling she could sense what I was going to do too.

I leaned across and placed a soft kiss on her forehead. "I love you, angel, and I am so fucking sorry," I whispered.

"Don't do this, Kyle!" Junior shouted as I headed toward the open doorway.

Cassie caught up with me and grabbed my elbow.

"I can't, Cassie. I'm sorry," I said, looking past her into the empty hospital corridor.

"If you love her, you'd stay," she said.

"It's because I fucking love her that I have to go."

Shaking her head, defeated, she loosened her grip and let me walk out of the hospital, feeling like the biggest dick on the planet and feeling like I might have just made one of the worst decisions of my life.

Chapter Thirty-One

ELLIE

I wasn't a difficult child, but I was stubborn to a fault and knew my own mind from an early age. I was basically like every other child in existence, but unlike a lot of children, I didn't have a normal mother. I never realised how threatened she was by me, but then why would I? I was a kid. I was a kid who craved a mother's love and acceptance, and I still craved it, was desperate for it, even the day after she sliced open my thigh with the buckled end of a belt.

Over the years, I became a shadow. I accepted defeat and everything that was thrown at me. Insults, emotional blackmail, not being allowed to make any real decisions on my own. It might not have come in the form of a beating, but my brain absorbed each and every spiteful comment like a sponge, until one day I was so full I could only think about squeezing every drop out of my overloaded system. But I couldn't get it out. Everything festered and became trapped inside like stagnant water. I discovered the next best thing. Alcohol. It might not have helped, but it numbed the pain. It helped me forget, albeit temporarily. It turned me into the person my mother always told me I would be. *A selfish bitch.*

During my time sleeping off my latest consumption, my life played out before my eyes like my own version of *The Christmas Carol*. It was a seriously messed-up dream, nightmare, vision, or whatever the hell you want to call it, but it did serve its purpose.

Jake starred as the ghost of my past, Cas was the ghost of my present, and both played their parts incredibly well. It was overwhelming seeing Jake's blue eyes again as they looked at me with compassion and love. Without saying a word, he took me back to a time long before I met him that night outside the club. He held my hand through every memory, through the heartbreak, through the pain, right up until we looked down on my prone form hooked up to drips and monitors after the accident. His ghostly form held on to my hand, and I could feel the gentle pressure as he squeezed. The sound of a feeble cry caught my attention and pulled my gaze away from myself in the hospital bed. I looked down at the pink little bundle now in his arms. Through misty eyes, I could see Jake's smile light up the room as he cradled our daughter. He looked so proud and very much the father I imagined he would be.

Lyla Rose was beautiful. I reached out and ran my fingers along her tiny little cheek. It felt like I was running my fingers through cool, heavy air. The sensation was surreal, but the smile and the twinkle of Lyla Rose's bright blue eyes, almost identical to her father's, felt very real as that familiar feeling of grief crushed my heart. Jake silently shook his head, running a cool thumb along my damp cheeks. Without words, he touched his heart and then mine before bringing his hand up to the side of my head, where I felt a gentle, comforting sort of pressure. As my tears continued to spill from my eyes, I nodded in understanding. He was telling me he would be forever in my heart and in my soul. He brushed a feather-light kiss against my forehead. I knew then it was time to say good-bye.

Seeing Cas in my dreams was harder than I would ever have imagined, but maybe it was because of what she showed me that made it hard. My subconscious mind likened her to the ghost of Christmas present because it kind of fit, but she too decided she wanted to show me a quick glimpse of my past. A past of her visiting me in hospital after the accident, her looking after my drunk arse every time I went on a bender, her looking after me every time I sank into the depths of a depression.

Our little journey ended up in the present, with me once again lying in a hospital bed, hooked up to monitors, but this time Kyle was the one sitting there holding my hand. My eyes misted over once again, but it was what I saw in his eyes that made me cry. I saw love, I saw compassion, but I also saw fear, hopelessness, and uncertainty. I knew the expression well because I saw it in the mirror every time things got tough. He was going to run. He didn't think he was strong enough to be with someone like me, and I couldn't blame him. I would have left me too. He was the type of person who liked control, liked having things mapped out. There was just black and white, and I very firmly sat in grey. I was the unknown.

I had no idea who represented my future, for they stood heavily clad in a thick black cloak that reached the floor as they towered over me. I didn't know whether to laugh or cry when I saw the figure in my dream, because the likeness to *The Christmas Carol* was uncanny at this point. Was I really that messed up my brain could only get the message across in the form of a classic piece of literature? Or maybe it was because *The Christmas Carol* was my father's favourite film, and in light of recent news, my mind was simply playing tricks on me. Whatever the reason, the slightly intimidating person in black showed me two paths, one of which didn't sit well with me. There was basically a headstone next to Jake's and Lyla Rose's with my name on it. I think the creepy figure made its point clear. I nervously laughed in my head. Maybe I should have added the prescriptive drugs with the alcohol on earlier drunken escapades? It might have just saved me a lot of heartache, and let's face it; my liver would have been grateful.

Two weeks had passed since I woke up in the hospital after my date with a bottle of tequila and painkillers. Two weeks had passed since Kyle decided to walk out that hospital door and not come back. I'd woken to a battered Junior and a red-eyed Cassie sitting vigil by my bedside. They didn't need to say anything about Kyle leaving, because I knew. They didn't question how I knew, but maybe they just thought their appearances were a bit of a giveaway. I decided against telling them I saw it in a dream, because I was certain this would have me carted up to the psych ward before I had the chance to finish the sentence.

For two weeks, that dream haunted me day and night as I tried to decipher the meaning behind it, but I suppose the meaning was clear. My self-destructive behaviour wasn't just hurting myself, but the people who did genuinely care for me. My true family. Cassie, Trix, Sadie, Junior… Kyle. Drinking until I was numb or running away from the past wasn't going to fix my problems. I needed to face them head on, accept them as being part of who I was, and not allow them to define me and my future, because then, and only then, would I be able to move on.

The flight home to England was uneventful. Well, apart from having to sit next to some fat bloke who really should have spent money on a double ticket. For the first time in my life, I was grateful for being shorter than most. I waited for my luggage patiently, my thoughts often drifting off to where I would go, what I would do. What I would say. I had spoken to my brother on the phone just before I got on my flight to London Heathrow, and he'd said he would greet me at the airport. I didn't know how I would react to seeing him, but at the end of the day, he was my brother, and my gut told me I needed to do this to help me move on. Our conversation was strained at first, but the longer we spoke, the more I realised he was just as much a victim in our fucked-up childhood. He was just better at dealing with it.

My black holdall with the print of blood-red roses entwined around a skull made its appearance. There wasn't another in the world like it. Turns out Paulie didn't just like hot doctors, boy bands, and hideous cars; she also had an eye for art and some kickass needlework skills. I scooped it up and headed toward the exit to where my brother greeted me with a genuine grin plastered on his face. The sight of him actually smiling stunned me into silence. The last time I'd seen him smile at me like that was when I was fourteen years old. I smiled a real smile and felt a small piece of the weight I'd been carrying around with me over the past eleven years leave my shoulders.

"Hey, Els. You look really good."

I raised an eyebrow. I was still recovering, and I knew I still wore the telltale signs of a major bender. My eyes were still slightly bloodshot, my skin pale, and I hadn't eaten properly in days because I couldn't keep much down. I basically looked like crap.

"Thanks," I replied, choosing not to argue. "So how's Dad?"

When I last spoke to him, he revealed my father had deteriorated. Years of smoking had finally caught up with him, and he was dying of lung cancer. Not that it would have probably made much difference; they'd caught it too late. No amount of chemotherapy or radiotherapy would help now, especially when it had spread to his bones, bowels, and liver. He'd recently been transferred to a hospice where he would live the remainder of his life under palliative care.

"Not good. Mum's beside herself."

I shot him a warning look. I told him I would come home on one condition. He wasn't allowed to speak about *her*. I would tackle that bridge when I came to it.

"You sure you don't want to stay at mine? Jules would love to see you."

I'd already booked myself a room at a local Travel Inn. Jules was lovely, but not my kind of person. Her sweetness would eventually rub me the wrong way, and I would end up telling her where to shove her "forgive and forget" beliefs. There was also the fact that he shared a student house with not only Jules, but three other eighteen or nineteen-year-olds, just a few miles away from where they attended uni.

"I'm good. Can you drop me straight off at the hotel?" I asked. He nodded as he took my holdall and carried it to the car.

The drive was short and sweet, which meant there weren't too many uncomfortable silences. He didn't slip up again and mention Mum. He asked me about my life in Vancouver, and I answered excitedly. I also found myself talking about Kyle. I couldn't help it. Apparently, I'd developed a bad case of verbal diarrhoea.

"He sounds perfect for you," he stated.

"What the hell does that mean?" I asked, not knowing whether to take it as a compliment or be offended. I hadn't mentioned Kyle's life in too much detail, but I suppose I gave enough information to give him reason to look at me questioningly from time to time.

"It doesn't mean anything." He sighed, clutching the steering wheel tighter. "I'm not like Mum. I'm not throwing insults, so you don't need to be so bloody defensive."

I relaxed a little and apologised. He relaxed too and nodded. I assumed that was also his way of offering an apology.

"I'm just saying I've not seen you this happy since…" He hesitated.

"Since Jake." I finished, gently touching him on the elbow. He jumped, taken aback by the simple gesture. I realised then he was probably just as unfamiliar with simple acts of kindness as I was.

"Yeah." He agreed. "But you seem different too. More confident somehow, but I get the feeling it's not all to do with this Kyle. Did something happen to you, Ellie?"

I looked out the window and ignored his question. I wasn't ready to share everything with him just yet. Maybe not ever. He sighed and suddenly looked older than his eighteen years.

"Okay, he doesn't sound like the greatest role model in the world, but I can see he's good for you, and I can see the move to Vancouver has been good for you too. I didn't think it would help, but honestly, I think it was a really good decision." I blinked back tears and continued to stare out the passenger window, watching the roadside rush by as I processed his comments.

"Thanks, but it doesn't matter now," I finally replied. "He's gone."

"No, Els. For what it's worth, I think he'll be back. Okay, I don't know him, but you've told me enough to make me think he probably has demons of his own to deal with, and once he's worked through them, he'll realise he's walked out on the best thing that has happened to him. I also think once you've faced your own shit, you'll realise you're worthy of being loved. You are worthy of that second chance of happiness." I heard him gulp nervously, so I turned to look back at him. He looked straight ahead as he drove, avoiding eye contact.

"I also hope you can give me a second chance too, Els, because whether you believe it or not, I've missed my big sister."

Through water-filled eyes, I looked at my kid brother and wondered how the hell he'd gotten so old. I reached across and touched his elbow again. This time he didn't jump.

Chapter Thirty-Two

ELLIE

You would think the smell of hospitals wouldn't bother me considering I worked in one, but going in one as a visitor? Different kettle of fish. The smell of detergent mixed in with sickness and death invaded my nostrils and had my stomach recoiling and heaving up what was left of my dinner. Unfortunately, it wasn't the first time I'd made friends with a toilet over the past few days. Maybe it was because of nerves, or maybe it was because I was still sick. I had no idea, but my reflection in the mirror told me I'd certainly seen better days.

I walked briskly down the corridor to room fourteen, where I was told my father was sleeping. My stomach tightened the closer I got. *Fourteen.* I just wanted to visit my dad and get this over with. Lucas had told me my mother wouldn't be there. She was off getting her nails done or whatever she did to pass her time, but no doubt she would turn up eventually, and I didn't want to be there when she did.

In so many ways, the hospice looked like a hospital, but the warmer colours, furnishings, and plants made it feel homier. There were also less people wandering around. Dad had his own room, which looked nice enough, although from the looks of him, I didn't think he could care less. The man lying in the hospital bed, hooked up to a morphine drip, oxygen tank, and various other bits and pieces, wasn't my father. He was just the shell of the man I once knew. He opened his eyes when I entered the room, and I could see them tear up instantly. I was shocked when I felt mine do the same.

"Baby girl," he wheezed out before violently entering into a hacking cough. "I didn't think you would come."

"Hi, Dad," I said, taking a seat next to the bed. I didn't hug him. I didn't hold his hand. I sat expressionless as I took in his sunken features. He'd always been such a big man, but now he was no more than skin and bones. It had been seven months since I left England, and in that time, he'd aged considerably. I knew only too well from seeing patients at the hospital what cancer could do to the human body, but I could detach myself. Seeing it first hand in someone I loved... no words can describe the feeling, but it made me realise no matter what resentment I felt toward him, he was still my father and I still loved him.

"I'm glad you came," he whispered, taking in a huge gulp of air, causing him to cough again.

"Shh," I said. Watching him struggle out his words and cough his guts up was agonising. I finally found the courage to hold on to one of his skeletal hands.

"I wanted to tell you I was…" He waved the other hand around as he tried to catch his breath. I grabbed hold of both hands and pulled them back down to rest by his sides.

"It's okay," I said, still holding them tight. I felt his hands turn and grip hold of mine with the little strength he had. Tears rolled down his cheeks more freely now, and I struggled to keep mine at bay. The man lying in the bed was very broken and sick.

"It's not," he choked out. "It's not okay. I'm so sorry for what she did. I'm sorry I wasn't there for you." He closed his eyes as the syringe driver gave him his next shot of morphine. He mumbled something else, but I couldn't focus on anything other than his apology. It was a lifetime too late, but I accepted the last words of a dying man.

"So am I," I whispered.

He'd drifted back to sleep, leaving me looking at the smooth skin of his face. It was like the worry lines had disappeared the moment he made his confession, freeing him of his burden, allowing him to move on. I let go of his hands, kissed him on the forehead, and walked out of the hospital feeling lighter than before I walked in. He never again opened those aquamarine eyes that were so like my own.

The funeral was a week later. During that time, I visited old colleagues and spent time with my brother. I hadn't spoken to my mother yet, and I hadn't been to the cemetery either. I knew if anything were going to break me, one of these two things would be it. The taxi pulled into the church grounds, and I sucked in a breath. I couldn't believe how many people were there. My parents didn't exactly have a social life to speak of, so they didn't have many friends. I guessed the people here were just nosy neighbours or your frequent funeral attenders. You know, the people who had nothing better to do and found comfort in other people's misery. People like my mother. I stepped out of the car and paid the driver, quickly scanning the crowd to make sure no one noticed my arrival. There was still some time before the service started, and there was somewhere I needed to go first. Sighing in relief that no one had seen me, I crept off quietly in the direction of Jake's and Lyla Rose's graves.

Their black granite headstones sat side by side, one large hand and one baby hand engraved into the dark stone, made to look like they were reaching out for each other. It was a nice touch, and I wondered who'd thought of it. I doubted it was anyone from my side of the family. I was surprised Lyla Rose's headstone didn't have *leaves a devoted grandmother* inscribed across the top of it in big letters.

Thinking about it, it was probably Jake's mum's idea. She was probably the only one comfortable enough to stand up to my mother when it came to making the funeral arrangements. Jake had an older sister, but she preferred a simple life and kept to herself, and obviously, I was still in a coma when the funerals took place, so I didn't get a say.

I didn't get to say a proper good-bye either. I placed the baby-pink carnations I'd bought on the way on top of her grave and settled some white roses on top of Jake's before sitting down between them, resting a hand on each side, on each of them.

"Hey, princess. I know this sounds strange, but I saw you with daddy and I know he's taking great care of you up there." I took a deep breath and swiped away the tears that were falling before returning my hand to my daughter's grave.

"You look just like him, you know. I think those beautiful blue eyes would have let you get away with murder if you had… if that silly man hadn't crashed into our car and taken you both from me." I finished slowly. The tears fell more freely now. I pulled a tissue from my pocket and wiped at my eyes and nose before sucking in another deep, calming breath.

"I'm so sorry I never got to hold you or say good-bye or… Oh God, I love you so very much. Mummy…" I cursed under my breath as I struggled to speak through the tears. "Oh, baby girl, I didn't think it was possible to cry anymore, but I was wrong, sweetheart. Thinking about not holding you or not seeing you grow into a beautiful young woman breaks my heart. I know it will get easier in time, but it still hurts. It hurts so bloody much," I said, running my hands over the soft green blades of grass.

"I will love you forever, my beautiful baby girl. You look after your daddy for me because he needs you just as much as you need him." I swallowed the huge knot that had formed in my throat and took a few more deep breaths. Dabbing my damp cheeks with my soggy tissue, I turned my attention to Jake's headstone.

"Hey there, gorgeous. God, I miss you so much," I choked out after a few minutes of silence. "You know, it's been one hell of a ride since you left me, and I know I would have pissed you off with my attempts at dealing, but… Aggghhhh!" I growled quietly. Everything was becoming too much. I breathed through the anxiety, the grief, the anger until my thoughts were calmer and I could continue.

"You would have been so disappointed in me," I whispered. "But you know what? I think I'm going to be okay now. I'm not going to be a disappointment to you anymore. I'm sorry it took me nearly killing myself to get the message, but hey, you know how I don't like to make things easy on myself." I tried to laugh, but I think I sounded more like a strangled cat.

I closed my eyes and looked up to the sky, feeling the autumn sun on my face, the breeze caressing my damp cheeks, but the tears had stopped falling now. Opening my eyes slowly, I stared at the clouds and exhaled. The overwhelming sadness was still there but was dissipating. I started to feel lighter somehow. Freer.

"I know I'm going to be okay, and you want to know why? I'm going to be okay because of you. Because five years ago, you found me in an alley and saved me. You then turned up in my dreams nearly three weeks ago and saved me again. I get it now. In my own weird way, you managed to show me what I needed to see." I ran my fingers through my hair and sighed. Ditching the soggy tissue back into my pocket, I wiped my face with my coat sleeve.

"Thank you for loving me, Jake. Thank you for giving me the strength to move on. Thank you for being there when no one else was." Kissing my hand and lowering it to his grave, I stood up to leave. After brushing myself down, I bowed my head at both graves and said a silent prayer.

"I will love you forever and always. Good-bye."

Chapter Thirty-Three

KYLE

After leaving the hospital, I disappeared off the radar, not wanting to be found. Junior had an idea of my whereabouts but knew better than to hunt me down. Saint tried once and ended up getting his lip stitched up for his troubles. Not that I got away unscathed. It was the first time I broke my nose. No, for now I was better off on my own, to run through my thoughts, the memories of the last couple of months, but the longer I spent in my own company, I realised I'd acted in haste. I used to pride myself in my strength of character, my ability to look after people, my ability to take charge, but when it had mattered most, I'd failed miserably. My kid brother was right; I was scared. Scared because she brought out feelings, emotions I never knew I had. Never knew I was capable of. I left when the woman I loved needed me most, just like every other person in her life. Okay, Jake and Lyla Rose had no choice, but I did and I chose to run. I chose to be a coward.

I stared at my dad's grave and wondered what he would have done. He loved Junior and me in his own way, but he never loved my mother. His life was the MC, and in the end, it killed him, but was he happy? If he'd found his own Ellie rather than my mother, would he have put his family first? I wondered if he craved the love of a woman just as much as the next man, but the poison that was my mother destroyed his soul. Ruined him for anyone else. I crouched in front of the headstone and stared at the intricate details of the angel wings carved into the black granite, desperately seeking the answers I was looking for.

"I thought you'd end up here."

Okay, maybe he didn't know better than to hunt me down. I ignored Junior as he crouched beside me.

"You know, Dad was a great man. I loved him and I'm sure he loved us in his own way, but the club was his life. The club always came first, and it led him to an early death. He's never going to see me graduate, he'll never see us get married, and if we have kids, he'll never see them grow up. And for what? Money? Greed? Power?"

"It's not like that." I lied. My voice was hoarse from not having spoken to anyone for a few days. It was also slightly disturbing he was voicing what I'd just been thinking.

"Like hell it's not. Don't get me wrong. I love my life. I want to be part of the club, but I don't want it to turn me into Dad. Or what you'll become if you carry on down the path you're heading. You were more like a father to me than he was," he said, nodding toward the grave. "That's how I know there's more to you than the reputation you've made for yourself. You have a heart, Kyle. Don't let fear get in the way of your happiness, and follow some of your own advice. Face your fears and don't let them define you." He got up to walk away.

"It's too late," I said quietly. He stopped but didn't turn around.

"Yeah. It might be. She's gone," he replied coldly.

Gone. Who would have thought one single four-letter word would have enough power to cripple someone like me? I would take a bullet over the pain now crushing my chest any day. *Gone.* I clenched my fists and swallowed the golf ball-sized knot that had formed in my throat. Taking deep breaths in through my nose and out through my mouth, I tried to calm the storm that had erupted inside my head, desperately trying to get out to cause destruction to anything or anyone in its path. I closed my eyes and thought of the one thing on Earth that could calm me. Aquamarine eyes, soft pale skin, and raven hair that felt like silk when I ran my fingers through it. *Ellie.* Why the fuck did I leave? She might deserve better than me and my life, but she made me want to be a better person. I knew I would never leave the club, because let's face it; that's not the way things are done, but she made me want to try and figure out how we could make things work. Have a future.

Junior had left by the time I pulled myself together enough to get back on my Harley. It roared as I kick-started the engine and brought it to life. I pulled out of the cemetery like my life depended on it, one destination in mind. If Ellie was gone, I needed to find Cassie.

Cassie didn't answer the door when I arrived at the apartment. It was two in the afternoon, but the curtains were drawn and there was no sign of life.

"She's at work," a voice shouted from the apartment next door. A little grey-haired old lady shuffled out the door in her nightgown and slippers. "You can bang on that door all day, but all you'll do is continue to piss me off. The blond one went to work. No idea where the other one is, but she hasn't been home for a few days." She shuffled back through her door without another word.

What the fuck? No matter how messed up my life was right now, I took a moment's break from my mini meltdown and laughed out loud.

I barrelled through the doors of the hospital and headed toward the ICU where I knew Cassie would be working. Sure enough, as I ran through the corridor, I spotted her blond hair as she wheeled a trolley into a private room. I didn't think twice as I followed her.

"What the hell!" she screamed, promptly pushing me back outside the room.

I spotted a young girl in her twenties with bright red hair, lying motionless and hooked up to various machines. I instantly felt like a dick for intruding. There was a guy inside who looked equally as shocked to see me before his shock morphed into anger. He stood and walked toward me aggressively, but Cassie held up her hand again. He sat back down obediently but still gave off the vibe that he would happily rearrange my face. He was shorter than Cassie and not that built, but something in his eyes told me I should leave quickly and not add fuel to his fire. My father always taught me you could tell a lot from looking at people's eyes because they're the windows to your soul.

As I stepped out of the room, Cassie forcefully pulled me by the arm into an empty side room. If looks could kill, I'd be taking the spot next to my father in a heartbeat.

"Where is she?" I barked, not giving her the chance to vent her rage. I knew she was pissed with me. She had every right to be, but I really didn't have time for any shit.

"Like you fucking care!" she snapped back, obviously not going to make things easy. I squeezed my lips together and clenched my fists at my sides. Cassie looked down at them without concern. A wicked smirk flashed across her face. "What you going to do? Hit me?" She challenged as she took a step forward.

Was she stupid? I'd never hit a woman and I never would, but hadn't she once told me she'd heard the rumours about me? They were likely to be true. My temper was unpredictable.

"I wouldn't," I said through gritted teeth, taking a step back. Looking at the anger in her face, it was probably more for my own benefit than hers. "I just want to know where she is, Cassie," I said, calmer.

"She went back home to England."

That horrible crushing pain reappeared in my chest. Not being able to stand any longer, I sat on the floor and leaned against the wall, defeated.

"Why?" I spoke into thin air. I wasn't looking at Cassie anymore, but I heard her sigh and felt some of the tension leave the room.

"Her dad was dying and she went home to see him. If you'd bothered to stick around, you would have known that was the trigger for her drinking that night. That and the fact her brother decided he wanted to take her for a trip down memory lane. It certainly wasn't because of you. Unfortunately, she had taken painkillers. She wasn't trying to kill herself, you know. It was just a shit freak reaction." Her tone was still laced with anger, but it wasn't as venomous. I was grateful she was calming down. Cassie was like a sister to Ellie, and this meant her approval mattered to me.

"When will she be back? What do you mean about memory lane?" I asked, needing answers to help dull the pain I was feeling.

"That's the thing. If her mother gets her clutches in her again, there's no telling if she'll ever come back."

"But she hates her mum," I replied, finally looking back up at Cassie, who was still standing by the door. Her anger had been replaced by confusion as she looked at me, probably trying to figure out what the hell was going on. If she had answers, I was happy to hear them, because I didn't have a fucking clue.

"Doesn't mean she won't do anything in her power to try and achieve the crazy bitch's love. She's been craving it since she was a kid. Not that it matters; she'll never get it." Cassie slid down the wall and joined me on the floor. She tugged her uniform down and started playing with the apron she wore.

"She needs to come home," I said.

"First fucking sensible thing you've said in a while." She nudged me gently on the shoulder with hers. She offered a weak smile and shook her head slowly. "Yes, she does need to come home, but it's up to her now, Kyle. You or I can't make her, and don't forget you left her, so even if she comes back, she may not want to see you. But for what it's worth, I hope she gives you a second chance, and I'm confident she'll do the right thing."

"Thanks," I replied, returning her smile. If anyone saw me right now, sitting down on the floor with my heart ripped wide open, my life would be over, but I didn't care. "You never answered my question about memory lane," I prompted, not sure if I really wanted her to answer my question, especially when I heard Cassie suck in a calming breath next to me.

"I'm guessing you saw the scars on her legs?" she questioned.

I did. There were some long red scars down her left hip and thigh, which I assumed were from the accident. There were more on her right thigh, but they looked different and were... silver. They were old scars. From how light they were now, I would guess they would have happened when she was a kid. *Shit.*

"Please tell me it's not what I'm thinking," I whispered.

"Yeah. I would say you're thinking along the right track. Ellie never told me, but I saw her notes when she was in the hospital. It didn't say who did it, but I know. The crazy bitch put her daughter in hospital when she was fourteen years old."

I'd never ever thought of hitting a woman. Until now.

Chapter Thirty-Four

ELLIE

Staring at the newly dug earth, wreaths, and flowers covering my father's casket felt surreal. The service was short and sweet. Tears were shed, including my own. I was surprised to see even my mother's eyes glisten, leading me to think maybe she had a heart after all, but then somehow I doubted that. It was all for show. She worked the crowd like she was attending a red carpet event and she was the star. You wouldn't have thought she'd just been widowed after thirty years of marriage.

He was gone, and I really didn't know what to think or how to feel. I was relieved he was no longer suffering, happy we'd made amends before he died, but I was still so angry he hadn't stood up for me as a child. As an adult. Angry that he preferred to stand on the sidelines and watch as his wife, the mother of his children, ridiculed his only daughter at every opportunity. Angry that it took a violent assault for him to finally step in, and angry he took a step back the first chance he got. The resentment still bore deep, right down to the marrow of my bones. He was dead. Did it make me a bad person to still harbour these feelings? Was it even healthy to still hold on to these grudges? It wasn't like he could come back and erase the past and fix everything for the future.

"Eleanor." The sound of her ice-cold voice had every hair standing up on end and muscles tensing I never knew I had. I suddenly felt like a child again. Scared. Alone. I hadn't actually spoken to her face to face since telling her to leave that day when I was still in hospital. We'd spoken on the phone a few times, each time resulting in me hitting the bottle, but that wasn't an option now. I'd made a silent agreement with Jake, Lyla Rose, Cassie, Kyle, and above all, myself that I wouldn't take the easy way out. I was stronger than that. I was a survivor. I wasn't a coward.

I turned slowly to face the woman who called herself my mother. She wore a tight-fitting black dress that finished just above her knees and a black shawl. Her black heels sank into the muddy ground, causing her to wobble as she tried to walk toward me. I went to step back but thought better of it. I wouldn't walk away from her. I wouldn't give her the satisfaction of seeing how much she still affected me.

I took in her hair, neatly styled in soft curls, framing her pixie-shaped face. I had really no idea what the hell was attached to the side of her head. I think it was meant to be a fascinator but looked more like the aftermath of a crow after being involved in an incident with a large moving object. Like a lorry. Her eyes narrowed into tiny slits as she ran her disapproving gaze over my body. I didn't really wear dresses or skirts or anything girly for that matter, so I can only imagine her disgust as she took in my black wide-legged trousers, black fitted top, and long cardigan that covered my arse. I think the final piece of my outfit had her breaking out in a sweat, though. I inwardly laughed at her sharp intake of breath as she spotted my black patent DMs sticking out from the bottom of my trousers. At least I'd decided not to wear my biker boots.

"Mother," I said without smiling. "You look well." I wasn't lying. She did look well, considering she'd just buried her husband.

"Of course I don't. I'm a mess. You'd know that if you hadn't gallivanted off to another country to do whatever it is you're doing while I was looking after your gravely ill father. It affected my health as well, you know. I'm on more medication for my heart. Anyway, you're home and look fine enough, so at least I can be grateful I don't have to fix any of your drama for the time being."

"I think you'll find, Mother, that I have done well enough coping on my own," I replied curtly, feeling my supressed anger slowly rise to the surface.

"Sure you have," she retorted dismissively. I clenched and unclenched my fists and willed myself to stay calm. "Anyway, enough small talk. Your old room is ready for you to move into. I'll get Lucas to bring over your things, and I'm sure we can arrange for your other things to be shipped back over."

Did she really just say my old room was ready? Did she really think I was going to move back home and act like the last twenty-five years of my life never happened? This time when I clenched my fists, my nails dug into my skin and I was certain to draw blood.

"Pardon?" Not the best of comebacks I know, but I think I was going into shock. I was certainly stunned speechless.

"I see you've still not got much between the ears, because I'm pretty sure you heard me," she snapped.

I could feel my blood boil as my anger surfaced again.

"No, I think I heard you just fine," I replied, finally finding my tongue and some backbone. My tone was cold, unyielding. "What I don't understand is why on earth you think I would be moving back home. Not just back to England, but moving back to *your* house."

"Because it is your home, and now that your father is gone, who else better than you to help look after me? Did you not just hear me mention my medication has increased because of my heart condition?"

I fought back a laugh. Not because it was funny, but because I was struggling to work out how she could have a heart condition when she didn't seem to have a heart, and the fact she said it with such sincerity made the whole conversation even more surreal. I couldn't help it. The laughter I was trying to contain erupted from my throat, and she looked at me like I was a mad woman. Maybe I was.

"Wow, you really are something else," I hissed. I could feel the heat rise to my cheeks and tears pooled in my eyes, but they weren't there because I was upset. They were there because I was angry. She must have noticed, because she suddenly looked uncertain and visibly took a step back. I approached her like a lion stalked its prey until I was standing in her face. We were so close I could smell the coffee on her breath.

"You know what, *Mother*? I suggest you back the fuck off and disappear back to the world of make believe or continue taking the drugs you must be taking, because I'm pretty sure you think you're talking to someone who gives a shit about your wellbeing."

I heard her gulp, and I'd never felt more empowered.

"Enough of this nonsense, Ellie. You don't know what you're saying. It must be the grief of losing your father and the guilt for not being here when we needed you," she said, clearly not as affected as I thought.

"Why?" I asked.

She knew what I was referring to, but she tried to mask her knowledge with a look of confusion. I could see through it. I was a master of disguise after all. It was probably the only valuable thing she'd ever taught me. How to force a smile and look happy when all I wanted to do was scream or cry. How to push back the tears and look strong and determined. How to pretend all was right in the world when all you wanted to do was curl up and die.

"I really don't know what you mean," she replied, putting her hand to her chest in mock hurt.

"Cut the crap, Mother. Why do you hate me so much? Why could you never love me? Why couldn't you be like a normal mother? Why did you beat the crap out of me that day? WHY?!" She flinched as I screamed, nearly stumbling on those ridiculous heels.

"I don't know," she whispered, and for the first time, I thought I saw real emotion on her face. Her features aged in front of my eyes as her eyes glistened with unshed tears. I wasn't sure how to react. Was I satisfied that I was able to evoke such a reaction? Was I happy or was I angry because she was surely trying to turn it all around again so the main focus was her?

"You have made my life a living hell. Do you know that?" She nodded in reply. "Do you know how much I resent you? How much I detest being in the same breathing space as you?"

A tear rolled down her cheek, and she delicately wiped it away. It was subtle, but I noticed her looking around to see if she had an audience. She was still trying to play the victim. I sighed. I should have known things would be no different, but strangely, it made what I had to do easier. I suppose deep down, I'd always known things wouldn't be any different. But I think it was the first time I saw everything for what it was clearly, and this time I accepted it.

"You'll never change, will you, Mother? You'll always be cold-hearted and manipulative, but despite all that, I do love you, you know. I just don't like you that much."

"Ellie…" she stammered.

I held up my hand to silence her, and she stopped herself from whatever she was about to say.

"I'm going home."

A huge smile broke across her face, like she'd just won the lottery. The tears she'd shed miraculously disappeared, and I silently berated myself for worrying when she shed her first crocodile tear, even if it was just for a little bit.

"No, Mother, I'm not going to *your* home. I'm going back to Vancouver. To Cassie and hopefully my new family, if they'll still have me. To people who love and accept me for who I am."

"You can't," she said with little emotion, her face unreadable, expressionless. Cold.

"Good-bye, Mother," I replied. I walked away from my mother for the last time and felt the weight finally lift from my shoulders. It was the freest I'd felt in years.

"So why even come back!" she shouted, not moving from my father's graveside.

"Closure," I whispered to the wind.

Chapter Thirty-Five

KYLE

"For fuck's sake, Kyle, sit your ass down. You're wearing a hole in the carpet," Saint snapped from where he stood at the bar, looking like he would like nothing more than to physically cause me pain. You could see he was struggling to hold himself back.

Tiny stood at the other end of the bar with Bear. He was trying not to bust a gut laughing, because no doubt he thought the way I was dealing with my current predicament was hilarious. Bear just looked his normal moody, expressionless self. By the sofa, Red bounced on the heels of his feet like a kid with ADHD, and the others, well, they just looked like they wanted to curl up in a corner and hide. Apparently, I was making people nervous. I didn't blame them. I was scaring the shit out of myself.

"Why now?" I barked to anyone who was listening and brave enough to answer.

"Hell if I know, but don't sound so surprised. You knew this shit was coming," Saint replied as I guessed he probably would. He knew the real reason I was prowling up and down like a hungry lion, and apart from Slade and now Junior, he was probably the only one who would dare stand up to me if he thought I was being a dick. Right now, I was acting like one. At least he seemed somewhat calmer now, but that probably had more to do with me having stopped pacing and not standing near anyone to cause damage if they decided to sneeze in my direction. It was fair to say I was strung tighter than a guitar and was ready to snap.

Slade had received a call from our chapter in Winnipeg this morning, requesting our help, and considering they'd helped us out of a tight spot or two in the past, we could hardly decline. This caused me somewhat of a dilemma, because today was also the day Ellie was coming home, and I had every intention of surprising her at the airport, regardless of whether she wanted to see me or not. I'd decided I would tackle that bridge when I got to it, but now it seemed I wouldn't even get the chance.

The door creaked open and we all froze. We'd all been waiting anxiously for Slade to come back into the room after speaking on the phone to his brother, the prez of the Angels of Death, Winnipeg chapter, for the last hour, and everyone was keen to hear what he had to say. Me especially.

I cursed under my breath when he said exactly what I was expecting. We needed to leave for Winnipeg within the next hour, therefore putting a halt to my original plans. I looked at my phone probably for the hundredth time in the last twenty minutes. Still no text. Cassie was supposed to be keeping me updated, but all I had heard so far was that Ellie had boarded the plane. That was nine hours ago. There was a good chance Cassie was ignoring me, though. She was expecting updates from me too, but I hadn't been so good at holding up my end of the bargain. Honestly though, what was there to say? No doubt whatever decision I made would piss someone off. I was just still deciding whose wrath I would rather face and whether I could live with the fallout. Cassie or the club?

"You look like shit." I hadn't even heard Saint stalk up beside me. Apparently, he'd been standing there for at least a couple minutes, saying my name, and like a crazed idiot, I'd zoned out and stood there staring into space. I ran my fingers through my hair, ignoring his comment. I knew what I looked like. That's why these past few days, I'd seriously avoided mirrors.

I watched on as the guys went about getting ready for the trip and then signalled for Saint to follow me to the bar. I grabbed a bottle of whisky and poured myself and Saint a drink.

"So what do you think? By the sounds of it, we might be gone for a couple weeks, tops. We'll need the normal supplies, maybe a few extras. Sounds like they're up against some heavy arsenal," I said to my

VP and best friend before downing the glass in one hit. I winched as the burn of the whiskey hit the back of my throat before it settled in the pit of my stomach. My drink of choice was usually a beer, but today called for the heavy stuff. Saint raised his eyebrow in question when I went to pour another, stopping me in my tracks. What the hell was I doing? Although I was hardly drunk, driving under the influence was sure to be a recipe for disaster.

"All sounds good. I've spoken to Sadie, and Slade has already instructed Big Mamma to keep an eye on Junior while we're gone."

I nodded, knowing this wouldn't be a problem. It wasn't like it was the first time she'd had to look out for him and it wouldn't be the last. He needed to stick to school, because there was no way in hell I'd let his grades drop any lower. The last few weeks had taken their toll on him, and despite being a bright kid, his academics had taken a nosedive. He might not have ever mentioned college, but I wanted him to have options. I never got the chance.

My phone chimed, telling me I'd just received a text. I pulled it out of my pocket, ignoring the intense stare Saint gave me. I tapped the screen and sighed in relief at seeing Cassie's name.

Cassie: *Oi, shithead. What the hell is happening? You meeting me at the airport or not?*

"That Cassie?" Saint asked, finally taking a sip of his drink.

"Yeah. Can you believe she just called me a shithead?" I said, somewhat amused.

"Yeah, because some days you are, and I suspect

from the way you downed that drink and the look on your face, she's about to call you a lot worse," he replied with a smirk. "What you going to do?"

I knew what he was really asking, but I had no idea. The only thing I knew for sure was he was right about Cassie. If she were here, I think she'd probably swing first and throw insults at me later, but I couldn't abandon the club right now. They needed me. I was the prez, and as much as I trusted Saint with my life, I couldn't let him take on what waited for us in Winnipeg, even though he would do it in a heartbeat. It wasn't a decision made lightly, but it was what I needed to do, and I felt like the biggest asshole on the planet.

Me: *Got 2 go away on business. Look after her for me.*

Cassie had some serious texting skills, or she already had her reply ready. Before I'd even put my phone down, it chimed.

Cassie: *U R a fucking arsehole.*

Saint downed the rest of his whiskey and shook his head. "You're an idiot. You know that, right?" he said, staring at me like I had two heads.

"I know, but this is what I do. If me and Ellie are meant to be, then she'll be waiting for me when I get back."

Saint slid down from the stool and took a couple steps away before stopping. We were the only two left in the bar now, the thunder of Harleys roaring to life outside like music to my ears. I didn't think the sound would ever grow old.

"Before we head out, I just want to say

something. Not as your VP, but as your friend. As your brother."

I nodded for him to continue but fixed my gaze at the door. I wasn't sure if I wanted to hear it, but something told me he would say it anyway so there was no point in arguing.

"The club may be my life, but I live for my family. Knowing my ol' lady and daughter are waiting for me when I get back is what makes me think about my actions more carefully, because I'll be damned if I ain't going to come back to see my little girl grow up. Take her first steps, say her first words, graduate from college, and I'm going to be the one who threatens to kick the ass of the fucker who takes her out on her first date. The thing is I know they'll be waiting when I get back because they're mine and they know where they stand. As for Ellie, *you* walked away. She has no idea how you feel about her. So what makes you think she'll be waiting for you when you get back? You need to ask yourself if you really want to risk it."

I couldn't look at him because then he would see I knew he was right, but I was an idiot, or rather a shithead and arsehole as Cassie so politely told me, so it was no surprise the only words that left my mouth as I shouldered past him and headed toward the door were, "Let's ride."

Chapter Thirty-Six

ELLIE

After I'd left my mother at the cemetery, I relieved myself of my stomach contents, and when my stomach was empty, my body thought it might be nice to get rid of its lining too. I pity anyone who stumbled across the mess I left behind a rather large 1920s headstone, because it really wasn't a pretty sight. I think I went into shock after realising I'd finally stood up to my mother and found the courage to leave my old life behind. I was then struck by a wave of anxiety when I realised I truly didn't have a clue what life was going to throw at me in the future, and I then made the decision that I really didn't care. Well, maybe that was a lie. There were some things, or rather people, I did care about, and I secretly hoped they would still play a part in my life.

Since being in England, I'd texted Cassie on a daily basis, but she didn't have much to report, just that the place was lonely without me, and Junior, Sadie, and Trix missed me too. There was never any mention of Kyle, and part of me wondered whether it was because he was still gone and there was nothing to tell or he really didn't want anything to do with me anymore. Thinking the latter felt like a kick to the gut, but looking back over the last few weeks, I wouldn't have changed anything. The last few weeks had been hell for not only me, but I couldn't have wished for a better outcome. If I hadn't faced those challenges, I would never have stood up to her. I would never have chosen to live, and for the first time in my life, I felt free.

My life with Jake had been perfect, but there was still always something stopping me from moving forward completely. Now I felt like there was no one holding me back anymore. There was absolutely nothing stopping me from taking the bull by the horns and ploughing right through. The feeling was bloody amazing, and now my mind was no longer consumed with guilt, anger, pain. I was bursting with ideas, dreams, and hope because I had every intention of taking advantage of this new lease on life by making sure I damn well enjoyed it.

I was going to see more of Canada, maybe tour around on my bike. I was going to enjoy life with Cassie and my new friends by doing whatever it is you're meant to do in a group of women. I wasn't overly keen on shopping and spa days, but I was going to bloody well give it a try even if at the end of it, I did want to poke my own eyes out with blunt needles. I was also going to actively attend AA sessions, because there was no way another drop of alcohol was going past my lips. I even considered that maybe one day, when I was strong enough, I would help people who had suffered through the same experiences as I, because some people don't have a Cassie. They don't have a Sadie, Trix, or Junior. They don't have a Kyle. They have no one to help pick up the pieces when their life goes to shit.

Two days after the funeral, Lucas dropped me back at the airport. This time, there were no nerves, and we actually parted by giving each other a hug. I did end up staying at his student house in the end, because apparently, he hardly slept in his room anyway, preferring to kip with Jules. Not that he would ever tell dear old Mum, of course. She'd have him back home before he got the chance to pull his jeans back up from around his ankles. It was nice to spend time with him and catch up properly. Being able to talk openly was difficult at first, and by no means was everything one hundred percent, but progress had definitely been made. There was still a way to go, but I hoped, given time, we could go back to being as close as we were when we were young kids.

The flight home was as uneventful as the flight to England, except this time I was able to sit more comfortably. I didn't think it was possible, but I think my neighbouring passenger was actually smaller than me, and no, she wasn't a child. She was old enough to be my grandmother. As the light pinged asking us to belt up for landing, I was hit by a sudden onslaught of nausea, and I wished I'd never eaten all those dough balls and pizza before I boarded. The little lady next to me must have seen I'd turned an odd shade of green and handed me a paper bag, a comforting smile on her face.

The worst thing about flying for me has always been the landing, but normally, I just suffer with popping ears and go deaf for about an hour. Oh, and I might also walk a little funny because my joints seize up, and that was before the accident. It has been known for me to be stopped at customs on occasion because I probably give the impression I'm smuggling something into the country, the make-believe item in question not being in my bag. I held on to the bag for dear life, feeling slightly better knowing if I were going to puke my guts up, it was better to do it in front of my new best friend instead of some hottie like Kyle.

Kyle.

Even now my mind drifted to him as I thought of those gorgeous brown eyes, his five o' clock shadow that made me want to run my fingers over his stubbly jaw. I thought about what it was like to lick every inch of his bulging muscles and using my tongue to trace the outlines of his tattoos. I thought about his hands on my body and the way he affected me with a single touch. Turned out there was no need for that paper bag. I'd become so lost in thought, I didn't even realise we'd landed.

"ELS!" Before I had time to respond, Cassie practically knocked me to the ground with an overly enthusiastic hug. "I've bloody missed you, hun," she said, still squeezing the life out of me.

"Have missed you too," I said into her chest. She finally let go when I started wheezing due to lack of air supply.

"He's not here, hun."

I hadn't even realised I'd been scanning the crowds for the one face I longed to see as much as my best friend. Trust Cas to notice.

"If it makes you feel better, he was planning on coming, but he's had to go away again."

There was no denying I was disappointed, but what could I say? It wasn't like we were together anymore, if we were even together in the first place. I suppose I should have been grateful she said he was intending on coming, because surely that meant there was still hope. I smiled, but the frown on her face told me she wasn't buying it.

"So what's new?" I asked, changing the subject as we headed outside the stuffy airport. Talking about Kyle was going to make me miserable, and it wouldn't be a good start to my new and hopefully stress-free life.

"Nothing much. Like I said on the phone, Sadie, Trix, and Junior have been calling for updates. Even Tiny popped around the apartment one day. He said he was checking to see if Trix was there, but I think he secretly misses you," she said with a wink and a playful shove in my side, making me stumble into a businessman with zero sense of humour. His reaction was so comical, we laughed hysterically like a couple of schoolgirls. I even had to stop and squeeze my legs together to prevent a little accident.

"I've missed them too," I replied finally. "It will be nice to catch up and let you all know the plans I've made in my head, and I've made lots of plans. We're going to have so much fun! There's also some other stuff I've decided, and I think you'll be proud of me, but right now, I need sleep or several cans of energy drink. Maybe we could all catch up tomorrow once I've fought off the jet lag?" I suggested excitedly and quite possibly without even taking a breath. I think I might have even clapped my hands and jumped up and down a little before catching a glimpse of Cassie's eyes glistening in the sunlight.

"Hey, Cas, what's wrong?" I asked, pulling her to a gentle stop by her elbow.

"I'm just happy, Els. It's good to hear you laugh like that. It's been a long time," she replied, wiping away a tear that had managed to escape.

"God, you're a soppy sod," I said, pulling her into another hug, not feeling awkward in the slightest. Who would have thought it possible for me to initiate a hug without turning stiff like a board? I think Cassie noticed this too, and her tears fell harder, but I got the sense my happiness wasn't solely the reason for her uncharacteristic breakdown.

"Come on. Let's get going. I have a craving for

chocolate ice cream, and I also don't believe those tears are purely for my benefit."

She wiped her face with her sleeves, still managing to look beautiful even with red puffy eyes and blotchy cheeks.

We made it to her bright-red little Jeep, and I chucked my bag in the backseat. Cassie had already gotten in the car and was reapplying her makeup. I opened the passenger door, but a distant noise caught my attention and stopped me in my tracks. Cassie even stopped applying her mascara and looked at me wide-eyed. A massive smile broke across her face when she realised what I'd heard.

"Okay, maybe he's not a shithead or an arsehole after all," she muttered.

"Pardon?" I replied nervously.

"Nothing, Els. It's a long story," she said, watching me closely. "What you thinking?" she asked, the sound of the approaching Harley getting louder. There was no mistaking the engine's rumble, and I think it was safe to say I could pick out the sound of Kyle's bike amongst a hundred others. My mouth went dry and an explosion of butterflies erupted in my stomach.

"I really don't know," I replied. He was nearly here, but I couldn't bring myself to turn around and watch as the bike pulled in. I was scared in case it wasn't him. Scared I would crumble.

Still staring at Cassie, I watched as her gaze looked past me to where the sound of Kyle's bike came to an abrupt stop. My heart was now hammering against my chest so violently I thought I would pass out. Heavy, confident footsteps approached me from behind, and I think I stopped breathing. He was so close I could smell the leather of his cut, the fresh air that clung to his body mixed with his cologne. He was close enough for me to feel his heat caress my back and engulf me like I was snuggled in a comfy blanket.

"I'll just go and… do something," I heard Cassie say as she quickly exited her car.

"Angel." His voice travelled through my body like highly charged electricity. Every part of me hummed with anticipation as he took another step forward and whispered in my ear, "You going to turn around for me?"

The warmth of his breath against my exposed neck sent goose bumps rippling across my heavily clothed skin. I slowly turned on the spot and came face to face with a wall of solid muscle. He was wearing a black long-sleeved top that clung to each and every contour like a glove. How the hell was he not cold? It was bloody November! Why did I even care, other than these thoughts distracting me from looking up at that gorgeous face I'd grown to love?

Scraping up my courage, I finally found the nerve to look up. I sucked in a sharp intake of breath. I knew he was like a walking Adonis, but somehow along the way, I'd forgotten how magnificent this man truly was, and by the way he was staring at me with those intensely dark-brown eyes, I didn't need to question his intentions. It was all there in the way he looked at me. Like I was the most treasured thing on Earth.

"Hey," I whispered.

"Hey, angel," he replied, staring longingly at my lips.

Wanting to kiss him as much as he wanted to kiss me, I stood on my tiptoes, surprising him as I curled my hand around his neck and pulled him toward my eagerly awaiting mouth. The kiss was hesitant at first but soon became fast and frenzied as our tongues tangled together hungrily. I clung onto his neck with one hand and his cut with the other like my life depended on it. As he lifted me, I wrapped my legs around his waist and squeezed. A loud moan of approval rumbled from the back of his throat. He gripped onto my arse tighter as his tongue continued to dance with mine.

Finally ending the kiss, we stood in silence as we tried to regain our breath. He slowly lowered me back to the ground. As I slid past his crotch, I instantly felt just how pleased he was to see me. My knees buckled, but strong arms held me up. I knew he would never let me fall.

"I'm sorry," we both said at the same time and laughed. I went to speak, but he held a finger up to his lips, motioning for silence before he rested his forehead on mine and sighed.

"Let me speak, angel," he said quietly before stepping back and tilting my face so I was directly looking at him.

"I was heading down the freeway when it hit me that I wouldn't be able to live with myself if I left you for a second time without saying a proper good-bye. I was an idiot for leaving you at the hospital, and I wouldn't blame you if you wanted to walk away." He looked at me seriously before adopting an extremely arrogant smirk that hit me right between the thighs. "Although, from that kiss, I would say all is forgiven." He chuckled when I blushed and applied a little extra force when I tried to look down.

"Nah, angel, I love it when you blush. Don't try and look away." He placed a light kiss on the end of my nose before turning all serious again. "When I heard you'd gone, I felt sick. For a moment, I literally fell apart, but it made me realise just how much I hated being apart from you. It made me realise how I feel. You mean everything to me, angel. I never in my life thought I would ever say this to anyone, but I love you. I love you so much. You. Are. Mine."

"Okay," I whispered as Kyle gently wiped away the happy tears rolling down my cheeks. He leaned down and led me into a soft kiss raw with emotion. He didn't need to say anything else. His kiss spoke to me in a million words.

"There's just one thing," I said, silently cringing at Kyle's sudden look of despair. He went to speak, but this time I motioned him to be silent. "Hold your horses. Let me finish."

"Sorry," he mumbled.

Not wishing to torment him any longer, I pulled him down toward me so I could whisper in his ear.

"Yes, there is no doubt I'm yours, but where I come from, old ladies have grey hair and are, well… just old. If I hear you call me an old lady while I'm in earshot, it will seriously piss me off and I might end up serving your balls up on a platter. Okay?" I placed a chaste kiss on the side of his mouth before releasing him. I silently chuckled at his shocked expression, which slowly turned into one of those *what the fuck* looks.

For a good couple minutes, he basically looked at me like I'd completely gone off my rocker. Maybe I had, but honestly, why would anyone want to be called an old lady at twenty-five years of age? Finally, he just shook his head and burst into a fit of laughter.

"Anything you say, angel. Anything you say." He grabbed my hand and pulled me toward his bike to take me home.

Home. Never in my life had one four-letter word sounded so good.

Epilogue

ELLIE

Do you remember the times I mentioned puking my guts up toward the end? Do you remember me saying on one occasion I craved chocolate ice cream? Bet you were all thinking the obvious, weren't you? Pity I wasn't so sharp on the uptake, but seriously, the thought never crossed my mind, because as far as I was concerned, I was on the pill. Pregnancy wasn't possible. You would think being a nurse, I would know the pill loses its effectiveness if you have diarrhoea and sickness while taking it. Okay, I might not have necessarily been ill, but I'd certainly nursed several hangovers over a period of several weeks, and this included me purging myself of my stomach contents on more than one occasion. Basically, popping those pills was about as affective as popping candy.

When I returned home from England, Kyle drove me home. We barely made it inside the apartment before we were ripping each other's clothes off and were at it like a couple of rampant rabbits. He then took off for two weeks to join his club in Winnipeg. During those two weeks, my sickness got worse, and it took peeing on five little sticks before I finally believed what the double blue lines were telling me. I was pregnant with Kyle's baby.

I was scared shitless. Cassie found me curled up in the foetal position on the bathroom floor, crying my eyes out. Don't get me wrong. I was happy, but I was also so confused. Was having another baby me trying to replace Lyla Rose? Would this baby be okay? Was it too soon to be having a kid with Kyle? Did he even want a baby? Unfortunately, he wasn't around for me to find out, sending me into all kinds of doolally. It turned out I didn't need to worry. As soon as he came home, I told him, and you would think I'd just told him he'd won the lottery. His grin was so big I was sure it would split his face in two. He pulled me into a hug, kissed the ever-loving shit out of me, and then I witnessed a grown man crumble as tears of joy pooled in his eyes.

Two weeks later, I was living with him and Junior in the suburbs, eating so much chocolate ice cream I was certain my normally pale skin would turn brown, and I was being treated with kid gloves. Don't get me wrong. At first, I loved being treated like the most prized possession in the world, but after two weeks, I think I was about ready to commit murder.

Eight months later, I found myself standing in the bathroom, staring at the puddle of water surrounding my feet. After I'd been to the toilet, I might add. I stood there for what seemed like hours but was probably only seconds before finally coming to terms with what just happened. My waters had just broken. It was disgusting, and I was completely alone. I grabbed a towel and shoved it between my legs and waddled into the bedroom to find my phone. I cursed loudly when I realised it had run out of battery. I waddled downstairs, towel still between my legs, and headed toward the landline in the living room. I anxiously dialled Kyle's number. Wasn't I supposed to be in pain right now? Things didn't appear to be going how they were meant to be, and I was starting to panic.

"Hey, angel, what's up?" Kyle finally answered.

I burst into tears.

Fifteen hours later, I was screaming and shouting so much Cassie threatened to knock me out. That was why she now waited with practically all of the Angels of Death MC members outside in the waiting area. Kyle grabbed my hand as another contraction overpowered me. He cursed under his breath as my nails broke his skin. It's not like I was unaccustomed to pain, but fuck me, it hurt like a son of a bitch. I threw ten tons of verbal insults in his direction and used language a sailor would be proud of. I think the message was clear, though. His dick wasn't to come anywhere near me again unless it had a bloody hat on. He laughed. I dug my nails in deeper.

"Okay, honey, you're doing fab. I can see the head. When you feel the next contraction coming, I want you to push right down into your bottom," the doctor said, staring openly at my vagina, which no doubt would never be the same again.

The next contraction came, and I think I literally raised the roof.

"That's great, Ellie. The head is out. Two more pushes, max," she said calmly. I looked at Kyle and, despite myself, laughed at his expression. The "slayer," the prez, the huge, tattooed, muscle-bound man who was no stranger to blood and pain was looking an odd shade of grey.

Like the good doctor said, my baby was quickly born. The look of bewilderment combined with adoration and pure unadulterated love on Kyle's face made my heart swell, but then something occurred to me. My body hit panic overload.

"Why is my baby not crying?" I asked, swallowing the huge knot that threatened to choke me. Kyle's expression looked worried, and he reached over and squeezed my hand. "Why is my baby not crying? WHAT IS HAPPENING?" I screamed through the tears that were now pouring.

The next few heart-stopping seconds felt like a lifetime as I watched the commotion on the other end of the room as the doctor rubbed my baby's back and placed a tiny oxygen mask over its face.

I didn't even know if I had a son or daughter. We'd decided to not find out the sex during the pregnancy. Not that it mattered. We'd decided on a name that would work for a boy or girl.

A piercing cry echoed through the room, and I finally let out the breath I was holding. The doctor walked over to the side of my bed, holding a bundle wrapped up snug in a plain white blanket. She leaned down and gently opened up the blanket, and Kyle looked like he was about to burst with pride.

"That's my boy." He winked, placing a kiss on our son's forehead before placing one on my own. The doctor handed over my little boy, and it took everything I had to hold myself together. Through misty eyes, I stared at the mop of thick black hair and rich chocolate-brown eyes, just like his father's. Lyla Rose had a baby brother, and he was the most gorgeous little thing I'd ever seen.

"Hello, little man, I'm your mummy," I whispered.

"What's his name?" the doctor asked.

"Lake," both Kyle and I replied at the same time.

Well, we could hardly call him Whistler, could we?

The End

Acknowledgements

Thank you to my gorgeous kiddies, Joseph, Katie, and Amy, who have made me go prematurely grey and cause me no end of stress but, in their own unique way, encouraged me to take the leap into the unknown and to write!

Thank you to Jacqueline Williams, who opened my eyes to the world of writing, and to Samantha Shaw, Erica Sands, Denise Higgs, Rachel Buxton, and all my other friends who have encouraged and supported me all the way. Your constant reassurances and "pick-me-ups" have been a godsend! You guys are the best—thank you for believing I could do this!

Thanks also to Samantha Good, who introduced me to so many fabulous authors in a genre I never thought I would read and enjoy, let alone write!

Cassie, thank you for editing my book! You have been absolutely fantastic! I truly appreciate all your help and look forward to working with you again in the future.

Mayhem Cover Creations, I LOVE my cover! Thank you for everything! You have been fantastic to work with, and I look forward to working with you again too.

Finally, thank you to you guys… the readers. Thank you for taking a chance on me and reading my debut book. XXX